LITTLE PAULA

V.C. Andrews® Books

LITTLE
PAULA

V.C. ANDREWS®

G
Gallery Books

New York   London   Toronto   Sydney   New Delhi

Gallery Books
An Imprint of Simon & Schuster, Inc.
1230 Avenue of the Americas
New York, NY 10020

Following the death of Virginia Andrews, the Andrews family worked with a carefully selected writer to organize and complete Virginia Andrews's stories and to create additional novels, of which this is one, inspired by her storytelling genius.

First Gallery Books hardcover edition February 2023

V.C. ANDREWS® and VIRGINIA ANDREWS® are registered trademarks of Vanda Productions, LLC

GALLERY BOOKS and colophon are registered trademarks of Simon & Schuster, Inc.

For information about special discounts for bulk purchases, please contact Simon & Schuster Special Sales at 1-866-506-1949 or business@simonandschuster.com.

Interior design by Erika R. Genova

Manufactured in China

10 9 8 7 6 5 4 3 2 1

The Library of Congress has cataloged the trade paperback edition as follows:

Names: Andrews, V. C. (Virginia C.), author.
Title: Little Paula / V.C. Andrews.
Description: First Gallery Books trade paperback edition. | New York :
    Gallery Books, 2023. | Series: The Eden series ; 2 | Sequel to: Eden's Children.
Identifiers: LCCN 2021062777 (print) | LCCN 2021062778 (ebook) | ISBN 9781982156404
    (paperback) | ISBN 9781982156411 (hardcover) | ISBN 9781982156435 (ebook)
Subjects: LCGFT: Novels.
Classification: LCC PS3551.N454 L58 2023 (print) | LCC PS3551.N454 (ebook)
    | DDC 813/.54—dc23
LC record available at https://lccn.loc.gov/2021062777
LC ebook record available at https://lccn.loc.gov/2021062778

ISBN 978-1-9821-5641-1
ISBN 978-1-9821-5643-5 (ebook)

LITTLE
PAULA

PROLOGUE

Daddy stole my baby.
   He and his girlfriend, Gabby, did it at night while Trevor and I were asleep. I was exhausted and completely unaware of their intention. The moment Daddy had found out I was pregnant, he forbade Trevor to sleep in my room. He sent him to the Forbidden Room, not realizing that for Trevor, sleeping there could never be a punishment.

   After our baby was gone, Trevor blamed himself for not waking, rushing into my room, and waking me. "Mama had the house trying to warn me with its creaks and moans. All the spirits of the ancestors who Mama told us lived on in our very walls were screaming. I'm sorry, Faith. I was already too deep in the darkness of fatigue and vaguely heard the frantic alerts in what I thought was a dream."

I was too upset to ask him to explain in more detail. He had never seemed so convinced that the house held voices. Little Paula had colic and for two days was constantly crying, especially at night, keeping not only Trevor and me awake but also Daddy and his girlfriend, Gabby, who slept in the bedroom that Daddy—Big John, as we often called him—used to sleep in with our mama, Paula. They constantly heard the baby's crying. Sometimes Daddy would scream, "Shut her up or take her downstairs!"

Daddy had recently returned from another long-haul trucking job with time requirements that caused him to violate safety rules and drive well over fifteen hours a day, sleeping and eating in his eighteen-wheeler. Gabby's brother, Nick, who was Daddy's best friend, often teamed up with him on jobs, though he couldn't this time because he had a new job himself. I knew Daddy was irritable because of his workload. Even his having both sides of the truck cabin proudly labeled EDEN TRUCKING didn't reduce the stress of the job. My baby's crying only added to his stress, but there was no doubt in my mind that Little Paula's colic wasn't what spurred him and Gabby to action. In fact, I now believed that they already had made that decision days after I had given birth to Little Paula, if not during my pregnancy.

Neither Trevor nor I saw any possible name for our baby but Paula. It was Mama's name, and she had planned for us to have a child and build a family in this very house. She'd had this in mind from the very day she set eyes on us in the foster home. Our biological mothers had deserted both of us. I could barely remember mine, but Trevor had a clear enough memory of his to wonder if he would recognize her on a street someday.

"Would she see me and walk right past me?" he sometimes asked aloud.

"How could a mother not know her own child?" I would say, but he remained skeptical. I understood his need to know.

We were empty vessels waiting to be filled with love. Mama saw this and saw Trevor's and my special relationship at the foster home. That was what made us perfect in her eyes, ideal to continue her family.

Nothing was more important to Mama than her family and the heritage that she had molded for us. She was confident that Trevor and I were the way to ensure it would all continue, because the affection and the need we had for each other were precisely what she said came with being part of a family. It was why she took such good care of us, homeschooled us, and taught us how precious her home and her legacy were to her. We weren't physically of her blood, but we would be spiritually.

"And believe me," she said, "that's more important. Blood-related brothers and sisters often grow up despising each other, competing, but you two won't ever hurt each other."

But that didn't mean our daddy wouldn't hurt us.

Little Paula was only three weeks old when they took her away from me. I quickly realized afterward that her being born in the house instead of a hospital was something Daddy and Gabby had planned as well. To make their intention easier for them, they had deceived me about my medical needs. Daddy always had been scheming ways to keep my pregnancy a secret and then find a way to make it seem as if it had never occurred. It was one more reason he wanted Trevor sleeping in another room.

So why would this abduction of Little Paula come as any surprise? Why wasn't I more suspicious, guarding my baby night and day?

"Trust," Mama once said, "is wonderful but dangerous. It makes you more vulnerable."

I wish I had remembered those words before it was too late.

Gabby had been taking me to see Dr. Lewis, an ob-gyn whom she claimed a friend of hers had recommended, which was why I had no idea of her and Big John's real plan. It seemed at first that they were doing everything they could to make all go well. I should have known something wasn't right when Gabby took me to Dr. Lewis, who practiced almost fifty miles away, instead of to a doctor nearby. There could be no local chatter, which helped maintain the secrecy Daddy wanted kept sacrosanct. No one knew me at the doctor's office; they didn't even know Gabby.

After I was showing at five months, I was forbidden to be outside where anyone could see me. No one but Nick was invited to the house. I was afraid, and Trevor was afraid for me should I be disobedient. Since Mama's passing, Daddy had no chains or doors confining his anger. I was sure his unbridled roar woke the sleeping ancestors. He could very well lock me up in the basement—or worse—so I didn't really complain that much or question their intention.

Daddy's size alone made him terrifying, even when he wasn't upset or irritable. It was why he was known as Big John, even to us. He lumbered through the house with his 240-pound, six-foot-four-inch body. I think the furniture even shuddered. When I was little, I definitely thought the earth shook. He wasn't unattractive, but he had facial features to match his size, his nose prominent and a little crooked, his lips thick, and his black eyes startling like bright ebony marbles with bushy dark brown eyebrows, eyebrows Mama always had to trim.

Gabby trimmed them now, and because she had once thought she'd be a hairdresser someday, she would cut his hair. She also did Trevor's reddish-brown hair, a shade lighter than Daddy's, but I didn't like her trimming mine. I thought her work was always uneven. Because mine was close to Mama's light brown, I felt even unhappier about it. I had wanted to look like her for Trevor and resisted as long as I could. It felt like it violated Mama, too, and if there was one thing I never wanted to do, it was add to the memory of her misery. But whatever resistance I had, it wilted when Daddy grimaced and said, "Let her do it. You look like a shaggy dog."

All during my pregnancy, I read and studied as much as I could about babies and how to care for them. "Oh, don't worry, don't worry," Gabby practically chanted. "Caring for babies just comes natural to a woman."

Nevertheless, I was anticipating more information and instruction from the doctor, especially as my birthing grew closer. "You don't have to keep seeing a baby doctor. You have to wait for your pregnancy to develop," she insisted. "You don't have any problems anyway."

Early on in my ninth month, however, I became a little suspicious, but Gabby did such a good job of allaying my concerns. Gabby had many excuses why she couldn't take me to see the doctor, but she constantly told me that I shouldn't worry. She said she had another close friend, Nina Stokin, who was a maternity nurse and would be here in a jiffy if I needed special attention.

Almost as soon as I began to have labor pains, Gabby told me they were nothing about which I should concern myself, that they weren't real, that this was common. Although she herself had never been pregnant, she constantly talked about her friends who had been and therefore claimed firsthand knowledge. She could be very sweet and convincing. It was hard to believe that, all along, she and Daddy were scheming. Every whisper between them should have lit my hair on fire.

Finally, because I complained so much, she had Nina stop by to examine me. Nina was a tall African American woman, almost as tall, I thought, as Daddy. Although she didn't smile much, she spoke with a confident tone that eased my concerns. She was just as confident as Gabby. She told me I was having Braxton-Hicks contractions, which were false labor pains women have before "true" labor.

"They're just your body getting ready for the real thing," she said.

I told her I had already had them at the beginning of the month. She finally smiled and assured me that I was still a good three to four weeks away from delivery and that being late was very common these days. She made pregnancy sound like some sort of modern phenomenon, and again, she reassured me that all was going as expected.

"I know three other young girls about your age who had babies. Seemed more like ten months, but of course, they probably lied about when and how they got pregnant."

I ignored her insinuation.

"The doctor told me I'd give birth about now, didn't he, Gabby?"

"Turns out, he's not all that good a maternity doctor," she said. "I didn't want to tell you and get you upset. Nina said she heard some bad things about him, didn't you, Nina? That's the real reason I stopped taking you to him immediately after she told me."

Nina just grimaced.

"Don't we have to find a new one, then?"

"Nina's as good. How many would you say you delivered, Nina?"

"Not counting my own, twenty, at least."

"See? Nothing to worry about," Gabby said.

They went off to have some wine and chat before Nina left.

Of course, I soon had good reason to doubt Nina, despite her assurances. The very next day, in fact, the pain increased, and the contractions were closer together. They began to last longer, too. I cried and complained, but Gabby and Daddy were drinking more since his return from his recent trip. They partied with Nick downstairs in our finished basement into the early hours and practically had to drag each other up the stairs when he was set to leave.

Hours later, I screamed.

Trevor came running in. I was already sitting on the edge of the bed.

"What's happening?"

"My water broke," I said.

He turned on the light, saw it, and ran for Gabby. She was quite dazed, still quite drunk, but the sight of what was happening woke her enough for her to call Nina. Nina told her things to do until she arrived. And Little Paula waited for her, waited to enter this world.

While the birthing was happening, Trevor was so terrified that he couldn't bring himself back into the bedroom. After nearly five hours, Little Paula was born in my very bed. Several times, I thought I would die.

At the end, I managed to say, "I thought you said I was having false labor."

Nina ignored me, cared for the baby, and left as soon as she could. She didn't even wish me luck. Again, I missed the signals between her and Gabby, signals that would have confirmed she was part of their plan.

After Little Paula and I were settled in, Trevor came to see me.

I was cradling our baby. Nina had left some instructions before she had gone home, and Gabby and Daddy couldn't wait to get back to sleep.

"How are you?" Trevor asked.

"Exhausted," I said. "She's beautiful, isn't she?"

I turned the baby toward him.

"Yes," he said. I knew what he was thinking. "It's almost as if Mama is here," he added.

I smiled and nodded.

Little Paula was sleeping, occasionally whimpering.

"She's probably having a nightmare that she was born," Trevor said. "I'm sure I did."

We both laughed, even though the memories of our own infancy were better left smothered.

I closed my eyes. Trevor kissed me on the cheek and, despite Daddy's warning, got into bed beside me. He put his arm around me, and I cradled my head against his shoulder. He kissed my forehead. I saw the smile on his face, but I was afraid to smile, too. It almost didn't seem right to be happy with Mama gone. I would forever blame myself. Both of us blamed ourselves.

Trevor had convinced me that Little Paula was going to restore both of us, bring light to the dark pain of sorrow. So comfortable and secure were we in each other's arms, I let myself believe it. But neither Trevor nor I could imagine, after the first happy night with Little Paula, how threatened our lives as a very, very young family would be.

ONE

When Little Paula started her uncontrollable crying a week or
so after she was born, I knew, even without the confirma-
tion of a doctor, that she had colic. However, nothing I had read on
the internet, no comments I saw from other new mothers, and not
even medical journals I had read seemed to have a definitive cause
for it or a perfect cure.

Some thought it was simply acclimation to the world outside
the womb, which could make babies irritable for some time. Others
thought they might be reacting to gas, having something called acid
reflux. Some suggested allergies. I tried all the remedies described,
especially laying her on her tummy, carrying her constantly,
and making sure to hold her upright after she fed. I massaged

her, gave her a pacifier, and even sang and hummed to her for hours.

Her crying even kept our cats, Moses and Becky, from coming upstairs. Maybe they thought she was another cat. They hadn't been behaving like themselves since Mama died, anyway. They'd stay away for days sometimes. Trevor went looking for them when they didn't return recently. If he had found them killed by some coyote or some other animal, he didn't tell me. I didn't want to look hard at him and see the truth. There was almost no other reason they wouldn't have come home by now. Daddy certainly didn't care or wonder. They were more Mama's pets than his. Besides, Little Paula was taking up most of my time and concern. There was a great deal I didn't think about, including my own appearance.

Last night, Gabby came into my bedroom and said she would give me some hours of relief and take Little Paula into her and Daddy's room for a while.

"Get some sleep," she said. "It doesn't do the baby any good if you're exhausted."

"Are you sure?" I had some trepidation, but I really was exhausted and had just finished breastfeeding her.

"Your father told me to tell you that," she said, which was a little surprising. Up until that moment, he rarely seemed to care about any difficulties I was having. He never came to look in on the baby and me and said almost nothing about her, about how beautiful and perfect she was. I thought maybe he didn't like the thought of being a grandfather.

If he had known Mama's true plan for us from the start, he either ignored it or, after some small attempts, just gave up caring. Most of the time, he returned home too tired to argue or wanting to save his energy for partying. However, we knew that from the

first day Trevor and I were brought from the Wexler foster home
to Mama and Big John Eden's home and were adopted, Big John
was opposed to us sleeping in the same bed. Trevor was nearly six,
and I was little more than four, but he still didn't think it was right.
Mama told him he was being ridiculous. There really wasn't much
choice when it came to where we would be, anyway: Mama already
had turned the other available guest room into a classroom for us.
She was determined to homeschool us. She had been a grade-school
teacher and was confident she could give us a better education than
what we would get in the "inferior" public schools.

There was one other possible bedroom in the house, but when
Mama was alive, that was kept locked most of the time, and we were
told almost from the first moment we arrived that it was the Forbidden Room. More than ten years later, when Mama and Trevor
caught me out behind the garage with our neighbor's grandson,
Lance, she had put me in the Forbidden Room and locked the
door. That alone was terrifying. Big John was on a cross-country
trip, though his being home wouldn't have helped. He surely would
have been quite angry, too, and wouldn't have interfered. In fact, he
might have beaten me with that thick belt he wore, something he
always threatened to do.

Inside the Forbidden Room, Mama had told me to go to the
unmade, stripped bed and wait. Neither I nor Trevor had ever seen
her so enraged. Whatever she had given me to drink put me in such
a daze that I didn't realize where I was or what was happening to me.
I spent two nights in a row like that. I had forgiven Mama for it and
forgiven Trevor for what she made him do to me while I was in that
room in my stupor.

As we grew older, and Mama still didn't give us separate
bedrooms, there was no longer any doubt that Big John under-

stood what Mama's intentions were. Neither of us ever heard him specifically say it, but it was like one of those blemishes or scars on someone's face that you pretend not to see. There is blindness that provides comfort.

I quickly realized that what terrified Mama was that I could become pregnant from being with someone else, someone she would consider outside our family.

Mr. Longstreet, our neighbor, had his grandson Lance visiting from New York City because his parents were in a somewhat nasty divorce proceeding. He was very handsome, and I dreamed of him wanting me to be his girlfriend and returning often to see me. Of course, if I had been a little more experienced, I might not have been so surprised to learn that he did have a girlfriend back in New York and was after me for one thing only.

Mama had been beside herself when Trevor revealed I was to rendezvous with Lance. Trevor didn't like betraying me, but there was never a doubt in my mind that he wanted to please Mama more.

Mama wasn't wrong about Trevor's and my relationship. There was always something very special between us. From the first day we were brought together at the foster home, both of us having been given up by our mothers, we stayed close to each other and practically ignored the existence of the other children. The Wexlers' daughter, a woman we called Nanny Too because she had been a nanny and now basically ran the foster home, was annoyed by this. She said we were so close that we shared a shadow.

We were ecstatic when Mama Eden decided she wanted us both. We weren't just getting a mother; we were escaping. And together!

Since we had been so close when we lived at the foster home, we thought nothing of having the same bedroom and sharing so much in Mama Eden's family house. She had met and married Big John after her parents were killed in an accident in their pickup truck on one of the winding Pocono mountain roads. She had resigned her teaching position as soon as she realized she was financially able to do so because of her inheritance. She had hated her job.

Mama tried hard to convince us that her family was built into our house, that their spirits roamed it and their concern for us would never weaken. I was always a little suspicious about there being family spirits in the house, but I wasn't afraid. After all, considering what we had already suffered in our lives, how could two little children feel any more secure and comfortable than we were?

We trusted her with everything, but I didn't want to be forced to have a baby, especially when I discovered what was in the Forbidden Room. I found that it was a room meant to be a bedroom and nursery, though not for my use originally. Her mother had become pregnant at a late age, and the intent had been to have a live-in nanny. There was a crib in the room, of course. Even before I looked into it the second day of my imprisonment, I felt the shock of what I would discover in that crib. It was as if I had always known what was there. Trevor admitted later that he had known.

No one was better at keeping a secret than Trevor.

Mama said the remains of the undeveloped baby, carefully bundled like a living infant, were the result of her mother's miscarriage, something Mama had caused with a so-called herbal medication to ease her mother's pain in her pregnancy. Her mother had miscarried in the bathroom in the Forbidden Room, and the room afterward had been turned into a shrine. Big John let it remain a shrine. I think he knew that she would have asked him to leave if he hadn't.

So afterward, after my two days of punishment, when she had insisted I return to sleeping with Trevor, I resisted. I knew what she wanted and knew what she had told Trevor to do, but I didn't want to get pregnant and maybe have as horrible a miscarriage as her mother had had. I had read that pregnancy for a girl my age was difficult. Undoubtedly, I was quite afraid of Mama's rage, but I wanted to sleep in Big John's den on the sofa bed, at least until he returned from his latest trip. I was hoping Mama would calm down by then.

Mama had broken her ankle falling from a ladder in a terrible rainstorm. She had intended to go onto the roof and fix a bad leak or at least plug it up temporarily. In a cast and on a crutch, she confronted me starting down the stairs with my bedding and tried to force me to return to Trevor's and my bedroom. She poked me with her crutch, attempting to drive me back, and in the process, she fell backward on the stairs and injured her head so badly that she died in the operating room.

Big John had his friend Nick Damien's sister Gabrielle come live with us. We didn't know at the time that Big John had been having an affair with her. Mama certainly didn't know. He had buried Mama's unborn sister in our Cemetery for Unhappiness, a patch of land on our property that Mama had designated as a place to bury terrible thoughts and comments so they would never haunt Trevor or me again.

I was surprised when Trevor voiced how guilty and responsible he felt over Mama's death. I had thought he would blame it all on me. But although Trevor didn't expect my relationship with Lance to go as far as it almost had, he admitted he had done more than I had to bring the other boy into our lives. He was responsible for setting up our internet connections, which Lance and I used for secret messages, so I understood why Trevor felt he had disappointed

Mama, too. Whenever I debate with myself about my pregnancy, about my willingness to go forward, I conclude now, and probably will until the day I die, that our having Little Paula was the only way to redeem myself when it came to what had happened to Mama. Trevor believed that from the very first moment.

Trevor, who had his driver's license by the time I had gone into my eighth month, woke up one morning, turned to me, and said, "Let's go show Mama what we've done."

We drove to the cemetery and stood by her grave so she would know that what she had always wanted was going to be. We were going to create a new family. I understood Trevor had made special promises to Mama, promises I had never known about.

The morning after Gabby had relieved me of caring for Little Paula, I awoke, surprised I had slept so late. Trevor had gone downstairs for breakfast and was already gone. He was attending the public school, which I was unable to do because I had become pregnant. Big John wasn't going to continue homeschooling, so Gabby had enrolled him. After he started, Trevor sent a chilling wave through me one day when he said, "Big John forbade me ever to mention you, and so no one knows you exist." Before I could ask, he added, "You know why."

It's a strange feeling to have, the feeling that so few people knew you were alive on this same earth. It empties you in ways you never experience otherwise. Sometimes I'd look in the mirror and wonder, *Am I still here?* During the days when Big John was on a trip and Gabby was at work at the insurance company, I'd hear no living voice other than my own in the house. I was talking to myself the way I remembered Mama often did. I even spoke to the imaginary ancestors, too, although I really wasn't sure that the creaks and moans in the house were their responses.

Whenever Trevor came home in the afternoon, I would vehemently insist that he sit and tell me about his day, every detail. Of course, I was most interested in how he saw the other students and how they saw him. He said they were suspicious.

"Of what?" I asked, thinking someone had found out about me.

"Of my doing well, being normal, because I was homeschooled all my life. It's going to take time to make friends," he concluded. "And Big John has already made it clear that I can't invite anyone here, not even to play basketball or go with me into our woods. He said I can't go to anyone's house, either, because they would then expect to be invited to mine."

"It's all because of me," I concluded, feeling bad for him.

"Because of both of us," he said, but he didn't sound despondent or unhappy about it. He looked happy, even proud. I was already three months pregnant.

While he was in school and Gabby and Daddy were working, I had to clean the house and use my free time to move ahead in the textbooks Mama had for us both in the homeschool classroom. I still dreamed of joining Trevor at the public school someday, somehow. However, Big John often threatened to throw out all the books, the computer, the microscope, and the desks so he could make it a guest room.

"We have friends we're going to want to stay over someday," he said. He seemed to growl more than talk these days. It was as if Mama had laid a punishment on him in the form of us, of me especially, and he was resentful of our very existence. I never spoke back, but my look probably spoke pages.

Perhaps she knew you were having an affair, I thought, looking at him. *Maybe, if you want to call us a punishment, we are. She used us for her revenge.*

Trevor and I enjoyed the days when Big John was off on a trucking job. Gabby was kind enough to us, but it was easy to see that she was almost as terrified as we were of disobeying any of Big John's rules when he was gone. She was so attentive to my needs and complaints during my pregnancy during the early months that I could never have imagined her cooperating with Big John when it came to getting Little Paula out of our lives.

That morning, Trevor was already gone before I rose, and hadn't even said goodbye. In fact, there was no one in the house. The moment I woke, the silence was like a clap of thunder. I sat up quickly and listened, and then, thinking Gabby was with Little Paula, I went to the bedroom she shared with Big John.

Knocking softly, I called, "Gabby?"

Greeted by silence, I opened the door and saw there was no one there. Now in more of a panic, I went to the top of the stairs, listened, and called, "Gabby?"

I hurried down the stairs to the kitchen. No one. To the living room. No one. It was spring. Gabby might have taken Little Paula out to see if fresh air would help soothe her, I thought, really hoped. But there was no one on the porch and no one at the side or rear of the house. I ran everywhere in my bare feet and nightgown, screaming for someone, and then I retreated into the house and sat stunned at the kitchen table.

I wept and put my head down on my crossed arms. What was happening? Shuddering and feeling a little chilled, I went upstairs, washed my feet, changed into a blouse and jeans, and went down again, this time waiting by the living-room window. I couldn't eat; I didn't even want to have water, but I did. Hours and hours went by. I dozed off, and then, finally, I heard Gabby's car pull into the driveway. I leaped up and hurried to the rear door.

Big John and Gabby got out of the car, but there was no sign of Little Paula.

"*Where's my baby?*" I screamed.

"Gone to where she'll have a real home. And now," Big John said, "you can be a teenage girl again, finish school, and either get a job or get married. You want to grow up fast, grow up fast. You should thank us."

He walked right past me, nearly bowling me over. I looked at Gabby. She tried to smile but lowered her head and followed him in. I collapsed on the step, embraced myself, and didn't move until Trevor returned from school. The realization was spinning around in my head and hadn't stopped. Little Paula was gone forever.

"What are you doing sitting out here?" Trevor asked when he came home from school and got out of what had been Mama's car.

"They gave away Little Paula," I said, and finally released my tears.

"*Gave away?* What does that mean?"

"I don't know," I said, and continued to cry.

He walked past me and into the house.

When I entered a moment later, Gabby was sitting in the kitchenette having a cup of coffee. Big John was having a beer. Trevor was standing off to the side by the doorway, his head down, looking ashamed.

"Where's my baby?" I asked as firmly as I could.

"I told you," Big John said. "You'd best do what I say now. I'm not gonna take to no whinin' and cryin'. We heard enough of that to last a year these past days."

Gabby looked up at me. "It's best, honey. You go up and rest. I'll find out what you do about . . . about the breastfeeding."

"Breastfeeding? Who am I breastfeeding?"

"No one, but there are things to do," she said.

"Go on," Big John said. "Do as you're told."

I looked at Trevor, who looked like he wanted to swallow his lips, and then I walked past him and up the stairs. Normally, anyone my age would surely not want to get pregnant and have a baby. They might even be grateful for what Big John and Gabby had done. I hadn't really thought hard and deep about what it would mean, but after Little Paula was born, I didn't regret her. Suddenly and completely, she had become my world. I was sure that only someone who'd had a part of her body lopped off would understand the dark emptiness that was rushing over me.

And what about our promise to Mama? I didn't like being forced to keep it, but it had been done.

Trevor came into the bedroom. I was in a tight fetal position, sobbing softly.

"There's nothing we can do about it now," Trevor said. "They're the adults. They make all the decisions for us in this house."

"They're not adults. They're monsters," I said. "Mama must be spinning in her grave."

He nodded and sat on the bed. Then he reached for my hand and gave me his determined glare.

"What?"

"Someday," he said, "somehow, we'll get her back, back where she belongs."

I stopped sobbing and looked at him. "Promise?"

"It's a promise we're making to Mama."

"Yes," I said, and sat up. Excitement was rushing over me. "You're right. That's what we'll do."

"For now," he said in his sly, Trevor kind of way, "let's let them think they've gotten away with it. Let them think we're settled;

we've accepted what they think must be. It's late in the school year, but maybe you will go to school for a while, while we plan."

"I couldn't now. All I would think about is Little Paula."

He shrugged his famous shrug. "Maybe you'll find another boyfriend." He smiled.

"Did you find another girlfriend already?"

"No. But sometimes," he said with a surprisingly melancholy tone, "sometimes, when I look at how happy and excited most of the other kids in my class are, I wish Mama had let us go to public school from the start and we were . . ."

"Were what?"

"Normal," he said. "Like have friends and go to parties and sporting events, everything we didn't have."

"Did you know they were going to do this? You did, didn't you?"

"I had a suspicion."

"Why didn't you warn me? I wouldn't have let her leave my side."

"They'd only find another way. What could I do? I'd have to quit school and guard the door."

"But . . ."

"Patience," he said. "Once they've failed at doing it once, they'll never do it again. We have special protection. You'll see, Faith."

I should have been surprised to hear him say such a thing. I should have been a little angry, in fact. Little Paula was gone. Even if she was gone for only a short time, it was still painful.

And how could he mourn about our lost youth? That was selfish.

But I wasn't surprised or angry.

I was suddenly even sadder, so sad that I was no longer sure if my tears were for Little Paula or for myself.

TWO

L ater that afternoon, Gabby rushed out and got me a firmer new bra with pads to soak up any milk leaking from my breasts. Nina told her to have me put cold gel packs in my bra to help relieve the aches.

"Nina said you should sleep on your back and use an extra pillow to support your breasts when you're on your side. You'll use this, too," she said, taking something out of a box.

"What is it?"

"A manual breast pump. Nina said that manual feels the most natural."

"Natural?"

"She breastfed her own two children at the start and then went to bottles so she could work. So she knows."

I glared at her. None of it would feel natural. How could taking a three-week-old baby from her mother lead to anything natural?

"Why didn't she at least come here to see how I was? I told you days ago that I still have some bleeding and headaches once in a while. I thought she was your good friend and cared."

"She is. She'd just . . . just rather not be involved anymore," Gabby admitted.

"Why not?"

"Don't ask me to state the obvious, Faith. You're a very smart girl." She smiled. "This will all pass in a few weeks, and then we'll talk about what to do next."

"Next? You mean my going to school?"

"We'll talk about it later. He's got to do a run tomorrow. He'll actually be gone nearly two weeks. Maybe you'll be all better by then and he'll be willing to talk about it."

"Better?"

"This will be over," she said sharply, not liking to repeat herself or sound ugly. "Just eat and do what you do normally. My advice is to pretend none of it happened."

"Like you two pretend? How do I do that? It happened to *me*."

She glared, told me the directions for the pump were in the box, and walked out.

I looked at the pump. This was to be my baby's lips? I wanted to heave it down the stairs, but I felt the pressure building in my breasts and instead read the directions. Maybe it was my desperate imagination, but I envisioned Little Paula when I began to use it. *Somewhere, wherever she is, she's feeding now, too,* I thought. Could she possibly be missing me as much as I was missing her? Was there the same emptiness in her heart? Surely, she was crying. Maybe whomever they gave her to was regretting accepting her and would show up on our doorstep with her. I imagined the scene with Little Paula screaming and reaching out for me.

"This was a terrible mistake," whoever held her would say. Both Big John and Gabby would look ashamed. I nearly fell asleep pumping my breasts and holding on to the dream.

Afterward, truly feeling exhausted again, I rested for nearly a half hour before I went down and saw that Gabby was sitting in Big John's den, watching her favorite soap, *General Hospital*. She had recorded it because she had to watch it when Big John wasn't here. Sometimes we watched it together, especially when she was home for one reason or another during the week. I used to wonder how she kept her job, because she wasn't sick. Whenever she raved about one of the actors in the show, Tristan Rogers, I would threaten to tell Big John.

Teasing Gabby had been fun before she cooperated with Big John to steal my baby. She was like the big sister I never had, often talking about makeup and clothes. Sometimes I thought Trevor felt the same way about her because she was so kind to him, often bringing home something she thought he could wear to school. Now, with the way she behaved, not putting up any resistance to Little Paula being given away, neither Trevor nor I would ever accept her as our stepmother if Big John married her . . . unless, of course, she realized how terrible it was and how terrible it made us feel and then talked Big John into bringing Little Paula back.

Was that the fantasy Trevor often accused me of having? Our surname was Eden. We'd joke about it sometimes and call ourselves Adam and Eve. Perhaps because we were so sheltered from the outside world, we were just as naive and vulnerable to serpents.

She turned, hearing me in the kitchen.

"All go well?" she asked.

I looked at her. "Do you think this is all like your soap opera? Today's episode?"

She turned away.

"If you don't wise up," she said without looking at me, "Big John will find a way to get you back into a foster home."

Right now, I wished he would, I thought, only the chance that Trevor and I would be separated was great. Anyway, we were legally adopted. How would he explain giving us up? Tell people that I ruined his life by getting pregnant? I didn't think so. Ironically, he was as trapped by having us as we were by having him as a father.

I gazed angrily at Gabby sitting so comfortably in Big John's chair. He was so big that his body was etched in the cushion. Sitting in his chair was like putting on his glove. She curled herself snugly, pulling her legs up and in. Maybe in her imagination she was sitting on his lap.

"Where is he?" I asked.

"He's gone to have some minor work done on his truck for tomorrow's trip," she replied. "I have a roast in the oven with some of Big John's favorite potatoes. Maybe you can do the salad. Nick always did our salads at dinner," she mused.

She told me that so often that I began to wonder if she really didn't miss that life. She wasn't cut out to be a homemaker, maybe not even a wife. Surely, she'd overcook the roast.

Gabby turned, her face softening. Her real name was Gabrielle. She was a buxom woman with raspberry-red hair. She was only an inch or so taller than Mama had been. When Daddy first brought Nick and her over to party in the basement, I thought that because she had so many freckles even at thirty, she had never gotten married and had short-lived romances. Men assumed there was something childish about her, perhaps. But I liked her back then. She had a smile that reminded me of a full-blown dandelion, one that caught and held the sun.

Would I ever see the sun in her again?

"My mother wanted us to have that baby," I said, practically blurted.

Her eyes widened, and she turned completely around, nearly jumping in the chair.

"What? That's ridiculous."

"To you, maybe."

"She told you that?"

"Not in those exact words, but both of us knew it was what she wanted."

I could see her grinding the information through her brain.

"Big John never told me anything like that. I know you're not really brother and sister, but . . . you've been brought up to think you are."

She shook herself as if she had just had a chill.

"The very thought of me and Nick having a baby . . ."

"It's not the same thing," I said. "Where did you take Little Paula? We have to bring her back. She belongs here. Mama wanted her to live here and keep our family going."

She turned completely back to the television screen and once again curled up snugly in Big John's chair.

"You did a terrible thing," I said, my eyes hazy with tears.

She didn't turn around. She made the television louder.

I walked out of the house.

Trevor had the hood up on Mama's car and was leaning over with a wrench in his hand.

"What's wrong with the car?"

He paused.

"Nothing. Big John's always after me to tighten hoses and such. Maintenance. Remember how he made me work beside him on his eighteen-wheeler's engine, greasing and oiling? Before Mama died, he told her I had the makings of a really good mechanic."

"How can you still think of that, think of wanting his praise?"

"I'm just recalling it. There were good days, too."

I nodded reluctantly. As difficult as it was to recall them now, after what he had done, there were.

"Anyway, he says a car is a responsibility, not a joy toy, and he told me if I didn't take care of it, he'd stop me from driving."

I stared at him. Trevor had shot up this last year and was either six feet tall or close to it. Maybe because Big John made him do so many of the heavy chores around the house, his shoulders were thicker and his torso leaner and beginning to ripple with muscle. I liked looking at him when he was naked and didn't know I was looking. I had the feeling he liked looking at me that way, too, unseen.

"Oh, Big John says to do it," I muttered. "That's gospel around here."

"I figure we should keep on his good side for now, at least, Faith."

"I hate him," I said. "He has no good side."

He nodded and returned to what he was doing. I walked around the garage. For some reason, I wanted to look at the place where I had met Lance that night, because in my mind it was where all this had begun. There was nothing especially evil or ugly to see when I envisioned our rendezvous. In fact, the memories titillated me, especially when I recalled his hands exploring my body, my nipples erect and tingling, and my thighs weakening and relaxing as his fingers glided over them to get at my panties. I could almost hear myself moan, or was I moaning right now at the memory?

"Hey!" I heard. Trevor had stepped toward me, wiping his hands with a piece of an old gray towel. "What are you doing? What are you looking at?"

"Dreaming of running away," I said. He stepped up to me, put his arm around my shoulders, tempting me to lay my head against his.

"That won't get Little Paula back to us."

"I know. I asked Gabby again what they did with Little Paula. She wouldn't answer. I thought she would be more sympathetic. She was so nice to me after Mama died. And to you, too."

"Working her way in," he said. "She's a conniver."

"What do you mean?"

He didn't answer.

"Trevor?"

"I met someone at school whose mother works for the same insurance company Gabby does."

"Who?" I asked, stepping away. It was just the tone in his voice when he had said "someone."

"Christina Grant. Her father's an accountant. Maybe because of that, she's a math genius or something."

I narrowed my eyes. "Is she pretty?"

"Hardly. She's short, almost a dwarf, with hair that looks like she dips it into an inkwell every morning before coming to school, strands leaking down the side of her head and over her forehead. When she talks to you, her eyes give you the feeling you're getting an X-ray."

"Sounds like you talk to her a lot."

He smiled. "I'm lazy. I steal her math problem solutions."

"She probably has a crush on you."

He shrugged.

"Anyway, when I mentioned Gabby, she told me Gabby has her job only because she had an affair with the manager of the insurance company, a married man. Her mother doesn't like Gabby. She says her mother calls her an empty sock. Not to her face, of course. I didn't reveal that it bothered me."

"You gave her the Trevor shrug?"

He laughed. "Yeah, something like that."

"I'd better get into that school soon, or you'll get into trouble," I said.

He really shrugged this time. Why wasn't I surprised?

"There's a little more than two months left to the school year, Faith. Maybe they'll want you to wait until the fall. I mean, you still have to go through some stuff."

"Right. Stuff."

"And then what will you do when we get Little Paula back? You can't go to school and care for her. And you certainly can't expect Gabby would give up her job to stay with her."

"Why did you even say I would?"

"I wanted you to be less sad."

"Eventually, I will, even after Little Paula's back."

He nodded, but not with confidence.

"We'll find someone else to help, maybe," I said. "A nanny."

"And pay her with what money?"

"Mama must have left us money," I said, my voice straining. I couldn't stand to hear anything negative, anything discouraging. "She planned for us to have a family. Didn't she?"

"Maybe there's money for us; maybe there isn't. We don't know anything about the costs and expenses of the house. We have a lot to learn that Big John isn't showing or telling us."

He paused.

"I know it's unfair for you to bear most of the burden. Believe me. I think about what it would be."

"I don't care if we can't afford someone. I'll sacrifice school until we figure it out. As long as we get Little Paula back."

"Right," he said. He didn't sound as confident as he had the first time.

"Were you just saying all that to keep me calm? I *will* run away if we don't get her back," I threatened. "Whether or not you come with me."

"Okay. Don't get yourself wound up. I wasn't just saying it. We'll get her back," he said with more firmness.

I looked toward the fieldstone wall that supposedly was built by Mama's grandfather, who had piled on rock after rock with hands she said had palms as rough as tree bark. The wall ran from the main road parallel to our house and a little farther than a half mile behind it. He had stopped six inches from someone else's property.

"Funny how Mr. Longstreet hasn't come by since Mama's death," I said, referring to our neighbor. "I liked him. Still do."

"Maybe he's afraid Big John blames him for stuff."

"Stuff again? What? Lance?"

"Let's not rake up what's buried in the Cemetery for Unhappiness, Faith. Don't look for trouble," he said. "Just be patient."

"Patient?" It stung. "You don't live without seeing anyone. You go to school," I said, and started into the forest, walking very quickly, practically jogging. I went right up to the stone wall and looked at Mr. Longstreet's house, hoping to catch a glimpse of him. Although I should have been ashamed of my being so naive and nearly spoiled by his grandson, I couldn't stop myself from wanting to revive some of those exciting memories.

Trevor walked up behind me.

I glanced back at him and then looked at the house. "I'm going over to say hello and see how he is."

"Better not. I really don't know why he hasn't come around. Big John might have threatened him and warned him to stay away from us."

"I don't care."

I started over the wall, and he put his hands on my waist.

"Please, Faith. If you make more trouble now, we'll have a harder time getting Little Paula back."

I paused. Maybe he was right. I turned and sat on the wall, facing him.

"Really, Trevor. How are we going to do this? How are we going to get Little Paula back? Are you just trying to keep me from doing something like visit Mr. Longstreet and causing more trouble, or do you have a real plan?"

"I have some ideas, but I don't want to say anything yet."

We locked eyes.

"You *do* have some ideas," I said.

Trevor and I really did have trouble lying to each other. Whether Mama was right about our spiritual ties or not, this much was true.

He reached for my hand. "Let's go back and put on the best performances of our lives every day for now, Faith. When their guard is down, they'll reveal what we need to know."

"Lie and deceive, just like them?"

"It's not like Mama is here, and neither of us really wants to deceive and be false," he added. "It's different now. You can see that, right?"

"Yes. Okay," I said.

We started back together. Before we reached the house, Big

John drove his truck in. Trevor paused, and we watched him get out, holding a puppy, cradling it in his arms; it looked like a golden retriever.

"Is he kidding?" I said. "That is supposed to replace Little Paula?"

Trevor smiled. "Mama wouldn't let him have another dog after a bear killed Critter, remember? She told him she'd end up caring for it because he was gone so much with trucking stuff. I'm sure he's gotten it for himself more than to make us feel better about losing Little Paula."

"I'll . . ."

"Go along with it, Faith. Remember what we're trying to do."

"Okay," I said, frustrated.

We continued to the house. It wasn't going to be difficult accepting and loving the puppy. Big John wanted him to have the same name as his other dog, Critter. He was adorable. Nevertheless, I was so tempted to be sarcastic and continue my rage. It was on the tip of my tongue to say, "What do you think? I'll breastfeed him?"

But I smothered any negative thoughts. I even managed some smiles. Trevor was better at it than I was, but I was good enough to wonder if I really would accept the loss of Little Paula.

"He's adorable," Gabby said. "How did you get him?"

"Fred Eckert's purebred had eight puppies. He had a 'Puppies for Sale' sign up. He gave me a discount because I use him for the truck so much," Big John told her. He looked at us. "You two better take care of him real good while I'm away."

Well, Mama would have corrected, but I said nothing.

"Sure," Trevor said.

He handed Critter to me. Maybe I had a natural love for babies of all kinds now, but I couldn't help being happy about him. Later,

I would chastise myself for loving anything, ever, until Little Paula was back.

Big John went back to his truck and brought in the dog food, a collar, a leash, and a bowl that had CRITTER written on it.

"How did you get a bowl with his name on it so fast?" Trevor asked him.

"It's not new. I had it in the truck since the day Critter died. Your mother wanted me to bury it in that Cemetery for Unhappiness of hers. Don't look so surprised," he said. "She had those crazy ideas before you two got here. Had me believin' every creak in this house was one of her relatives, moanin' or somethin'. It's a wonder I'm not kooky between things she done and what you two done."

I looked at Trevor. Were we going to let him beat on us forever?

He kept his lips pressing down on the words I was sure were jamming up in his mouth.

"I'll make the salad," I said, to break the silence and avoid hearing any more of his complaints about us.

"Let's eat in the dining room tonight," Gabby said. "Feels like some sort of celebration with the new Critter."

Big John grunted his agreement and put the collar on Critter. Trevor helped Gabby set the table. As usual, Big John plopped himself in his easy chair in his den, waiting to be told everything was done and ready. Critter followed him and lay at his side.

The dog couldn't love him that fast, I thought. *He's just aware of who reigns as king here.*

Everyone became a different person in his or her life, I mused as I worked and listened to his television blaring. Some changed a few more times than others. Both Trevor and I were so different from who we were ten years ago, and not just because we were infants then. A new life, new sounds, new things to do and taste remade us. Mama remade us.

Even Big John was once much happier and even a little loving. He approved of adopting us, and for a time, he was truly the father we'd never had or known. He would bring us gifts from his trips and enjoyed the wonder of us. I think he had always wanted children, perhaps to counter his own troubled childhood living with an alcoholic mother and no father. He especially loved to tickle me and pretend to be a monster, chasing me through the house until Mama made him stop. And he loved grabbing Trevor by the ankles and swinging him around upside down. Trevor screamed, but he never cried. It was his fun-fair roller-coaster ride. Even Mama would laugh sometimes and then tell him to be more careful.

When we were smaller, we would crawl over him and try to tickle him whenever he sprawled out on the living-room floor. Mama said it was like Gulliver in the land of Lilliput, but we'd have to read *Gulliver's Travels* to understand. She promised that we would, and at least I did. Trevor wasn't as much of a reader.

Who was this man now in his den, looking bitter and unhappy so much of the time, even before the birth of Little Paula? I wondered.

Was he planning to leave and live somewhere else with Gabby? Desert us? Maybe when Mama died, his conscience nagged at him. He was still in her family house, no matter how much he ridiculed the idea of ancestors living with us. Maybe he heard them at night. Perhaps that was why he was eager to drink too much and lose himself in a stupor so often. I wasn't even sure whether Gabby was making him happy half the time. How could a woman who feared you more than loved you make you happy?

How different our lives would be now if I hadn't been defiant and angry on that stairway. Big John would have left us for sure, but all three of us, Mama, Trevor, and I, would be raising Little Paula. I could go to school. Mama would have told everyone she was her daughter. I would have had everything, my child and a school life with friends. Perhaps in the end, Trevor and I would have found someone else; perhaps not, but it was fun to imagine.

I realized that Critter had returned to the kitchen. He sniffed around me and whined. I lifted him and held him just the way I would hold Little Paula. Then, as if I realized I was enjoying it, I dropped him hard on the floor, and he yelped. I wanted to pick him up again, but I didn't. When I looked up, Big John was in the doorway, looking like he was growing bigger and bigger every second.

"You hurt that animal and I'll hurt you," he threatened.

Trevor hurried back in and picked up Critter to pet and calm him. I returned to the preparation of the salad, my heart pounding, while Big John stood there glaring.

"The roast is ready," Gabby declared.

It looked dried out, but Big John wouldn't complain, at least in front of us. I knew that he wanted to prove his life was better with Gabby than it had been with Mama.

Everyone was sickeningly quiet at dinner. I recalled our earlier meals when Mama was alive. She talked so much that everyone was long finished with their meal before she was even halfway through. Trevor would get Big John to describe his road trips. When he knew where he was going, Trevor would look up the places he had to drive through and ask him questions about them. Most of the time, we realized Big John didn't half look at the scenery. He was like a robot, driving his eighteen-wheeler and listening to talk radio. He smoked his cigars, something Mama wouldn't let him do anywhere in the house but the den.

Now he smoked wherever he liked. Gabby said nothing. I was

sure our ancestors squirmed and grunted at the odor that seeped into the walls and the furniture. I was afraid of criticizing him or reminding him it was something Mama hated. I once mentioned her in a similar way, and he quickly snapped back, "She'd be alive and be here, 'cept 'cause of you."

He could bring tears to my eyes faster than a bowl of onions.

He's pretending, I thought. *He doesn't care about her being gone. But swallow your thoughts, Faith*, I told myself. *Study how Trevor does it, and do the same.* I often had nightmares of Big John standing above me at night after Mama had died. Like some creepy shadow, he spilled over the walls and ceiling. Before I'd given birth, I would instinctively press my palms protectively over my belly and wake with a start. Trevor was always asleep and never believed Big John would haunt me, haunt us, like that.

"Don't make him out to be any worse than he is," he advised. "It only comes back at you. Try not to think about him that much."

Maybe that was the solution: *Don't look at him; look through him; don't hear him unless he's telling you something to do. Ignore him.*

Later that night, when we were in bed, Trevor began to whisper.

"After he leaves on this trip, we'll start to explore."

"Explore?"

"I'll pretend to be sick one day and stay home from school. When Gabby leaves for work, we'll look for whatever paperwork they have on Little Paula. Clues."

"So we can find her?"

"Yes."

"But he won't let us bring her back here, Trevor."

"One thing at a time," he said.

"You know something else, don't you? You wouldn't even think of this if you didn't."

"Just sleep on it for now, and dream of having her back," he said, avoiding my eyes.

My breasts began to ache.

"I've got to use the pump," I said. "I'll go to the bathroom."

"You don't have to," he said. He sat up. "Go on."

I turned on the light and lowered my nightgown. He looked mesmerized.

"I'm imagining her," he said.

"Me, too."

"Mama talks to me," he suddenly said. "Even when I'm in school."

"What?"

"I hear her, Faith. Just like she heard her relatives, her ancestors. You've heard them."

I stared at him. I thought I had, but I could have been imagining it. I wasn't afraid of frightening him as much as I was of frightening myself.

"Haven't you?" he asked, almost angrily.

"Yes, of course," I said.

He nodded and lowered himself to the pillow again. Often, he did look like he was listening to Mama speaking. He looked that way now.

I finished and put out the lights. In the morning, I remembered what I thought had been a dream. In it, I heard Trevor stir, slip on some shoes, and very, very quietly slip out of the bedroom. I would swear I heard the stairs creak. But I was too tired to see if he had just gone to the bathroom or somewhere else. When I woke in the morning, I saw he wasn't beside me.

"Trevor?" I called. I sat up in a small panic. Could he have run away? Would he go without me because he thought Mama had told him to do that?

I let out a deep breath when he appeared in the doorway, dressed. I glanced at the clock.

"You're up too early for school, aren't you?"

The sun was just coming up. Shadows reluctantly retreated from the room and the hallway.

"He's leaving very early today," he said. "We should both have breakfast with him. Make him think we're sorry he's leaving and wish him a good trip just like we used to, Faith. C'mon. Get up and get dressed quickly. I think he's already gone downstairs."

"I'm not that good of an actress," I mumbled, then rose and washed and dressed.

The two of us descended.

"Gabby is still sleeping," I whispered. "She's not rising earlier than she usually does just to say goodbye to him. Mama always did."

"They said their goodbyes in their room because she's not an early riser. Probably," he added as we turned toward the kitchen.

Big John hovered over a bowl of his favorite cereal and sliced bananas. Critter was lying there, but raised his head as soon as we appeared.

"So where are you going this time?" Trevor asked him, just the way he used to on the mornings he left on a trip.

"Jacksonville to Biloxi to Beaumont, Texas, and back. I expect you to take good care of things here, includin' Critter."

"Oh, we will," Trevor said.

Big John stared at him a moment and then fixed his gaze on me.

"You do whatever Gabby tells you to do and get yourself on your feet."

"I'm on my feet," I said, almost laughing at him. "I'm not sick. I gave birth."

"Pour me a coffee," he ordered. "You used to get up with your mama and have that ready and waitin' when I was startin' a trip."

I poured his coffee. Trevor got a bowl and sat. I stood off to the side. If Big John saw my face, he'd never believe we were going to be obedient.

"You work on that car like I told you?"

"Oh, yes, sir," Trevor said.

I sat with a cup of coffee. Critter whined, so I leaned over to pick him up.

"Give the dog some exercise, but don't let him roam free, hear?" he said.

"Yes," I said. "I'll wait for Trevor to come home from school."

"Good. Stay on our land," he added.

"Have you seen Mr. Longstreet recently?" I asked. From the way he was glaring back, I didn't think he would answer.

"I seen him from the road, but I got my own problems now. Don't need to hear the neighbor's."

"What problems does he have?"

"Whatever, it's none of your business. You got plenty to take care of here. We don't need nobody nosin' around." He looked at Trevor. "You make damn sure of that."

"Oh, I have enough on my plate at school," Trevor said. "Which reminds me, Dad, I need some money for school lunches and such while you're away."

"Don't know why she don't make your sandwiches," he said, nodding at me.

"She's had a lot to do mornings."

"Not anymore." He grunted and reluctantly reached into his pocket, took out his wallet, and gave Trevor forty dollars.

"Thanks. I was thinking I'd clear out the garage enough for me to get Mama's car in at night with Gabby's."

"Don't leave junk layin' around. This house looks like it belongs in a museum as it is. Your mother wouldn't let me paint new fresh colors, nothin'."

"Oh. I'd be glad to help you do that," Trevor said enthusiastically.

I glanced at him. He'd never do that, I thought, but he was sure a good liar when he wanted to be.

"We'll see. Might sell it and move closer to the action. Make Gabby happier," he said, and finished his coffee.

A surge of cold panic shot through my chest. Sell Mama's house? Trevor said nothing; he just stared coolly at Big John.

Before anything more could be said, we were surprised to hear Gabby coming down the stairs.

"I was going to make Trevor breakfast before he went to school," she moaned, as if we had stolen her way to impress Big John. She rarely ever did that.

She was wearing what I knew was Mama's robe. Mama had been much slimmer than Gabby, or I had no doubt she would wear some of her other things. Big John had taken most of it to drop off for the homeless. I wanted to protest, to say I'd want to wear Mama's clothes, but he seemed determined to rid the house of any reminders of her. He had taken down all her family pictures. We had no idea what he had done with them and the pictures of her and him. Gabby had changed all the bedding in their room and was talking about new window treatments.

Big John rose. He never simply stood there, I thought. He always loomed over us.

"Got to get goin'. I'll call you like I said when I land somewhere

tonight," he told Gabby. Those were the usual words he would say
to Mama.

"Have a good trip," Trevor said.

The way Big John looked at him made my heart skip beats.
Could he see Trevor's sarcasm?

"You just do as I said," he replied. "Both of ya."

He reached for his light leather jacket and started toward the
door. Gabby followed him, kissed him goodbye, and whispered
something. Then, after she looked back at us, she decided to follow
him out to the truck. We heard the big engine start. Not that long
ago, we'd be out there with Mama to wave goodbye as he turned the
eighteen-wheeler and drove onto the highway. Trevor had longed to
go with him back then, but Mama had said he wasn't ready.

We could hear the gravel crush beneath the big wheels. And
then the truck shifted gears and disappeared, the roar of its engine
dwindling behind it.

"Well, at least he's gone for a while," Trevor said. "Easier for us
to work on Gabby."

He took my hand, smiling with that self-confidence of his.

Sometimes Trevor could make me believe it was day when it
was night.

THREE

"I can't pretend to be sick today," Trevor whispered when Gabby stepped back into the house. "She's already seen I'm all right."

"Don't worry. I'll start looking for clues when she leaves."

Critter came over to us, and I picked him up and put him in my lap.

"What are you two whispering about?" Gabby asked with a suspicious smile. "And right after your father leaves?"

"I thought I might build a doghouse for Critter while Big John is on his trip. Faith will help as much as she can. We wanted it to be a surprise for Big John. So please don't tell. The old doghouse is out in the back, rotting away."

"Oh, what a great idea. He'll love it. That's very nice of you to think of it for him."

"It's for the dog," I said dryly.

She looked at me, missing my sarcasm completely, and laughed.

"It would have to be one helluva big doghouse for Big John," she said. "In the meantime, we'll keep him in the den at night after we all go to sleep. He doesn't go upstairs. John's orders."

"He'll mess," I said.

"We'll put down some old newspaper, and then one of us will clean it up. I promised him that we'd work on getting him housebroken while he's away. You'll help, right?"

"Right," I said. *I'll just forget you took my baby and concentrate on a dog*, I thought, but kept my phony smile.

"Well, since you already got your breakfast, I'm going up to shower and dress. You have a good day at school, Trevor. And don't worry about Faith. I'll take good care of her until you're home."

"Aren't you going to work?" I asked, trying not to sound disappointed.

"Oh, didn't I tell you? I'm on a sort of leave of absence until everything is right with you. I had other excuses for it, so don't worry," she said. "No one knows anything they shouldn't know."

I looked at Trevor, who shook his head gently to warn me not to do or say anything that would show my disappointment.

"Well, that's very kind of you," I said.

She smiled.

"We'll have some good times, and," she said sotto voce, as if Big John was still here, "we'll watch all my *General Hospital* recordings today and catch up completely. You don't have to do your home-school work or anything." She thought a moment. "How do you know what to read and study anyway now?"

"Mama created the syllabus for all our high school studies."

"Syllabus?"

"It's like a map of what you should study."

"Oh, that was very thoughtful planning."

"Planning? She didn't know she was going to die," I said.

Trevor poked me.

"Of course not. Anyway, let's have a girls' day."

I forced a smile as she left to go up.

"Don't take any big risks," Trevor warned me as soon as we heard her start up the stairs. "There'll be times when she's out while Big John's away. We'll plan for it, and I'll take those days off."

"Maybe I'll drug her," I threatened, looking toward the stairs. "There's still some of Mama's old medicine in the cabinet."

"Don't dare. Don't do anything now that will raise their suspicions about us, Faith. Promise?" he said.

Reluctantly, I did.

"I know this will be hard for you, Faith, but try not to talk to her about Little Paula. Talk about anything and everything else unless she brings it up, which I doubt she'll do. The faster she thinks we're over it, the faster she'll reveal something, and if she does, don't acknowledge it. Pretend you didn't hear it, and tell me later."

"What about Big John? Do you think he'll believe we're over it? Ever? Even if she tells him?"

"He won't care after a while," he said with his usual confidence. "I'd better get going. Are you going to be all right?"

"No, but I'll pretend to be," I said. It brought a smile.

That's something we haven't done for weeks, I thought, *smile at each other.*

He leaned over to kiss my cheek.

"I'd better take Critter out to do his business," I said, "and start on the housebreaking. Otherwise, I'll be cleaning up doo-doo for months. She's too dainty to do it."

I put Critter down so I could get his leash.

"Don't dare go over to Mr. Longstreet's," he added, after he picked up his book bag. "You heard Big John. They must have had words."

"Don't worry. Just don't . . ."

"What?"

"Talk to any pretty girls."

He laughed.

"Go on. I'll walk out with you," I said. When we stepped out, I asked him if he was really going to work on the garage.

His face flushed with the anger that always seemed to be boiling just beneath the surface since Mama's death.

"Mama's car should be in there, not hers. I'll make room for them both."

"Okay. Then I'll help. What about the doghouse?"

"I might be able to do something with the old one. The roof's not rotted. She won't know the difference. Okay. I'll be on my way back as soon as the final bell rings."

Critter did his business while Trevor was driving out. He beeped the horn, turned, and disappeared. I stood still looking after him, longing for the time when I would be able to drive out and go to school, or anywhere for that matter.

"C'mon," I told Critter, and went back in, took off his leash, and let him wander about the house.

Almost as if he had heard and understood Gabby, he ended up lying on the den floor but watching me as I started to clear away the breakfast bowls and cups. *I wonder*, I thought, gazing at him at the foot of Big John's chair.

I listened for Gabby a moment and then went to the den. Would there be anything helpful hidden away here? I looked in the small table next to Big John's big easy chair first. The top lifted for storage of small items. There were papers that looked mostly like old receipts from the hardware store and the drugstore, a pack of his cigars, and his cigarette lighter. I took out each piece of paper and checked. There was one slip of paper with just a name, Lydia Couch. It wasn't Daddy's handwriting. I had never heard that name. Could it have something to do with Little Paula? Maybe it was just something to do with Eden Trucking.

I put it all back and closed the table quickly just as Gabby was coming down the stairs. I was afraid she would see the guilty look on my face.

"Get hold of yourself, Faith Eden," I whispered, pulled myself up, and took a deep breath. "You can handle her."

I quickly returned to the kitchen sink and began wiping the bowls dry and started on cleaning the counter.

"Oh, let's not do any housework today, Faith. I told you. It's a girls' day," she said, and poured herself some coffee. "We can take Critter and go for a walk in the woods, and you can tell me things you learned about nature and stuff. Although Nick and I lived here all our lives, I was never much of a country girl."

She opened the refrigerator and took out some jelly to put on a roll before she sat.

"You never went in the woods? Even when you were younger?"

"Not really. Nick tried to get me to go hunting with him and his friends for years. I think he was trying to make me the brother he wished he had. He got over that as soon as I started developing breasts. I thought they'd never stop growing. His friends started calling me Dolly Parton."

"Who's that?"

"Forget it," she said.

I turned and watched her gobble down her roll. Then she leaned toward me and whispered, "My mother was jealous. She never had the figure I had. My dad actually told me that."

"What really happened to your parents?" I asked, and leaned back against the sink. "Neither you nor Nick ever mentions them, or haven't when Trevor and I were around you, so we know only that your father had a heart attack and your mother smoked and drank."

"Yes, my father died young of heart failure, and my mother remarried when Nick was in his twenties and I was nineteen. Wasn't long after that she and her new husband moved to Kansas, where she died of lung cancer. People used to tell me they thought our house was some sort of factory because of all the smoke coming out of the windows."

She laughed. "Neither of us went to her funeral."

"What? Why not?"

"Even before my father died, she treated us like weights around her neck. I think we were both mistakes. She never really wanted children."

"So you never had a loving relationship with your mother?"

"Certainly not like you've had with yours." She laughed, nervously, I thought. "I doubt any girl really had one like yours." She paused, and then, with a slight smile, said, "It's not always a good thing."

"Why not?"

"Some mothers make their children their whole lives, so much so that their husbands begin to resent their own children. It was just the opposite with mine. I was a daddy's girl. My mother always put us in the same sentence."

"What does that mean? What sentence?"

"You know . . . whatever I did was 'you and your father's fault' or 'your father and you are responsible for this.' He wasn't even aware of what she meant or what she was accusing him of doing half the time, but if he was there when she said it, he would be angry at her. When he died . . . I thought my mother was almost happy about it. She didn't wait that long to find another man. Neither Nick nor I liked him, but she couldn't have cared any less about it. She ignored us when they were together. Like I said . . . weights around her neck."

She looked at me and smiled. "I mean, I could understand how she felt sometimes."

"Why?"

"You're too young to realize what you would be going through all your young life if you had a child to care for, especially at this age. No parties, no fun. Children turn you into a slave when you become a mother. That's what my mother was fond of saying, and to be honest, after seeing other young women my age with children, she was probably right. Thanks to her, I doubt I'll ever have children."

"Oh," I said, and put my hands on my aching breasts. I almost said, *Little Paula needs to be fed.*

"What?"

"I've got to . . . go do it," I said, turned, and hurried up the stairs.

I thought I heard her say, "It's not like you can hear her crying."

When I returned, Gabby was already watching one of her recorded soap opera episodes. She was so into it that she didn't hear me. I stared at her a moment and then turned quietly and tiptoed back up the stairs. Trevor would be upset, but it was an opportunity,

I thought, and went to her and Big John's bedroom. I hurried to his side of the bed and began to look through the top drawer of his night table. Under a pile of insurance receipts and such, I found a thick manila envelope with no names or addresses on it.

My fingers trembled as I undid it and reached inside.

It made me gasp.

In my hand was a stack of hundred-dollar bills. There were at least ten thick stacks in the envelope. Why would he have so much money in a night table? Maybe this and the name I had found, Lydia Couch, had something to do with Little Paula. I couldn't wait to tell Trevor all of it.

"Faith, are you doing okay?" I heard Gabby call from the bottom of the stairs.

I rushed to put it all back and close the drawer. Then I hurried to the top of the stairs. She was staring up.

"I was starting to worry about you." She paused with those suspicious eyes. "What were you doing on that side of the upstairs?"

I started down the steps, keeping my head down. Trevor always told me I had a face like a window.

"Don't tell Big John," I said, taking a breath and raising my head. My tears were real, maybe more tears of fear.

"Tell him what?" she asked. "What have you done?"

"I can't help it. I can't help thinking about Little Paula when I use that pump."

"Oh." She flipped her hand as if that was so easy to fix. "Well, time will change that. You'll stop having to use the pump, and as Big John said, you'll get on with your life. I'm putting on another episode. Before today's over, we'll be caught up, and tomorrow or the next day, we can watch a fresh episode."

"Tomorrow or the next day? How long can you stay away from work?"

"Two weeks, at least," she said. "My boss is . . . considerate," she added, and laughed. "The other girls who work there are jealous. Long ago, I learned how to play a man like a puppet. Every man has strings to pull. You'll learn."

When I reached the bottom of the stairs, she paused to turn to me.

"Once this all gets less intense, we'll go shopping, too. You need new things, and I love looking at what's new. I'll take you to this new sandwich shop at the mall for lunch, and we'll sit and gossip about everyone around us. It's time you became a girly girl."

"What's that?"

"Thinking about yourself, your hair, your nails, your clothing and makeup. I have no doubt that when Big John lets you go to school, you'll have boys with their tongues hanging out, looking like Critter there. But first, I have to remake you so you don't look like some girl from *The Walking Dead* or something.

"My mother never did much to help me look pretty, just like yours didn't do much for you," she continued. "I bet she never showed you how to do makeup. Mine didn't. As I said, she was jealous of me, but I wasn't going to curl up and become some plain Jane. I studied and learned on my own about makeup and hair. Men don't have to work as hard at it as we do. They think the stench of beer or whiskey is enough cologne. Just don't go out with boys who have dirt under their fingernails. Ugh."

"Daddy doesn't wear any special scent," I said.

"I'm working on Big John. I want him to get some new clothes now, and I'm going to stop cutting his hair and stuff like your mother did. He needs to go to a real hairstylist and have a manicure, too. I decided I don't want to pursue that career. Or any career. We have enough money to live well. Besides . . . I'd rather have people working on me than me on them."

She laughed.

"When he returns, I want you to help me with all that. If I bring something up at dinner, don't be afraid to agree. We'll gang up on him," she said, and gave me an excited smile. "I want us to be close friends. It's like having a younger sister."

She threaded her arm through mine.

"Let's get back to *General Hospital*, make a great lunch, and then take Critter for a walk before Trevor gets home."

We marched through the kitchen, but just before we sat and she started her recordings, the phone rang.

"Don't worry," she said. "If that's one of my girlfriends, I'm not going anywhere with them. Although we do have a lot of fun," she said, and picked up the receiver. "Hello."

She listened a moment and then said, "I'm his fiancée."

As she continued to listen, the blush left her cheeks. Her face paled as pure fear worked its way into her eyes.

"When is that?" she asked. "Yes," she said. "Thank you."

She cradled the phone as if it was made of breakable glass and stood there staring at it.

"What?" I asked.

"Big John's truck missed a downhill turn. They're not sure why yet. And it went over the edge, flipping and tossing him about in the cab."

"And?"

"He was brought to the hospital."

"Where is he?"

"Harrisburg," she said. "Pinnacle Health." She looked wobbly and put her right palm against the wall to steady herself. "Nick's coming back from a trip. I'll call him and let him know what's happening. I don't know how close he is to home. I hate going to hospitals."

"We'll get Trevor. He'll drive," I said. "Call the school, and tell them why he has to come home."

She looked stunned.

"Gabby, if you want to go to him, we'd better get ourselves organized. We might have to stay nearby. I'll get Trevor's things together, what he'll need, and my own. You do the same for yourself."

She nodded but didn't move.

"Call the school," I said. "It's better if you call and explain who you are and why you need him."

She widened her eyes, like someone who had just regained consciousness.

"Yes, of course. You're so smart."

Critter whined as if he understood something was suddenly very wrong.

"We'll take the dog," I said. "We may be gone a while, even a day or so. It'll be fine."

Trembling a little myself, I hurried to the stairs. Maybe it was selfish to think it, but without a mother and maybe now without a father, what would happen to Trevor and me?

I gathered the clothes we would need if, as I suspected, we had to stay over a night or so. Mama used to say forethought was the most valuable of all thoughts.

Then I filled another bag with the things I would need. I'd probably have to use the breast pump in the car or while we waited in the hospital.

When I came down with everything, Gabby was still standing in the kitchen, looking like she was in some hypnotic state or something.

"Didn't you get your things together?"

"What? No, not yet."

"Did you call the school for Trevor?"

"Yes. Whoever it was who answered was very nice. I called Nick, and he said he'd be home by eight tonight."

"Well, we can't wait, right? Didn't they say to come right away?"

"Yes," she said. She looked like she couldn't think, let alone move.

"Okay. So we'll use your car. It's newer," I said. "I'll take Critter out to pee so we won't have to stop. Where are the keys to the car? I'll put one of the bags in the trunk."

"They're in the car," she said. "He's a big man, stronger than anyone I know. He'll be fine. Right?"

"Right," I said. "Get your stuff. We'll leave as soon as Trevor arrives."

She started toward the den.

"Where are you going, Gabby?"

"What?"

Did she think we were returning to *General Hospital*?

"Oh. I hate hospitals. I mean, I don't mind watching programs about them, but going there . . ."

"Don't we have to go?"

"Yes, of course."

She turned and headed toward the stairs. I went out, found her keys in the ignition of her car, and put our clothes bag in the trunk. I left it open for her to put her things in and then went back inside, gathered Critter's bag of food and his bowl, and brought those to the car. I brought him out and let him sniff until he found his toilet.

I looked into the woods. The afternoon shadows seemed thicker, wider, and deeper. I really wasn't sure how I felt about Big John being in an accident and taken to the hospital. I had kept myself busy up till now so that I wouldn't think about it, but now that I was catching my breath, I found my feelings or lack of them curious. I was so angry at him for what he had done, for taking Little Paula away. Surely, that was part of it. But the truth was that I didn't think Trevor or I had ever felt as close to him as we had to Mama.

When I was younger, every time he had done something that frightened, annoyed, or even revolted me, I would remember Mama's stories about her courting Big John, as she had called it. The man she had described was much softer and more considerate than the man we knew, now especially. Those images of their falling in love, their early days, when they went out and went boating on the lake, seemed enough to smooth over the way things had become. I had hoped to feel some of that gentleness she had described in Big John. Maybe there were flashes of it, but as time passed and we grew older and Mama made us more and more her world, he did drift away. He grew colder and harder when it came to us. Trevor even stopped longing to go on a trip with him. I thought Mama and Big John had become two different people since they had courted.

The truth was, he was gone so much when we were growing up that it was difficult to have a real relationship. Sometimes, and I think Trevor even said it more than once, we felt like he thought of us as pets. Maybe Mama did hover over us protectively, and maybe, just as Gabby had described from the many soap operas she watched about new mothers and their husbands, Mama concentrated on us so much that Big John began to resent us, resent how much time she would spend with us even when he was home. Trevor had once said, "He was glad she found us, because she wouldn't nag him as much when he was here or care as much about how long he was gone. He did try a little to be a father, but Mama was too . . ."

"Possessive," I said, finishing his thought. "There wasn't much room for him."

"Yes."

Despite how much we loved Mama, I think we both felt sorry for Big John back then. We wanted a father. That was certain, but now . . . now, how could we ever love him? Just the other night, I told Trevor that when Big John looked at us, he saw Mama and felt guilty for how he had treated her by having an affair with Gabby and how he'd taken her into our home.

"Maybe he wishes we would run away," I said.

Trevor thought a moment and then angrily said, "This is our home, Mama's home. It's our family home, Faith. Let *him* run away."

I wanted to agree with him, but I also wanted to find Little Paula and run away.

What would we do now?

Trevor drove in and parked.

"Where is he?" he asked, practically leaping out of Mama's car.

"Harrisburg. I wrote down the name of the hospital."

"Yeah, that's about three to four hours. What else do you know about what happened to him?"

"He went over the edge of the road at a turn at the bottom of a hill. He was probably going too fast."

"Umm," Trevor said.

"Like what happened to Grandpa and Grandma," I reminded him.

He looked at me. He narrowed his eyes as his thoughts went deeper, and then he almost smiled.

"Yeah. Makes sense," he said in a weird way. It was like he had heard someone else talking instead of me and was reacting to that. More and more lately, he looked like this, I thought. I hated how we were drifting apart in little ways, ways unnoticeable to anyone else, since he had begun school. His world had expanded, but mine remained where it was, caged in this house and our forest, especially since I had become visibly pregnant.

"What makes sense?"

"Nothing. What are we doing?"

I nodded at the house. "She's a mess. I have all your things with mine in a small suitcase in case we need to remain nearby."

"Thanks."

"I'd better go see about her," I said, and handed him Critter's leash.

"We're taking the dog?"

"We might be there a day or so, Trevor. We don't know. I have what we need."

"Right."

He turned toward the woods with Critter. I hurried inside. Gabby wasn't downstairs. I rushed up the stairs. She was sitting on the bed, staring at the floor.

"What's wrong?" I asked. "Why haven't you come down?"

She looked up slowly, her eyes covered with a thick film of tears.

"My father didn't die quickly. He was in the cardiac unit for almost a week. I was there every day, watching those machines and the nurses and smelling the odors and seeing other sick people in the hallways. I hate hospitals."

"Well, what are we going to do? We have to go, right?"

"I'm not really his fiancée. I just said that so they'd tell me what was happening. You two are so grown-up, and you're his children."

For a long moment, I was speechless. I knew what she was saying between the lines, but it didn't seem possible.

"You want us to go without you?"

"Well, you could call me, and I could come later with Nick," she said.

"But if he's awake, he'll surely wonder why . . ."

"Oh, you could say I wasn't feeling well. I'm not, really. I'm so nauseated, and I feel like I would only be trouble."

"But we're *kids*. I don't think we can get a place to stay if we have to. We don't have money, anyway. We don't even have credit cards."

"Oh. Yeah. There's money," she said, rising quickly. I knew where she was going. She took out the manila envelope and pulled bills from one stack. She handed me what was easily thousands of dollars.

"You will find a place to stay near the hospital. Just explain why you need to, and when you show them the money, they won't turn you away."

I took it slowly and studied her face.

"You're not telling me everything, are you?" I asked. "What else did the hospital say?"

"The man who called said he's going into a critical operation. That's all he said. But don't you see? He won't know if I'm there or not for a while, anyway, for sure. I'll wait for Nick. We'll follow."

She kept nodding to convince herself.

"That's the best idea for now. You can leave the dog. It'll make it easier for you."

I stood there looking at the money and then at her. If I didn't agree, she'd surely burst into tears or get even more hysterical.

"Maybe you should make some sandwiches so you don't have to stop," she said, nodding. "I can help do that."

"We're not going to be hungry before we find out what's what."

"Oh, sure," she said.

"We'll need your mobile phone. Not just to call you but to use the map application."

"Oh, sure," she said. "I left it in the den, on the table by the easy chair."

Clutching the money, I hurried down the stairs, found the phone, and went to the rear door.

"Bring Critter and his things inside," I shouted to Trevor.

"How come?"

"Gabby's not coming with us. We can leave the dog home."

"Not coming?"

"I have her mobile phone," I said, holding it up. "We'll use Google to find our way to the hospital." I almost added, *The way Lance showed me on his phone.*

He brought Critter, but, still disbelieving me, he entered the house and unfastened the leash. Critter looked disappointed.

"Where is she?"

"Upstairs. Let's just go," I said. "She gave me this."

I showed him the money.

"So much? Where did she get that?"

"I'll explain it. We're still taking her car. Let's just go, Trevor."

"Okay."

"We're leaving," I shouted, and followed Trevor out.

"Explain," he said when we got into the car. He started it, and we drove onto the road.

I began by telling him about her parents and then described in more detail how she was behaving right now. But none of that was on my mind. I paused and looked back.

After our house was long gone from the rear window, I realized I was finally going somewhere.

And for a while, I didn't even think about Big John.

FOUR

As we rode and I saw the scenery and people, it was as if I could suddenly breathe. For almost all my life, excluding the foster home, the four walls of the rooms in the Eden house and a patch of woods on our property were my entire world. I was so unaware of what buildings, restaurants, and shopping centers were minutes from our house. Mama never took us for rides. It was as if she was afraid that someone might see us, remember we were their children, and take us from her. Mama never took us to try on shoes or clothes. For all our lives here, we saw the world through two windows, really, the ones in our room and television.

For a while, I couldn't turn from the car window. When we started on the main highway, Trevor was quiet for long periods. From the way the afternoon sun blinked on his face, he appeared to be smiling. Without an iota of surprise, he had listened to my description of Gabby and her reaction to what had happened to Big John.

"Doesn't what I'm saying upset you? It frightens me. And Gabby is beside herself. I was afraid she was going to have a nervous breakdown or something right in front of me."

"I've really never gotten used to her being his girlfriend," he said. "I don't know about you, but even with the way he and Mama were right before her death, there seemed to be more of a relationship between them than what Big John has with Gabby. Sometimes," he continued, now really smiling, "she was as much of a mother to him as she was to us."

"Yes," I said, recalling how she would bawl him out and make him do things the way she would make us.

I did remember the times they were close and loving but also the times she would rip into him and send him practically crawling off to hide in his den until she calmed down from whatever he had said or done.

"You know what I call Gabby, now that she's living with us, when I think of them?" Trevor said. I shook my head. "His bed warmer. Something like a heating pad. Neither of them really shows much affection for the other in front of us. I hear him complain about her poor cooking constantly. She's a terrible shopper. She always seems to be out of something he wants. If you ask me, he spends at least seventy-five percent of his time grumbling about her to her, at least as much as he complains to her about us."

I sat back and thought how dark all this was. Gabby had nothing legally tying her to us if Big John didn't marry her. Really. What could happen to us if something terrible had happened or was going to happen to him?

"Yet despite how she yelled at him and threatened him," Trevor said, "Mama would have been out the door when that call came from the hospital. She wouldn't have waited on us, and she certainly wouldn't have remained behind whining about how she couldn't stand to go to hospitals. Mama always said, when you know you have to do something, you swallow it down and do it, no matter what. Mama would say Gabby doesn't have the grit. She's lucky she doesn't have to remember to breathe."

He turned. "You still haven't explained that fistful of money."

I described my opportunity to search a little and the two things I had found.

"Lydia Couch?" He thought and shook his head. "I don't remember hearing that name."

"Me, either."

"Of course, she could be one of Gabby's friends—but why just her name on a slip of paper? Gabby is so . . . haphazard. Who can make sense of her?"

I was tired of talking about Gabby.

"Little Paula is getting lost in all this," I said, more to myself than to him, but he heard it.

"No, she's not. We're not going to let that happen. Everything . . . everything provides an opportunity, whether we make it for ourselves or not. You'll see."

We drove on. A little under four hours later, we turned into the hospital parking area and found a space. I couldn't stop the trembling rumbling down into my legs, movement emanating from the anticipation of tragic news. Even after the things Trevor had said, criticizing her reluctance to come to the hospital with us now, I suddenly appreciated Gabby's fear and trepidation, especially with her father's history. The hospital building loomed, a constant reminder of how fragile we all were. Few people went through life without having been brought to a hospital at least once, even if that once was the end of their lives.

"C'mon, Faith," Trevor said, taking my hand.

We walked silently over the walkway and into the hospital lobby. There was a sliding window ahead of us. As we approached, Trevor took out his wallet and flipped it open to his driver's license, as if he had been here and done this at least a dozen times. The slim gray-haired lady behind the window was standing with her back to us and filing some paperwork. The lobby looked at least half full, with everyone gazing curiously at us. When the receptionist turned and saw us, she smiled and took her seat, sliding the window open.

"And how can I help you two?" she asked, smiling, as if we were grade-school students who were maybe lost.

"Our father was brought here in an emergency after a truck accident," Trevor said. He slipped his license out of the wallet and put it on the counter. "His name is John Eden. We were informed and came as soon as we could. We live about four hours away."

She quickly lost her smile, tilted her head, and looked at his license. Then she pressed a button on her phone, but slid the window closed as she talked. We could barely make out her words, but I heard her say Daddy's name and Trevor's. She listened, and then hung up and slid the window open.

"Where's your mother?" she asked.

"She died," Trevor said, "months ago."

"There's no one else with you?"

"No, ma'am," Trevor said. He hesitated and then added, "My father's girlfriend was unable to come. She'll come later."

She pressed her lips together, with her disapproval practically floating out of her eyes over the word "girlfriend." Trevor had preceded it by saying our mother had died only months ago. Maybe he did it deliberately, I thought. My brother could easily be a good chess player.

"Is this your sister?"

"Yes, ma'am," Trevor said quickly.

"What's your name, young lady?"

"Faith Eden," I said.

"Just a moment," she said, and closed the window again while she used the phone. She listened, and then she began writing on something. After she hung up the receiver, she opened the window and put Trevor's license back on the counter with two visitors' badges. Trevor quickly put his license back in his wallet.

"Mrs. Wegman will greet you at that door," she said, nodding at a door to her right. "Wait for her. She will then take you to a waiting area near the operating room and post-op suite. The operation on your father was completed a half hour ago. She'll explain everything she can and see if your father's surgeon can speak to you soon. Good luck," she added with a slight smile, and closed the window as if she was grateful she could separate herself from our and any other visitor's misery. Perhaps she had to do that to survive in this job, I thought. I probably would.

Trevor looked at me. The reality of all this dropped a dark shadow over us. My heart, if it had a voice, would be roaring, I thought. He quickly took my hand, and we started toward the door.

Neither of us spoke. We stood there staring at the small window. When Mrs. Wegman opened the door, it felt like all the air was being sucked in, us along with it.

"Trevor and Faith Eden?" she asked. She looked to be at least in her forties, with a face that showed more age. She looked stern, efficient, but with a glimmer of compassion.

We both nodded. Trevor showed her his badge, and I showed her mine.

"Okay, follow me, children."

She walked slowly. "Where are you from?" she asked.

"We live in Lake Wallenpaupack," Trevor said.

"Oh, quite a ride. So," she said at the elevator, "you know your father was in a very bad truck accident."

"Yes," Trevor said. "His truck flipped."

"Well, he needed emergency surgery. He's still under sedation, but I've had Dr. Lau informed that you have arrived. I'll show you where to wait for him. Is anyone else coming?" she asked when we stepped into the elevator.

"Later, my father's girlfriend and his best friend will be here. He's her brother and just arriving from a trip himself. He's also a truck driver."

She nodded, probably wondering why Gabby hadn't come with us but looking like she wasn't going to spend too much time thinking about it. Perhaps all nurses and doctors had to be behind the same wall the receptionist downstairs built for herself, a wall to keep them from becoming too involved with patients and their families. All that emotion could smother them.

When the elevator opened, she took us to a small waiting room and told us where we could get water.

"Is he going to be all right?" I asked quickly when she started to turn.

"We need to listen carefully to the doctor," she said. She flashed a smile but walked away before I could ask anything else.

"He's always been a careful driver," I said. "How could this happen?"

"He hasn't always been careful. Remember the times he drove

too long, pushed his trips? Mama often scolded him." He was quiet for a moment and then added, "He hasn't been himself lately. You know he's been drinking too much. Maybe he drove drunk. Who knows? We're here, but he's not our favorite person right now. Of course, we have to pretend he is."

I looked down and clutched my hands. I didn't even want to look at the hospital walls. Everything Gabby had said about hospital odors, other patients, and the tension replayed in my mind. How would we explain her absence to him? Would he blame it on us somehow?

My breasts began to ache, but I pushed it from my mind. Trevor was suddenly sitting so calmly, staring blankly ahead. Why wasn't he as nervous as I was?

After what seemed to be hours but was probably minutes, a door opened, and a man a little shorter than Trevor looked at us and started toward us. He was Asian, so I assumed he was Dr. Lau. He was still dressed in his hospital fatigues. The expression on his face revealed nothing, I thought. It was almost as if he was coming to ask us how Big John was doing. He paused and introduced himself.

"I'm his son, Trevor, and this is his daughter, Faith," Trevor told him.

"Your father was in a very, very bad truck accident. For whatever reason, according to the police, he wasn't wearing his safety belt, and consequently, he was tossed and bounced about in that truck cab quite severely. We had to operate immediately because there was internal bleeding. The most serious injury was to his spinal cord. He might need another operation, but I feel certain he has suffered paraplegia because of this injury."

"What's that?" Trevor asked.

"Paralysis from his hips down. His legs. The extent of this is yet to be determined by our neurological department. For now, we've stopped all internal bleeding. He has other injuries, not as severe."

"His spinal cord?" Trevor said as if the words had just reached his brain.

"L-one to L-five," I said.

I looked at Trevor. I knew he understood, but he finally looked a little terrified, too.

"Exactly," Dr. Lau said, almost smiling.

"We were homeschooled, and our mother spent a great deal of time teaching us about our bodies," I said.

This time, he did smile and nod.

"I wish I had better news for you. I believe his upper body will remain as strong as it was, and he will be able to manage a manual wheelchair."

"Wheelchair," Trevor repeated.

I could almost see the visions playing in his eyes, fear the brightest. Was he already imagining how difficult it would be to live with him, not that it wasn't these past few months? For a moment, he looked like he had completely zoned out. That only increased the anxiety that had taken hold of me. Our silence seemed to affect the doctor. He looked sorry he had told us even this much.

"I feel he is out of critical danger, but you have to prepare yourselves for what's to come. He will need to be in therapy, and there will be a psychotherapist helping him with all this, too. For now . . . I'm afraid it will be some time before you can visit with him. He'll be quite disoriented. There's much to be done in the recovery room. I would suggest your returning late tomorrow morning."

Neither of us spoke. I thought the silence was beginning to annoy him. He was surely thinking about giving all this information to children.

"Isn't there someone else from your family coming to the hospital?"

"His girlfriend and his best friend," Trevor said. "Our mother died."

"I see. All right, I will consult with you all tomorrow. We should know a great deal more then. Just ask for me at the desk when you're all together, and they will inform me of your arrival."

I thought his meaning was very clear now: he would rather speak with adults, although I was having more and more trouble thinking of Gabby as an adult. *Wait until he meets her*, I thought.

"For now, take care of yourselves. Your lives will change," he added with the assurance of a biblical prophet.

It felt like the last nail was being driven into the coffin of our childhood. We were being jerked forward into a darker adulthood, whether we liked it or not. For a moment, I couldn't smile to thank him or anything. I turned to Trevor.

Suddenly, there wasn't an iota of fear in his face, whereas I imagined I appeared more like a porcelain doll shattering.

"We'd better find a place to stay tonight," he said.

"What about Gabby?"

"Wait until we're outside, and then call the house on her phone and give her the news."

He rose, and I followed him to the elevator.

Shouldn't one of us say this is terrible? I thought. *Maybe he's just being brave. Maybe I still don't believe it.*

"Go call," he said when we were in the lobby again. "I'll find out what's available nearby."

I hurried out and called the house. It took four rings for Gabby to pick up. I almost ended the call, thinking she and her brother had started out for Harrisburg.

"Hello," she said. I was sure I heard the television in the background.

"Isn't Nick back yet?" I asked first.

"He's close. I've just been trying to do everything but think. How is he?" she asked, the terror resonating in her voice.

I began to explain it. Only one word seemed to have stuck in her mind.

"Wheelchair? For sure?"

"Yes, Gabby, for sure."

"For the rest of his life?"

"Yes. It's permanent damage to his spine."

She was silent so long that I thought she'd hung up.

"Gabby?"

"Well, if you can't see him until the morning, there's no point in Nick and me going there until tomorrow. We should give Nick some rest from his trip."

"I'll call you in the morning, and you can tell me when you expect to arrive," I said. "We'll wait for you in the lobby before we ask to see the doctor. We'll have to take turns seeing Daddy, I'm sure."

I thought she laughed.

"He'll think I was always there," she said. "Nick's going to be very upset," she added, as if she wouldn't be.

"Yes" was all I could think to say. I heard her begin to sob and take deep breaths.

"I'll talk to you tomorrow," she said, almost in a loud whisper, and hung up.

I turned when Trevor appeared.

"There's a Hilton nearby and a Radisson. Let's try the Hilton first. They said it was more expensive. Might as well enjoy this money. So what did she say?"

"Nick wasn't there yet. She was stunned when she heard about his being in a wheelchair forever. She said they wouldn't come until tomorrow. Big John would think she was always here anyway, so why not let Nick rest first from his trip?"

Trevor smiled as if he had anticipated nothing different.

"She's right. Surprised she's that thoughtful. I'm starving. I haven't eaten since breakfast. Let's get dinner at the hotel after we check in," he said, as if that was that. He started for the car.

How could he have any appetite after all this? I wondered. I felt like my stomach had done flip-flops the whole time. Trevor had gotten driving directions, and we were at the hotel in what seemed like five minutes.

Apparently, the woman working at reception in the hotel was used to people who had loved ones in the hospital staying there. She was surprised we were paying in cash, and her eyes widened when Trevor took out the folded bills and handed the night's cost to her. We booked a room with two queen-size beds. After we brought our things up to it, we went down to the restaurant. I told him I couldn't eat much.

"Hey, you have to keep your strength and your health up, Faith. You're still a mother and will be for a long, long time."

I sat back. He amazed me. Despite my giving birth and caring for a baby for three weeks, Trevor seemed to have leapfrogged over me into maturity. I had already sensed that was happening after he had begun public school and started driving. Mama had assured me that girls matured faster than boys, but it didn't feel that way now, especially because of the way he spoke to people and comported himself. It was probably because my contact with other people was so limited, I thought. I couldn't help feeling weaker and less confident than he seemed, especially at this moment.

When we were growing up together, I was the one who had the answers and who negotiated with Mama for anything we wanted. I never doubted that she loved him more than she did me, but I always sensed her expectation that I would be in control, I would make sure he did this or that.

Now, whereas what had happened to Big John left me frightened and feeling helpless, Trevor seemed to slip easily into the role of head of the household, at least until Big John was recuperated enough to return home.

Trevor ordered dinner for us and then began to describe what we would do, as if he had thought it all out during our ride to the hospital. It was almost as if he had known all along that we'd hear such bad news. I could only tremble at the possibilities of Big John's injuries. He was already planning around them.

"There are some slabs of wood in the back of the garage that were left over from some job Big John had done on the house. They're still good. I'm going to build a ramp to the back door so he can wheel himself in and out of the house. Also, just like we did for Mama, we'll fix up the den to be a bedroom so he doesn't have to be brought up and down the stairs. I mean, who could carry him up those stairs, anyway?"

He thought a moment and nodded.

"We could bring down the bed from the Forbidden Room and replace the sleep sofa with it. Whatever, there's plenty of time to make the changes, I'm sure. He'll be here at the hospital a while."

"How could you think of all those things so fast? I'm just getting used to the idea of him in a wheelchair."

"Remember what Mama said. You do what you have to do. I wonder," he said, "how Gabby's going to react to becoming his caretaker and nurse, because that's what she's going to be . . . if she stays."

"I don't know," I said, my mind whirling with all he was saying. If she left, would it all be in my hands? How much would I have to do? How much caretaking would Big John need? It was all so daunting, but Trevor didn't look very disturbed. If anything, he looked a little amused.

The waitress started to bring our food.

"I'm starving," he said. "You see the desserts?"

"What about Little Paula?" I asked when the waitress left.

He paused and then smiled.

"This is going to make it easier for us to get her back, Faith."

He started to eat.

Was it?

Could I be happy such a terrible thing had happened?

"How?"

"Big John doesn't rule our world as much. You'll see."

"How long are we going to stay here near the hospital?"

"We'll go home after we see him tomorrow. Got work to do, and I don't want to miss too much school."

"You're making it all sound too easy, Trevor."

He shrugged his famous shrug. "It is what it is."

We went right up to our room after dinner. Trevor took a shower while I used the breast pump. Afterward, we watched television until we were both asleep. I called Gabby at breakfast, but there was no answer.

"I'm sure Nick made her set out early," Trevor said. "He and Big John have been best friends for a long time."

Trevor thought we should wait until almost checkout to give Nick and Gabby time to arrive. He thought staying in our room and watching television was better than sitting in a hospital lobby. I was amazed at how clearly and calmly he thought of small details, especially now, the day after we had heard such terrible news, now that it was all sinking in. My thoughts were twisted and turned every which way. What about Little Paula? We still didn't know where she was, let alone figured out a way to bring her back. What could happen to us? How would we adjust our lives to accommodate what had happened? Would I really ever go to public school? How would Gabby react to all this? There was a cascade of questions.

When I brought some of this up, Trevor said, "We'll think about it all later. One thing at a time."

He laughed about something on television, checked his watch, and said, "Okay, let's go."

I was so frightened of what we were about to see in the hospital that I nearly tripped over my own feet going to the elevator. Trevor checked us out of the hotel, and we put everything back in the car.

"We have to get gas before we start back," Trevor said as we entered the hospital parking lot. "Remind me."

"You really think we shouldn't stay another night? What if Nick and Gabby want to stay?"

He looked at me as if to ask, *So what?* We parked and went into the lobby. Trevor had timed it well. We were there barely ten minutes before Nick and Gabby entered. Although she looked white with fear, she wore one of her prettiest light pink dresses and a light blue shawl. Her hair looked like she had just come from a beauty salon, and she had obviously spent time on her makeup. She clung to her brother's arm as if she were blind and had to.

Nick Damien wasn't a small man, by any means, but we really only saw him when he was with Big John, and Big John could make anyone look smaller than he really was. He wasn't quite six feet tall, and was stouter and softer-looking than Big John, for sure. He had close-cut hair a shade darker than Gabby's, and although he didn't have freckles like she did, he was someone who would always cling to his youthful look, with his green eyes and very light facial hair. I remembered him telling Mama that he didn't need to shave but once a week. It was always easy to see that he idolized Big John. He'd laugh when Big John laughed and grew angry at whatever angered Big John.

Trevor used to call him Big John's half-pint shadow.

Now he stepped over to us ahead of Gabby and embraced us both.

"This is so terrible," he said. "For us all."

"Is he awake yet?" Gabby asked. She clutched her purse in her right hand like a drowning woman clinging to a life preserver. I could see the veins embossed as she tightened her grip.

"I don't know," Trevor said. "We've been waiting for you. We have to let the doctor who saw us last night know we're all here. He said he'd meet with us, and then we could go in to see Big John. But I saw that they let only two visitors in at a time."

Nick nodded, kept his arm around Trevor's shoulders, and walked with us toward the receptionist's window. Trevor stepped forward and explained who we were and who we were there to see. She provided visitors' badges for us and called the surgery recovery room to tell the nurses we were here and to inform Dr. Lau. Trevor led the way to the elevator and the waiting room. It was as if he had been here a hundred times.

"We wait here," he explained. Nick looked quite impressed with him.

Gabby was already starting to sob quietly.

Nick chastised her. "You have to put on a brave face for him, Gabby. I told you that all the way here, practically."

She sucked in her breath, wiped her eyes, and nodded, before sitting beside me and taking my hand, as though I was the one who had started crying.

"It's all right. It's all right," she said. I suspected she had been chanting that to herself ever since she had woken up or been woken up this morning.

Trevor rose first when Dr. Lau appeared. He immediately introduced Nick and Gabby. I stood beside him.

"Well, the news is a little better this morning. He's definitely suffered serious injury to his spine, which has caused paraplegia, specifically loss of the use of his legs, but we believe he'll have control of his bodily functions."

He paused to let that settle.

"He can't be cured?" Nick asked.

"I'm afraid not, but he's obviously a very strong man. He'll be wheelchair-bound but eventually capable of doing almost everything but walk, run, and dance. There are so many accommodations for this disability.

"Of course, he'll be here recuperating, and we'll start his therapy. There are services available closer to his home, and arrangements can eventually be made to have a therapist once or twice a week. Some psychological counseling is necessary," he added. "We'll start that here, too. So . . . why don't we start with his children visiting first? He's kind of foggy yet, but he has been able to understand what's happened. Okay?"

No one spoke.

"Sure," Trevor said. He took my hand. "We'll visit first."

"Obviously, not long visits right now," the doctor said.

Trevor and I followed him into the surgical recovery area. I had to look down to be sure I was actually walking. My body felt that numb. Where was my anger when I needed it? I thought.

He took Little Paula away from us. Why wasn't that my strongest emotion?

Despite his size, or maybe because of it and how we had seen him all our lives, Big John looked small in the hospital bed. He still had an oxygen feed and an IV inserted in his big forearm. There were blotches of black-and-blue marks along his cheekbones, his chin, and what we could see of his neck. He looked barely awake. He didn't smile at the sight of us. He looked like he had stolen all my anger.

"We were here last night," Trevor immediately said, as if that might make things better.

He closed his eyes for a moment and then opened them. He started to speak but so low we had to practically lean on the bed to hear him.

"What?" Trevor said.

"Your mother did this to me," he said. He tried to nod, but obvious pain in his neck restricted his movement.

Trevor looked at me. I would swear forever that he was smiling even though his lips were tight. I could see that smile I knew so well. It was floating in his eyes.

FIVE

"How was he?" Nick asked when we came out of the surgical recovery area so he and Gabby could go in. He was already grimacing and bracing himself for the unpleasant news. He and Big John had spent practically all their free time in Lake Wallenpaupack together. Mama had thought that they each encouraged the other to do "unspeakable" things. She rarely joined them in the basement to drink with them or watch them play pool and drink. Prophetically, she once commented about Nick, "That man desperately needs his own woman and family. Taking care of his flighty sister is ruining his own life."

When the opportunity arose, Nick had probably hoped Big John would marry Gabby and officially take her off his hands. I felt certain that this was another reason for his disappointment.

He stared at the doorway to the recovery room as if he was looking at the entrance of an execution chamber. Of all people, Nick Damien would realize the total and devastating impact Big John's injuries would have on him. Our father had stood like a living Paul Bunyan. Mama had told us he was so impressive in size and strength that he captured the awe and attention of every man when he stepped into a room. She had told us that Nick cherished being beside him, sharing that spotlight. It wasn't difficult for me to imagine that Big John, being torn down from that pedestal, would despise himself, being wheeled about all his remaining life. All hopeful smiles and words of consolation would fall and melt like flakes of snow around him. Nick knew it; he'd rather be anywhere else.

"He's very angry," Trevor told him.

Nick nodded. "I bet."

Gabby whimpered.

"Faith and I will head home now," Trevor said. "There's a lot to do around the house, and I should return to school tomorrow. We'll plan on returning to the hospital as soon as we can spend some real time with him. Maybe you can find out when he'll be moved to a room."

"Yeah, sure," Nick said. "I'll be around to help around the house. I already checked on his truck. It's pretty much totaled. I'll look into the insurance for him. Don't worry about any of that."

Gabby had her head down as she took deep breaths, her shoulders lifting and falling. She looked like someone about to dive into a bottomless pool of sadness, I thought. She wouldn't do Big John any good if he looked closely at her face. Whatever promise she made would be thin air. As soon as he looked at her, he would know she had nothing like the inner strength Mama had possessed. To talk of any real future together would be to bathe in false hope, but I was sure no one would come right out and say it, not now.

I kept my head down, afraid Trevor would blurt out what we had heard Big John say about Mama.

"Drive carefully, and don't speed," Nick warned. "We'll be heading right back after our visit."

The way he said it made me wonder if there had been any doubt raised. Did she tell her brother on the way here that she couldn't live in the house with an invalid? Did she declare she wouldn't become Big John's nurse? Did she want to go straight home with us without even seeing Daddy? Did Nick tell her she had to think of us and not herself? Having her around reluctantly would surely be worse than her leaving.

Trevor nodded and took my hand. "See you soon," he said to Nick.

I looked back. It seemed to me Nick was practically dragging Gabby into the surgical recovery room.

"Why did Daddy say that about Mama?" I asked after we had gotten into the elevator.

"Conscience," he replied.

"What does that mean?"

The door opened, and he stepped out.

"What does that mean, Trevor?" I repeated, following him.

He kept walking. I practically had to run to catch up.

"Trevor?"

He stopped. "He always made fun of Mama talking about the spirits in the house. He'd say things like, 'They must have creaks for voices.' One time, he pretended her great-grandmother was accidentally flushed down a toilet. I remember she didn't get mad. She just said, 'One day, you'll see, and you'll be sorry you ever doubted.'

Well, that day must have come. I bet he'll tell us he heard her voice in the truck when he was losing control of it."

"I'm not sure I understand."

"He believes she's getting back at him," Trevor said. "Don't you see?"

I looked back at the hospital as if I could see Big John.

"If he blames Mama, won't he blame us somehow?"

Trevor shrugged. "Probably. We have more reason to blame him. Forget about it right now. We have things to do. As soon as we get home, we'll start searching for some clue as to where Little Paula is. We'll check out that name, Lydia Couch. Maybe we'll find out more. Mama will show us," he said.

He started for the car. Did he really believe that? I wondered. He had said it with such eerie confidence. I had always trusted Mama when she said our ancestors lived with us. When I was little, even though I might have imagined it, when I had seen a light and a shadow falling a certain way on a wall, I told Trevor I had seen one of the spirits. He either nodded as if it was no big deal or widened his eyes and smiled, often adding, "So did I. Mama didn't lie or make up a fairy tale for us."

Now as I recalled, it was always true. A passing breeze became the wisp of a spirit moving by in a hallway or on the stairs. The sound of a pipe straining under the force of more water pressure was the moan of someone who had died unnaturally, before his or her time, perhaps a baby born dead. Although our dreams, especially mine, would have been horrible nightmares to most children our age at the time, Mama told us they were gifts.

"They're letting you in. You're opening doors most can't even see. That means they'll protect you, care for you, and accept you as family. Never cry or scream or come running to me when that happens. You could drive them away," she warned.

I tried to be as brave as she wanted me to be, but sometimes, ashamedly, I'd cower under the covers and move just a little closer to Trevor, who either wasn't seeing and hearing what I was or had already learned to accept and welcome it.

No. Trevor was right. It was not that big of a stretch to believe what Big John had told us in the recovery room. Mama had been with him in that truck cab. But if he told anyone else, he or she would think it was simply a delusion coming from his injuries and his horrible experience. No one would believe it. No one but us.

"You forgot to remind me to get gas," Trevor said as soon as I got into the car.

"I didn't have a chance. You're practically running away from here."

He started the engine and drove out of the parking lot without denying it.

After we got gas and started for home, he said we'd just drive straight home and not stop for anything to eat. The gray skies were opening to reveal light blue. At least we wouldn't be driving in the rain, even though the day felt dank and dark.

"How long do you think they'll stay with Big John?"

"From what you've been telling me Gabby said and the way she was reacting in there, I'm sure she'll try to get out of there as quickly as she can. Nick will stop for lunch, though, so we should have a good few hours by ourselves."

"And Critter. Don't forget him. He must have messed by now."

He looked at me and smiled. "In Big John's new bedroom," he said. He lost his smile. "He'll probably want to get rid of the dog now."

"Why?"

"He can't walk him or run with him or do anything much more

than watch him feed and hear him bark and whine. No, he'll want to give him away, unless we decide we want to keep him. I always wanted a dog, but Mama insisted all the work would fall on her. I used to think he'd bring one home anyway from one of his trips."

"I guess I'll take care of him."

"You'll be quite busy, Faith. We're getting Little Paula back," he said, his eyes narrow and his lips tight.

"Okay," I said. I wanted to feel happy about that, but I couldn't help wondering whether Trevor wanted her back because he loved her as much as I did or because retrieving her would be somehow defying and taking vengeance on Big John. Maybe it didn't matter as long as we had her again.

He drove faster than he had going to the hospital and at times was well over the speed limit, but I was afraid to say anything. He hovered over the steering wheel like a race-car driver and wore such a look of determination that I knew he would snap back at me. Along the way, I had to use my breast pump. I was hungry but decided to close my eyes and ignore it. I must have fallen asleep, because next thing I knew, Trevor was poking me to tell me we were minutes away from home.

I was hoping to see Mr. Longstreet when we reached his house first, but he was nowhere to be seen.

"Now I'm starving," Trevor declared when we pulled into the driveway. "Let's throw together some sandwiches and then get started with the search."

As I feared, Critter had messed and Gabby had forgotten to put down paper. It didn't do my appetite any good to clean it away. The dog was so happy to see us, to see anyone, I thought, that he wouldn't stop jumping and barking until I finally held him while Trevor worked on our sandwiches.

"I'm going to start in his closet," Trevor said as we ate. "Search through all his jackets and pants. You go through every drawer, and look again where you found the money."

"Okay."

When I gazed around our kitchen and looked back at the den, I suddenly felt weak and sick. The vision of Big John in that hospital bed and remembering the way Dr. Lau described his diagnosis thickened the dark pall that had fallen over this house when Little Paula was taken. Even if we were able to find her and bring her back, what sort of happiness would we find here? What kind of a home would this become? How could she grow up under all this sadness and anger? She would never know whether Big John was smiling or grimacing at her and looking at her with bitter envy when she started to walk. No matter how I explained him, she would see him as an ogre, terrorizing us even from his wheelchair. That's the way I imagined him to be.

This wasn't some far-fetched fear. Because he was so enraged by what had happened to him, it was difficult to visualize Big John ever smiling again. I was sure I would have nightmares about him wheeling forward and grabbing hold of either Trevor or me to shake the life out of us. Imagining Gabby at the center of it all was impossible. She'd be crying all the time, and he'd be ranting at her. Although I would never say the words, they were there in my thoughts: *Should we let Little Paula go? Do we really want to bring her back into this world now?*

"What are you thinking so hard about?" Trevor asked.

"How horrible it's going to be here."

"Not for us," he said. He smiled. "It's going to be better for us. I can see Mama sitting right there beside you, nodding and smiling. When we bring Little Paula back, our ancestors will celebrate. Maybe it will be dark and dismal in that corner of the house," he said, nodding at the den, "but not in ours. Let's get started with the search."

He rose, brought his glass and dish to the sink, and headed for the stairs. I followed, Critter trailing behind me and then whining at the bottom of the stairs.

"Just wait there," I told him, and hurried to join Trevor in Big John and Gabby's bedroom. He was already pulling out Big John's pants and jackets and throwing them on the bed. I watched him a moment and then went to the drawer that contained the envelope of money. He opened it and began to count it.

"There's at least fifty thousand dollars here," he said.

"How do we know for certain that this money has anything to do with Little Paula?" I asked.

"We don't, but I have my suspicions. Wait."

He pushed aside some shirts.

"Here's Mama's legal papers. We'll keep these in our room. Check all the slips of paper in the envelope. Look for names, addresses, anything."

I sifted through everything carefully while he dug into the pockets of all the jackets and pants on the bed.

"There's nothing here," I said, "nothing in with the money."

He continued raking through the clothes and then stopped at a piece of paper that looked ripped from a larger sheet. He read it and looked at me, his eyes brightening.

"She never asked you to return her phone to her, did she?"

"Gabby? No, she didn't, and I didn't think of it, either. It's in my purse."

"Let's go get it," he said, hurrying out of the room. "C'mon!" he screamed from the hallway. "They're not going to be that far behind us. You'll see."

We went back to the kitchen. I opened my purse and took out the phone. Trevor practically seized it and began to explore.

"What are you looking for?"

"Seeing if she has this name and phone number in the phone, a recent call," he said, giving me the piece of paper he had found in a pair of Big John's pants. "Voilà!" he said, and showed it to me.

"You think . . ."

"Let's go on the internet to find the address, and we'll know when we go there."

"We're just going to go in and get Little Paula?"

"No. We'll stake it out first. First be sure that she is there."

I looked back toward the stairs, envisioning all that money in the envelope.

"You think . . . you think they sold her to this person?"

"We'll see. Let's not get our hopes up too high until we investigate. Maybe it's nothing," he said, pointing at the slip of paper. "Maybe this is just someone they know, one of Gabby's girl-friends. In the meantime . . . let's not act like we're even thinking about it. I'm going to go check out that lumber for a ramp. Better take Critter out for a while, too. If I'm right, they'll be here soon, and the best thing we could do is get them to believe we're trying to do the right things and prepare for Big John's return."

"Okay."

"When they're here, I'll suggest Nick help me change the furni-ture around. There's a closet in Big John's den. We'll empty it of all his junk and start bringing down his clothes tomorrow."

"Will Gabby stay with us?"

He thought a moment. "I think Nick will make her, at least until Big John is brought home. They're probably arguing about it all the way back. But how would she look, deserting us at this point,

Faith? Even though you're practically taking care of her most of the time, she's the legal adult. We have to take advantage of that."

"What do you mean? How?"

"Be as nice to her as we can. Sympathize with her, make it seem as if we're sadder for her than we are for ourselves. Actually, that's not so far from the truth."

We were both quiet, contemplating what the next few weeks of our lives would be like.

"Our main goal is to find and bring back Little Paula," Trevor said. "Whatever we have to do to maintain our lives here until then, we'll do. Okay?"

"What made you so brave and grown-up?" I asked, almost resenting him for it.

He smiled. "Not *what*, but *who*. Mama, of course. Look at all she taught us in homeschool, moving us faster in our studies. Sometimes in class, I have to pretend I'm just learning something and be careful with my answers when the teacher calls on me."

"Why?"

"The other students still find me . . . different. Everyone assumes I'm supposed to be behind them. I've had some of the boys tell me they'd hate having to be at home all the time, and there's always the talk about girls. I think that's another reason you shouldn't be so concerned about the girls I talk to or who talk to me."

"What?"

"They're still not sure about me. I think too much. I can't help it sometimes. I act years older. One thing you'll learn about kids in public school when you do attend someday: being too different is not a good thing. It either frightens or makes the others feel somehow inferior, and the easiest solution for them is to avoid you."

"Is that what's really been happening to you?"

"Yes," he said. "I told myself not to care, but that's lying to yourself. Everyone wants to belong, be popular. You'll see."

"Maybe they'll feel sorry for you when they hear about Big John."

"Maybe. You can be sure I'll take advantage of it, especially with my teachers. Let's make sure Nick and Gabby feel sorry for us when they arrive. Practice crying."

"I don't have to practice."

He laughed. "Crying about him, not Little Paula—although that's a good idea."

"What is?"

"When you put on a sad face or do cry, think about Little Paula," he said. "Until we get her back," he added.

"Okay."

"I'll get to the lumber. I'd like Nick to see how considerate and forward-thinking we are. It will make him feel sorrier for us. Take Critter out."

I went for his leash.

While Trevor rummaged through the garage, I started into the woods with Critter. For almost all my life, this area of the forest had been part playground and part classroom but also, as it had been for Trevor, the place for my make-believe. Trevor had been the only boy in my life, but as I grew older and read more about the romances men and women had in the stories, I couldn't help envisioning myself in such a relationship.

I knew my naivete had led me into a near disaster with our neighbor's grandson, Lance, but even now, I often found myself dreaming about it and the way I had wanted it to be. I didn't think I was hurting Trevor. Part of my vision for the future was imagining that he would find a more romantic love of his life than I could be.

We were too used to each other to create fantasies about each other. It would be dreadful to tell him, but I couldn't foresee his kissing me the way Lance had, despite Lance's deceptive motives.

Mama used to tell me to beware of romantic love. "Big John and I began with passion so strong that I was convinced it would live forever. In a way, we used each other, so I can't blame it all on him, but he drifted just like a boy in a candy shop would, going from this to that, always calling the new discovery the best ever but always looking for something better. Romantic love is the match that sets your relationship on fire, but to make it lasting, you have to have constant recommitment. Do you understand what I'm saying?"

I didn't, so I shook my head.

She smiled. "You will. You'll come to see that what you have with Trevor is bound by more than that spark of passion. You'll become so much a part of each other that you cannot fathom being apart. That is love."

As I stood looking through the trees toward Mr. Longstreet's house and remembering the way Lance would come, leaping over the stone wall, I knew in my heart that Mama was probably right.

But I also knew that I didn't want her to be.

Would I ever?

I turned as I heard Trevor bringing out the boards to make Big John's future ramp.

"Do you really know how to do that, Trevor? Maybe you should wait for Nick."

He dropped the wood and turned to me, smiling.

"I researched it. Don't worry."

"When?"

He paused.

"When you were sleeping in the hotel. I went down and used the hotel's computer."

"It just came to you to do that?"

"I thought . . . remember forethought, the best of thoughts?"

I stared at him, amazed and waiting for those words to follow. Somehow I didn't want to hear it. It was beginning to frighten me to hear it.

"Mama put it in my head. Just the way she got into Big John's in the truck."

Even though I was skeptical, I knew that if Trevor thought I didn't believe it, believe that Mama was really here with us, he'd never find a way to bring Little Paula back. He'd tell me I didn't deserve her.

We both turned at the sound of a car entering the driveway. It was Nick and Gabby.

"Sooner than I thought," Trevor said, looking at them. "I guess she had no appetite." He smiled. "As Mama would say . . . like reading an open book of secrets."

I started out of the woods and greeted Nick and Gabby with him. She had obviously been crying. Her eyes were red, and her complexion was the color of a fading calla lily. Nick, visibly upset, slammed the car door and looked at Trevor.

"Be a while before we need that," he said. "But good thinking. We'll need to be sure that wood is thick and strong enough. I can get some fresh lumber."

"How was he with you?" I asked.

Gabby looked up, and Nick paused.

"He wanted to die, but we assured him we'd be there for him, and you two would as well, right, Gabby?"

She looked up fearfully at us. "Yes," she said.

"There will be a lot to do around here to make it comfortable for him. We have to imagine him moving about in a wheelchair. We saw the doctor again. He'll be in therapy and such for weeks yet. Lot of healing to do, inside and out. They'll move him to a room in two days, so returning next weekend would be good. We'll all go together. I don't have another job for about three weeks.

"You guys got to grow up fast, do good in school, and definitely not get into any trouble."

Was everyone just going to pretend Little Paula had never happened?

"We were thinking we should turn his den into his bedroom and avoid stairs," Trevor said.

"Yeah, good idea. We'll clean it up real good, right, Gabby?"

"Yes," she said weakly.

"Over the next few days, we'll bring down everything he needs, maybe move the bed from . . . from the other guest room and take the sofa bed out. It's not that comfortable," Trevor said.

"That's pretty good thinking, Trevor. Big John is going to be proud of you, maybe not for a while, but he will be eventually."

Nick turned back to his car.

"I stopped and picked up some fried chicken and biscuits for us. Gabby will warm them up."

"Sounds good," Trevor said. He looked at me.

"I'll get the table set," I said, and we all headed for the back door.

Just before we entered, Gabby put her hand on my arm, and I turned to her.

"He'll hate every moment," she said, and walked in ahead of me.

Trevor heard her say it. "Don't pay attention to her right now."

"She won't stay, Trevor."

"Let's just make sure she does until he returns. After that, I wouldn't want her here anyway. She helped him take away Little Paula."

He walked in ahead of me. I stood there a moment and looked back at the woods, at the shadows that had seeped in between the trees and had begun a slow, steady crawl toward our house. Maybe it was because Trevor was saying it so much, or maybe it was real, but I was sure I saw her, Mama, looking toward the house, looking toward me, and smiling.

Critter leaned against my leg.

The shadows deepened, and what I thought I saw was swallowed up in the darkness that was falling rapidly and chasing me quickly into the house with Critter.

Anyone who had stepped in with me would see that Trevor was the most enthusiastic and energetic. He glanced at me and smiled.

I wouldn't even have to tell him what I thought I had seen in the woods.

He'd say he saw her first.

SIX

At dinner, it was mostly Nick and Trevor who talked, making plans about changes around the house and completing all the necessary preparations for Big John's return. Trevor suggested condensing or moving some furniture to the basement so that Big John could navigate his wheelchair easily through the house. He had even looked up something called a stairway chair lift.

"We can get him a second wheelchair that we leave in the basement. I bet he can still play pool with you and even throw darts," Trevor said with convincing excitement, so convincing that I had to give him a second look. He moved his eyes to reassure me that he was just placating Nick.

Then he turned to Gabby and said, "Big John's never going to be as happy as he was, but at least we can all help to get him halfway there."

"Of course we can," Nick said. "Those are good ideas, Trevor. I think he'll be proud of you when he finds all this."

"Then let's get it done, soldier," Trevor said, sounding like the army commander he used to pretend to be when he played in the woods, charging at invisible enemies hiding behind bushes and trees. Just like then, he looked back at me, urging me to come along.

Nick smiled and nodded.

Gabby was mostly quiet throughout the dinner and ate very little. I could see from the way Nick looked at her from time to time that he was not happy about the way she was behaving. Her face seemed to be folding into itself, a shelf of tears icing over her eyes. The whole time Nick and Trevor talked about things they would do to make Daddy's life as close as possible to what it was, she sat with her head down, her fingers weaving in and out of each other.

All this talk about how to make the house comfortable for someone with paraplegia obviously disturbed her. I felt sure that if she could, she would get up and bolt out the door, never to be seen again. In the end, that wouldn't matter to us, as long as Big John was home and was serving as our legal guardian.

"So let's give it all a little time," Nick declared at the end of our dinner, "and take things slowly." He looked at me. "After he's settled in, you can concentrate again on your schooling and such."

"I'm not in school yet," I reminded him.

"Oh, right."

I was anticipating his saying something about Little Paula, but he didn't.

"Well, I'm sure there's all sorts of paperwork to do in order to get you registered for school. Either Gabby or me probably got to become your guardian, I think they call it. For the time being, at least. I got a friend whose brother's an attorney. I'll ask him for some advice tomorrow. No worries for now," he said. "I'll come back in the morning, Trevor, and we can start on that ramp. Over the next few days, we'll rearrange some furniture, see what we can store away just as you suggested."

"I'm going to school, so it will have to be in the afternoon," Trevor said. "I'm back at quarter of three."

"Oh. Right. Well, I got a few things to do around my house anyway in the morning, changes I have to do there, too."

I saw the way Gabby was looking at him, probably wondering if he meant he'd have to get it cleaned up for her to move back. I was betting she probably hoped so.

"I'll get the fresh lumber and what we need for the ramp and be over in my pickup," Nick said. "I'll just check in with Gabby in the morning to see what else you need in the way of groceries and such." He turned to Gabby. "Unless you're up to going shopping."

"No. I need . . . some rest," she said. "I don't want to see anyone or anyone to see me."

"Yeah, sure. Faith will be a big help in the meantime," he said, without even looking at me. The possibility of my having a life, too, wasn't his concern. The absence of Little Paula, even from their thoughts, angered me. It was a fait accompli, but I kept it under the lid like a pot of boiling water.

He paused, glanced at Big John's den, and shook his head. "Can't imagine him confined to a wheelchair."

Gabby looked up, the fear and horror exploding over her face like a cracked egg. "I can't lift him in and out of it," she said.

"He won't need you to do that. Once he recuperates, he'll still be able to lift you over his head, I'm sure."

"But I have to go back to work."

"Really, Gabby?" Nick said. "You think you're going back to work?"

She looked at us and then down at the table again. The silence felt like a funeral was about to begin. Everyone was to suck in his or her own sorrow.

"Just an all-around bad day today," Nick said. "We'll all have to get a good night's sleep," he added, looking directly at Gabby. "We don't want to make him feel any worse than he does when we see him again. You give someone like this hope, not sympathy, and certainly don't show him any pity, hear?"

She sighed deeply. She looked trapped, caged in by what was the right thing to do. For a moment, I felt sorrier for her than I did for Trevor and me. Then I thought, *Good.* She should suffer as an accomplice to the stealing of Little Paula. Long ago, Mama had taught me that sins were meant to fester until your conscience begged for forgiveness.

Gabby rose and began clearing the table to avoid Nick's angry eyes. I rose to help her. When Nick started to leave, she stopped working and followed him out to his car. Trevor and I looked at each other knowingly.

"We need her," he reminded me. "For a while. So don't do or say anything that will give her an excuse to leave."

I nodded, and we both went to the window to see if we could hear their conversation. It was clear that whatever she was saying was getting Nick angrier.

"How could you even think of putting more pressure on this family right now?" he shouted.

We heard her sobbing. Whatever he said after that was clearly an expression of disgust. He got into his car and slammed the door, started the engine, and drove off quickly. She stood there watching him and clutching her hands close to her throat. Then she turned and started back into the house.

"Remember, Faith, she has to feel sorrier for us than she does for herself," Trevor said. "Anytime you feel sorry for her, you remind yourself she helped him steal Little Paula."

"I know. I already thought of that."

He took my hand, and we sat on the sofa. She came in slowly and looked at us holding hands and staring down at the floor as if we were both still quite stunned. Actually, I was. So much could change in your life in minutes. I had never wished more that I had Mama's inner strength.

Trevor looked up first at her. "Faith is very, very frightened," he said. "She's afraid Big John will do something to himself now."

"Oh, no," she said. "He wouldn't."

"Neither of us is eighteen," he reminded her.

That spoke pages. She understood.

"Of course. Don't you two worry. I'm here for you. We'll all get through this together. My brother is a big, big help. He's always been there for me."

"Yeah, Big John's lucky to have him as a friend," Trevor said.

She started to stand straighter, unclutching her hands. Whether it was an act or not, demanded by her brother, she was going to look stronger for us.

"The best thing is for everyone to help do the things you and Nick discussed. Tomorrow, Faith and I will clean out that den while you're in school, and we'll work on his clothes, too. Right, Faith?"

"Yes," I said, smiling through real tears, tears born of fear and sadness. Despite it all, I actually felt sympathy for Big John. Maybe Mama was punishing him justly, or maybe it was simply a bad truck accident, but it was difficult to be totally unsympathetic toward him given his injuries now. If I were in his place, I'm sure I would have uttered a desire to just die, too.

"Well," Trevor said, rising and tugging on me to stand. "Nick's right. We should all get a good night's rest. Tons of things to do ahead of us."

"Okay," she said. "I'll look after the kitchen and Critter. You two go up to bed."

"Thank you, Gabby," Trevor said. "We're so happy you're here for us."

"Of course," she said.

"And for Big John," Trevor added.

I smiled and nodded, too.

"Oh, yes," she said. "Yes."

We started for the stairs. With his back to her, Trevor was smiling with his wide, impish grin.

Later, after we were both in bed, he lay back with his hands behind his head and spoke, staring up at the ceiling.

"We have to be careful that we don't reveal what we really want to do," he began. "I'll scout out the address after school, maybe tomorrow, maybe the next day, and check on this name, Lydia Couch. Then we'll plan around Gabby and Nick. Nick will be here as much as he can be, but despite what she said at dinner, Gabby will find ways to get out and about. She'll want to be with her friends to soak in their consolation. She'll milk it, for sure. The key," he said, turning to me, "is our being patient."

"What if that's not where Little Paula is?"

"We'll work on Gabby after Nick is gone. She'll tell us something. I have some ideas for how to get information out of her. Maybe one night we'll all get drunk together."

"Drunk?"

"We'll pretend, but she'll really be drunk."

"It's funny, but I never realized you were such a plotter, Trevor Eden."

I could see his smile in the light of a quarter-moon sidestepping clouds.

"Mama taught me," he said.

"What did she teach you?"

"She said, 'Sometimes it's better if you don't let your right hand know what your left hand is doing. Deception has its proper place.'"

I silently searched my memories for when she had said anything similar to me.

"She told you a lot more than she told me, it seems."

"You had your face in a book lots of times. The truth is . . . I think you were always more independent than I was, Faith. I grew up here practically hanging on to Mama's apron strings."

Yes, I thought, *he's right*. At least he was honest about it.

"You always seemed to be confident and full of curiosity, always wanting something more," he said. "Always wanting to have girlfriends, be out and about. You had dreams of traveling. There's always been that hunger in you, more than in me."

"Really?"

Funny, I thought. Even though you might look at yourself in the mirror all day, you wouldn't see things about yourself that others saw. You could literally die never knowing who you really were. But you wouldn't believe anything anyone said about you without trust. There was too much jealousy and competition. I didn't have to be out and about in the world to know that. Maybe Mama had taught me that; maybe I just realized it instinctively.

"Of course, really. You were the one who pushed us to go to

Mr. Longstreet's house and meet his grandson, weren't you? You were hungrier for company than I was."

He laughed. "And here I am, the one in public school."

"I don't forget it," I said. "And I don't forget that Mama wanted it that way."

He instantly realized what he had said had saddened me. "I know. Sorry."

He leaned over to kiss me on the cheek.

"Don't worry. You'll have what you want, everything you want. I'll make sure of it. Mama would want it that way."

He leaned back and closed his eyes.

Why was it that what Trevor was saying made me happy and frightened at the same time? I fell asleep with my arm curled as if I had Little Paula cradled there.

I woke before he did, but I lay there, feeling the weight of yesterday. I was half hoping that when I had woken, it would all have been a bad dream, starting with the stealing of Little Paula. I wished so hard for that to be true that I was sure I heard her cry.

Trevor woke with a start and got out of bed quickly, not even gazing back at me. It was as if sleep had been like chains restraining him. He rustled around for his clothes and hurried to the bathroom just like he did most mornings. He didn't check to see if I was awake. When he appeared again, he looked bright and full of energy. It was almost as if he had completely forgotten all that had happened.

"Gabby's not up," he said. "I expected it. Probably wants to stay in bed all day and not face the music."

"What music?"

"Preparing for Daddy's homecoming, satisfying Nick, comforting us."

"I'm not crazy about getting up, either."

"C'mon. Remember our plan. You try to avoid talking at all about Little Paula and be concentrating on what to do around the house to make it comfortable for Big John. As I said, I might not be able to check on that address today because Nick will be waiting for me to start work on the ramp."

"Every day she's away getting used to a new mother . . ."

"I know, but don't worry. I'll figure something out soon. I'm going to get some breakfast."

I rose and dressed slowly, wishing I had half his energy, optimism, and enthusiasm. The door to Gabby and Big John's bedroom was closed. I didn't hear a sound. Trevor had taken Critter out and was just coming back in when I entered the kitchen.

"Pretty cloudy," he said. "I think it's going to rain most of the day. Try to be cheerful with Gabby."

"Cheerful?"

"Look, life here is looking miserable for her."

"It's not exactly joyful for me."

"The less she sees of that . . ."

"I don't know if I can be that deceptive."

"You have to be," he said. He squeezed my arm gently and left the house. I watched him from the window.

Something's changed him, I thought. The darkness and depression that he had after they had taken Little Paula seemed to have morphed into a faith in himself that brought him happiness and hope. It was almost as if he welcomed all our new challenges so he could prove himself a man. There was no doubt in my mind that Mama would be proud of him, proud of how he was handling everything, but that still didn't quiet the rumbling trepidation I felt in my heart.

He drove off, and I fed Critter. I was nearly done eating my breakfast when I heard some movement upstairs just before the phone rang. I heard myself gasp. Was it the hospital? Had something fatal happened to Big John? Gingerly, I lifted the receiver and said, "Hello."

It was Nick.

I could tell from his tone of voice that he was very upset that Gabby wasn't up, dressed, and downstairs with me. She was supposed to tell him what we needed. I rattled off some of the basics like milk, juice, butter, and bread.

"Okay. You tell her I'll be there for lunch," he said. It clearly sounded to me like a warning.

After another good five minutes, she came down and entered the kitchen. I was cleaning up. She looked dressed to go out. Her hair was pinned and neatly flowed down behind her head. She was wearing lipstick and a little rouge and had on a belted black pantsuit. She clutched a matching black bag with a decorative gold circle.

"I'm sorry I didn't have breakfast with you," she said, "but my girlfriends texted me last night and invited me to have breakfast with them at the Lake Club. I know they all just feel sorry for me and want to cheer me up."

"I thought we were going to work on the den and start moving his clothing."

"Oh, we will."

"Nick just called and said I should tell you he'll be here for lunch," I said.

Her smile faded. "Lunch? I thought he was busy all morning. Okay, I'll pick something up on the way home. Keep him occupied if I'm a little late. I'm sure you'll be all right. Don't worry about changing things in the house. We'll do it, but I'm sure John won't be home for quite a while."

She avoided looking at me and went to the door.

"Shouldn't you call the hospital to see how he is?" I asked.

"Nick said he would do that," she said, smiling. "I'm sure he'll have a report for us when he's here. Oh," she said when she opened the door, "it's starting to rain. How dreadfully depressing, today of all days."

She reached to the side where we had an umbrella, stepped out, and closed the door. The silence that followed was like the aftermath of a gunshot. It seemed to reverberate in echoes.

I went up to use the breast pump.

Before Little Paula was born, I was often alone in the house. Big John would be on a trip, Gabby would be at work, and Trevor would be at school. I tried to keep busy with my studies and taking walks. I read that this was a good thing for a pregnant woman to do. I knew I had to stay far enough from anyone driving by. I went into the darker areas of the woods and sometimes sat on a tree stump until it felt uncomfortable. My imagination always played tricks on me. I'd hear someone in the house or imagine Mama was standing just outside the back door watching for me. Sometimes I'd talk to Little Paula in my womb, describing the world she was soon to be born into.

I wondered how she was reacting to being somewhere completely different now, hearing a different woman's voice. Did she recoil from it? Did she trust it? Was there a place in her infant's mind for her to miss me? When she cried, was she crying for me as well as for milk or comfort? Whoever held her and cared for her right now surely wanted to keep her healthy and well, but that wasn't enough. She wanted me. She wanted to be home.

It was difficult to think of her without feeling so much emptiness in my heart.

And when I did, I didn't feel sorry for Big John, not at all.

Mama was probably angry whenever I did, anyway.

The rain grew hard at times, the drops tapping like long fingernails on the windows. I worried about the leak that had caused so much damage and led Mama to her injury, which eventually resulted in her death. Close to eleven o'clock, it became a steady drizzle. I tried to read, but I couldn't concentrate on anything and finally just sat in the living room and waited for Gabby's return, hoping she'd be here before Nick. For me, it was more difficult to lie and pretend with him. Gabby welcomed lies, like someone afraid the truth would burn her, always burn her deeply.

I wondered if most unmarried women her age were like that. Were any like me? Once I did get out in the world and meet other girls, would I be so different that none would trust me or care to know me? Would they think of me as the girl who lived in a cave?

Unfortunately, Nick arrived before she did. I rose and quickly went to make some fresh coffee.

"Where is she?" he demanded the moment he opened the door and saw me. He had seen that her car was gone.

"She went to have breakfast with some friends." I looked at the clock. It was twenty after twelve. "I'm sure she'll be back any moment. I have some coffee going."

He closed the door sharply.

"I have the groceries you told me you needed," he said, putting them on the counter.

I started to put them away.

"Did you call the hospital?" I asked. "She said you would."

"Yeah. He's still in a lot of pain, so he's heavily sedated. No way he could talk on a phone. It's a long haul, for sure."

He slammed himself into a kitchenette chair.

"My sister has never been one to face unhappy things. When our father took seriously ill, she wouldn't go to the hospital. He died without her seeing him, and she was definitely his favorite."

"She never went to the hospital?"

He shook his head. I almost said, *But she described how horrible it was.*

"No. She stayed home, crying in her room and doing just what she's doing now, sucking up sympathy from her friends. It's my fault. I've always protected her. My mother was too into herself to care."

"How did you get her to go see Big John in the hospital, then?"

He looked at me and smirked. "She went . . . but she was worthless. She stood behind me and didn't say a word to him. He was too out of it to notice or care. I'm not going to let her just fluff him off on you two," he vowed. "Time she took responsibility for something."

I nodded. *Yes*, I thought, *time she took responsibility for stealing Little Paula, too.*

"She was supposed to get us food for lunch, but I can make you an egg sandwich if you like."

He thought a moment. "Yeah, sure. Thanks."

I began.

"You two are quite mature compared to kids I see today," he said. "I have no doubt you'll handle the new situation quite well. Your mother would surely be proud of you both."

I kept my back to him and debated whether I would mention Little Paula. My mother wouldn't be proud of that. He complained about his sister ignoring ugly things, but he was deliberately ignoring her being stolen from me and given away. *Don't do it,* I could hear Trevor warn. *Don't give them reason to become suspicious.*

"Your mother wasn't that fond of Gabby," he said, "but I imagine you knew that."

I didn't respond. He was right, of course, but how could reinforcing that help things now?

Just as I served him a cup of coffee and his sandwich, we heard Gabby drive in. The rain had slowed until it was little more than a faint drizzle. I saw her get out with a bag of groceries and start for the door.

"This is delicious," Nick said just before she entered.

"Oh, you didn't wait. I bought you some pastrami," she said.

He glared at her. I held my breath. Was he going to chastise her in front of me?

"Take out a slice. I'll put it in the sandwich Faith made me," he said.

She rushed to do it, smiling at me nervously.

"Nick called the hospital," I said, before things turned too nasty. She didn't look like she would ever ask.

"Oh?"

"Not much change yet," he muttered. "Still heavily sedated."

She nodded and gave him the pastrami. He ate and sipped his coffee.

"You want a sandwich?" Gabby asked me.

"Not yet," I said. "You go ahead."

"Oh, I'm not hungry. We had one of those breakfast buffets at the Lake Club." She smiled at Nick. "You know how I have to taste everything. Mother complained all the time about how much I wasted. No one complains at the club. I could have a pinch of this and a pinch of that and just leave the rest. I'll just have some coffee and sit with you while you eat."

He smirked and sat back. "The Lake Club. Just la-di-da, even now."

"Well, what am I supposed to do? Lock myself in the room and cry?"

He shook his head and looked at me as if to say she was a lost cause. Then he stopped eating and looked troubled, thoughtful.

"John has such a great driving record. I don't recall him ever tapping someone's bumper. Driving was his whole life. I don't think there was anything he took more seriously. And as far as I know, he wasn't pushing his hours this time."

"Maybe he was drinking," Gabby said. "I've seen beer bottles in his truck cab."

"That was only for when he slept in the damn thing," he shot back at her, as if he was the one being accused. "You know he doesn't drink when he drives. You heard him complain about the other drivers that do. And besides, they'd have checked the alcohol content in his blood."

He stared hard at her.

"What?"

"Did you upset him before he left?"

"No. He upset me, giving me a list of things he wanted done in the house, rattling them off like he was a drill sergeant and I was in the army."

"And? Go on. What did you say? Did you complain, make a fuss?"

"Well, I'm not a maid here, Nick."

"You're not a maid at home, either," he snapped. "Ma cleaned your diapers until you were twenty."

"Oh, that's such an unfair and disgusting thing to say." Her eyes teared. "You can't find a way to blame me for all this. You're always finding ways to blame me for something. You should see him at home," she told me.

He looked a little sorry when I turned to him.

"All I'm saying is a man with his experience knows how to navigate going down a hill and approaching a turn," Nick said.

"Maybe something broke," she said.

"He takes really good care of his truck, better than I do mine."

"Not anymore," Gabby said. It came from her lips like a thought unbridled.

He looked at her sharply, his rage bringing crimson to his cheeks and some whiteness to his lips.

"That's just the kind of talk and thinking we want to avoid," he said.

She looked at me. I had suddenly become the judge and jury for both of them. She saw that I wasn't going to leap to her defense.

"I know. I know. I'm sorry. I'm upset, too." She looked at him. "You always think you're the only one who can get upset." She dabbed at her eyes with a napkin.

"Somehow everything always rolls around to center on you. Daddy spoiled the hell out of you," he said.

Nick finished eating with a vengeance, his eyes on her. I didn't want to say a word and start them at each other again. She stared down at her coffee, her lips trembling as she held back her tears.

"I got to pick up a few more things," he told me. "Tell Trevor I'll be back about the time he comes home."

"Okay."

He rose. "Thanks for lunch. I'll unload my materials in front of the garage and leave." He looked at the den and then at Gabby. "You work on this place as if he's coming home tomorrow, and do the things he asked you to do. I'm not going to put up with you running away from trouble this time."

He turned and left.

"He'll find a way to blame all this on me," she said to me. "Just wait." She took a deep breath. "He acts like we can make things hunky-dory just by rearranging furniture." She wiped away the few tears that had escaped and then smiled. "At least I had a good time this morning. It was so good to get out and see people who care about their appearance."

She sighed deeply when I didn't offer a supportive comment.

"Okay, I'm going to go change to help, not that it will make my brother happier."

"I think he's just taking it all hard, Gabby. They're such close friends, right?"

"You don't know the half of it. I've always been his punching bag when something upset him."

I looked away. After all that had happened in our family, I wasn't exactly in the mood to feel sorry for her. Try as hard as she could to get me to, she realized I wasn't going to spend any time on this.

"Maybe I'll start working on John's clothes, what we'll be bringing down to set up the den as his new bedroom. There are some things that should have been thrown out a long time ago, but he wouldn't. I'm sure he won't care now."

"Okay," I said.

She looked at the door through which Nick had just left. "I wish he'd get another trucking job tomorrow and leave us alone for a while."

She headed for the stairs.

Leave us alone for a while? What did she think we were going to do? Have parties? Invite her friends? What about Big John? What about Little Paula?

She's not going to last, I thought, *even with her brother breathing down her neck making her.*

She didn't come out of her room before Nick returned and Trevor drove in right behind him. The sky had cleared to partly cloudy. Neither came into the house. They went right to work on the ramp, as if Big John really was coming home tomorrow. I watched from a kitchen window until I heard Gabby's footsteps on the stairs.

She wore jeans and a light pink athletic shirt, her hair as put together as it was this morning. I was surprised at how much makeup she had on, too.

"I meant to come down sooner, but I lay down for a rest and fell asleep. Can you imagine? We never know how tired we really are. I hate that just-slept look, don't you?" she added, justifying her makeup for sure.

"There's rarely anyone here for me to impress one way or the other," I said.

"I know. I really have been thinking about you. While John's recuperating, we'll do more than just get everything prepared for a crippled man. We'll work on getting you ready to face the world."

"I don't think John or anyone like that enjoys being called crippled."

"Well, what do you call them?" she asked, her hands on her hips.

"Disabled."

"Same thing to me," she said. "He still can't stand on his own two legs, and I'm hardly strong enough for him to lean on. Few people are."

"Those words are the same thing to you because it's not you," I countered, a lot more sharply than Trevor would have wanted. "My mother told me that when people are injured like that or born with a disability, they don't like to be treated as inferior. You wouldn't."

"Oh." She thought a moment. "I guess not. Well, let's not think about it until we have to. You're always quoting your mother. When it came to something like the . . . *disabled*, my mother would say nothing's ugly if you look the other way."

Ugly? Shut your mouth, Faith, I told myself. *Dig up your phony smile.*

"Very wise for some people," I said. *And cowardly*, I thought.

"I'm so glad you agree."

Agree, I thought, almost laughing. *She hears what she wants.*

She clapped. "We're just going to get along real good until your father comes home."

Was she really too blind to see it? It wasn't my father's return I was thinking about daily. I know it was either my imagination or my wishful thinking, but I heard a baby's cry.

"Soon, Little Paula," I whispered. "Soon."

"Did you say something, Faith?"

"What? No. Just scheduling the housework, things we must get done, in my mind."

"You're so organized all the time," she said, as if that was a fault.

"Right."

I closed my eyes. *Ignore her*, I thought. *Think only of Little Paula.*

Was I doing what Gabby's mother preached, fooling myself?

Or was Trevor fooling me by making me believe we would get Little Paula back when all the time he knew it was impossible?

The answer wasn't going to wait much longer.

SEVEN

After Nick gave him another beer, Trevor joined him enthusiastically to celebrate the work they had already accomplished for Big John. They faced each other in the kitchen, both still with their sleeves rolled up and their hands dirty. Mama would explode at the sight of them like that in her kitchen. She was always after Big John to wash up and change his clothes the moment he returned from work.

"You'd better treat this house like a cathedral," she'd told him. In the early days, I remember him only doing what she asked. Toward the end, he'd make snide remarks like "If this is a cathedral, I'm an atheist." And he was in no hurry to clean up. He'd always have his beer first and often leaned against the counter, just like Nick was doing, almost in the same spot.

He and Trevor drank and toasted each other. The ramp was firmly installed. They talked about adding banisters on both sides, making pathways in the woods so Big John could wheel himself in and out of nature, and lowering shelving to make it possible for him to reach for things without calling for help.

"You know, we could even put a motor at the top of the ramp by the door, a motor with a chain to attach to his wheelchair and pull him up if he wanted," Trevor suggested.

"Hey, that's a good idea," Nick said. He finished his can of beer, crushed it in his hand the way Big John would, and tossed it into the garbage.

"I'll look into it on the internet," Trevor said. "There are probably sites for the disabled, showing other things to make life easier."

"Yeah," Nick said. "You kids and your computers are changing the world."

Why was Trevor thinking so hard about all this? I hadn't seen him as happy since he was able to get his driver's license. He was so celebratory, in fact, that for a while, I actually wondered if he had forgotten what our real purpose was supposed to be during these days and weeks. Suddenly, he was Nick's best friend, stepping into Big John's shoes. I saw he liked the way Nick was treating him more as an adult than as a high school boy, drinking beer with him, sharing off-color jokes and who knew what when they whispered.

"I think I'll hang out here a little after dinner," Nick told Gabby. He turned to Trevor. "You and I can shoot some pool. As I recall, you weren't bad at it."

"Big John taught me when I was only ten."

"Mama didn't like you down there so much," I reminded him. "She always said it was too damp."

"It's not that bad," Nick said. "My basement is a bit of a rat hole. It still has a dirt floor. My father never put any money in it. He never did that much with our house at all," he said, and looked like he had sunk into a pool of angry memories. Then his eyes brightened. "What's for dinner, anyway?" he asked Gabby.

"I bought some hamburger. Everyone likes that, right?"

"You don't know how to cook a hamburger," Nick said. "Trevor and I will barbecue. You two do the salad, potatoes, and vegetables. What do you say, Trevor?"

"Sure. I'll just go wash up." He looked at me but didn't signal anything but satisfaction.

Moments after he left, I said I would do the same and started to follow him. Almost as soon as I stepped out of the kitchen, Nick started to criticize Gabby for how she looked.

"Dolling yourself up while John is suffering. Why are you wearing makeup here? And why did you bring up the idea of your returning to work in front of the kids? You don't want them thinking you're going to desert them now, do you? That'd be a bigger mess than we have and put more worry on John."

I listened for a moment and could hear her sobbing and his intolerance of it.

"You know you don't get anywhere crying in front of me, Gabby. I'm not our father. Don't start pulling that stuff on me."

I hurried up the stairs. I really didn't want to hear any more about their family life. Mama was right about them. Even though they didn't live in one, Mama was keen to call them "trailer trash." It usually started a nasty argument between her and Daddy. In the months before she died, Daddy was no longer putting his hands up and walking away. He'd argue, slam doors behind him, or go out and drive away to meet Nick at some bar.

Trevor was already undressed, with a towel wrapped around his waist, and heading for the shower when I stepped into our room.

"Why are you getting so buddy-buddy with Nick?" I asked. "He had to have known what they were planning for Little Paula. He's Big John's best friend."

"Definitely knew about it," he said, as if it meant nothing. "When we were working on the ramp, he started with 'I hope you appreciate what Big John did for you by finding a proper home for the baby.'"

I gasped. "What did you say?"

"I said it was a little shocking at first. 'But necessary,' he said. I didn't say anything except 'As long as it was a good home.' 'Oh, you can be sure of that,' he said. I was hoping he would say more, but he got into the work on the ramp, and I didn't want to push it and make it too obvious. He'll let something out that we can use as long as he trusts me, feels comfortable." He paused, obviously deciding whether to add something.

"What?"

"He doesn't trust you."

"How do you know?"

"Just from the way he spoke about you. You have to stop looking so . . ."

"So what?"

"Sad. Anyway, I found out who Lydia Couch is. She's the wife of Forster Couch. He owns Couch Foods. They live in a gated mansion on a hundred acres outside Aberdeen. Very wealthy people. I don't know for sure they're the ones we're looking for, but it's looking like a real possibility.

"Lots of questions, though. How would either Gabby or Big John get in touch with them, know them? I'm thinking either Nick or Big John did a haul for Couch Foods or maybe more than one. But I'm still not sure why they would want to take Little Paula. Why not just do it legally through an adoption agency if they wanted a child? I'm sure they could afford the money that's in that envelope, but there must have been another reason."

I felt guilty now for accusing him of forgetting about Little Paula and enjoying Nick's company.

"Well, that's good information. Nice, Trevor."

"Yeah. Either Nick or Gabby will slip up and give us more details. He wants all four of us to visit Big John next weekend, by the way. He said he might have a short haul for a few days after that."

He started to close the bathroom door.

"Do you think Little Paula will get so used to a new mother that she'll cry for her when we take her back?"

He paused, thinking. "She'll never forget her real mother. That's family. Remember what Mama said about unseen ties to those you love."

"Even a baby?"

"Sure. Family's family, no matter what the age," he said. "Let's keep up the peace here among us."

"What if they hire a nurse? How will we explain Little Paula?"

"What's to explain? She's our baby, isn't she?" he said, looking frustrated by my questions. He closed the door and went for his shower.

I stood there a moment and then decided to change my clothes, just because that was something Mama had liked us to do, dress for dinner. We didn't have to wear anything formal, just as long as we didn't eat in the clothes we had worn all day.

I went to the Forbidden Room bathroom to wash up, and when I stepped out, I just stood there gazing at the old crib. When I was little, I used to think that if you thought about something hard enough and envisioned it well, it would happen; it would be there. Mama had liked that. I remembered her saying, "I do that, too. See, you're already part of this family."

Shadows played with my imagination. I drew closer to the crib to be sure I was seeing nothing. Standing there, looking down to where I had found the remains of Grandma Eden's baby, lost to her in a miscarriage, I was sure I could hear the tiny whimpers and cries of Little Paula from wherever she was. Did this dark and frightening room possess that power? As Trevor might say now, *Our memories are soaked into these walls. Our ancestors are crying as well.*

I leaned and pressed my hand against the wall. Any way I could, I wanted to be close to her again. I welcomed the shadows, the voices, anything that would help me embrace her. Although I did think about the things Gabby had said, that having Little Paula would prevent me from having a young woman's life, I didn't let that diminish my love for and need for my baby. None of that seemed more important, especially now.

I whispered a promise to our ancestors. "None of that matters. I won't think of it. Only she matters."

I paused, then whispered again, "Bring her back to us. She belongs with her family."

I didn't hear voices as Trevor did, but I hoped I was being heard.

Trevor was already dressed and downstairs when I stepped out. I could hear his and Nick's voices below and then their laughter.

When I went down, they went out to the barbecue, and Gabby was peeling potatoes and sniffing as if she were peeling onions.

"What do they want, fried potato slices?"

"I don't know," she said, more like wailed. "Nick is so short with me. Whatever I do is going to be wrong."

"Trevor likes it in olive oil. I'll do it. Are we eating at the dining-room table or here?"

"I don't know." She looked frantic, as if this was a life-or-death decision. I almost laughed at her.

"We'll eat here. It's easier," I said. "Take out the salad ingredients. I'll set the table."

She looked lost. I could hear her thinking, *What if I forget an ingredient?*

"Okay, okay. I'll do that, too. You can just sit and talk while I work," I told her. She nearly jumped at the opportunity to do nothing.

I started to work on the potatoes first.

"I never really thanked you for helping me with the breast pump and all," I said, with my back to her.

I sensed she was very vulnerable, constantly on the verge of tears. She'd want to confide in me. I'd be her only friend here, even though, as Mama would say, it would be stuck in my craw, which she had explained meant that whatever it was, it was against one's conscience, one's beliefs.

"I felt sorry for you and wanted to do whatever I could to make things better," Gabby said.

Oh, I thought. *Now she's admitting she felt sorry they had stolen her away from me?*

I turned. "Thank you. I appreciate it."

She leaned toward me. I was holding my breath. *She's going to tell me something important, some detail that eventually will bring Little Paula home.*

"That's why I don't think I'll ever be pregnant," she said, and sat back. "I just can't go through it." She laughed. "I'm just too selfish, I guess. Maybe I'm more like my mother than I think I am."

I tried not to show my disappointment, but the truth was, she really was thinking more of herself than she was of me, maybe had been from the very start of all this. She was worried I would complain and disturb Big John, who would then take it out on her.

"Why?" I asked, turning back to the food. "Did Big John mention having more children?"

"No," she said, snapping back. I looked at her, surprised at the sharpness. She brushed her hair back. "He hasn't even mentioned marriage. Nick makes it sound like I'm so important to John. But I'm not worried. I have other men hanging like apples on a branch just waiting to be plucked."

"So you'll leave Big John, move out?"

"No, I didn't say that," she quickly replied, her eyes on the door. "I'm just not . . ."

"Finished with your love life?"

She laughed. "Something like that."

After only a moment of hesitation, I said, "I don't think it was your idea to sell Little Paula. You just went along with it like you went along with anything he said or did, right?"

If Trevor had heard me, he would have screamed.

I could see she was reviewing how she would reply, but before she could, Nick came in.

"I need more of that barbecue sauce," he said. "We were both a little careless. The ants will have a feast."

He laughed. He had already had one beer too many, and there

were a lot more to come, I thought. I hoped Trevor wasn't getting drunk. Just like Nick and Gabby could slip up and say something about Little Paula, Trevor could slip up, too. I fetched the sauce for Nick. He looked at Gabby and at me, realizing I was doing all the preparation while she sat.

"My father spoiled her." He took a step toward her. Even I thought he would slap her. She cringed. "You'd better keep thinking how lucky you are, even in this mess," he told her, and went back to the grill.

"He's always been like that," she said as soon as he closed the door. I knew she was embarrassed. "Taking any bad news out on me. He's more my mother's child than I am. She was just like that." She looked at me. "Don't keep asking about the baby. You don't realize how lucky you are, being able to up and leave to see the world whenever you'd like."

"How can I do that?"

"John told me how your mother left almost everything to you two. He was real bitter about it. You'll own fifty percent of the house as well as money. John said she thought if she died, he might remarry, and his new wife would be entitled to half the house. The money she left you is put aside. He's just a . . ." She searched for the word.

"A what?"

"Custodian until Trevor's eighteen. Then you get your share, Faith, when you're eighteen. It's the way your mother had her lawyer write it up. But don't let Nick talk you into becoming John's maid and caretaker forever. I'm not going to be," she muttered. She rose. "I think I'll have a beer. You want one?"

"No, thank you," I said.

She couldn't see my smile as I worked on the salad and then the potatoes. Trevor was right. Get their trust, and they'd reveal things.

Trevor and I would have money, and eventually, Daddy wouldn't be able to stop us, not that he could do much now. Maybe he would never have told us any of this until he had to.

"Hungry?" Nick shouted when he came in with Trevor. He held the tray of hamburgers up.

"Starving," I said. Trevor looked at me. He could see I had something to tell him. We'd never stop being able to read each other's thoughts. Mama had been right about that.

She had been right about most everything.

And as Trevor would say, she still was.

"This is one fine meal," Nick announced at the table. "Better salad than I make, and these potatoes are something. I hope you watched her work, Gabby," he said. He pointed his fork at her. "She'd starve if it wasn't for me. How do you boil water, Gabby?" He laughed and poked Trevor, who smiled.

"Stop it, Nick," Gabby said.

Nick returned to his beer and his meal.

I felt my throat close up. The kitchen suddenly seemed too small, stifling.

Maybe I was imagining it, but the walls seemed to ripple. Something within them was stirring. All I knew was that fear was closing its hand around my heart.

"Excuse me," I said, and then rose and hurried to the stairs.

I went to our bedroom and sat, actually terrified that I might hear Mama's voice or maybe someone else's in her family. Trembling, I closed my eyes, embraced myself.

I didn't hear Trevor come in. He was standing right beside me, but I didn't open my eyes until he touched my shoulder.

"What's wrong?" he asked. "Nick's asking questions. Why did you hurry out before you finished eating? You've got to control your emotions, or they'll never say anything, give us any details that will help us. What happened?"

"With their arguing and all and her constant complaining, it just felt a little claustrophobic. Sorry."

"You have to be stronger. We've just got to be patient, Faith. Feel for Mama whenever you want to give up. She's always been our strength."

"I know. Gabby told me something," I said, to change the subject quickly. "She said Mama had left half the house to us and put money aside until we reach eighteen. You get your half sooner than me, of course, and Big John is only a custodian of our money. She said Mama thought he'd remarry if something happened to her, and she didn't want his new wife to get interest in the house."

"Ha. Mama could see the future, couldn't she? Good work. Let's find the paperwork she filed with her attorney."

"I almost had her say something about where they took Little Paula."

"Don't worry. We're going to find out everything, or enough to do what we need to do. Maybe tonight. He's got her cleaning up, and we're going down to play some pool. I'll see what he reveals after another two or three beers."

"Just be careful. You're drinking too much, too, Trevor. You could slip and say something you wished you hadn't."

"Naw. I'm fine," he said. "Go down and help her. Maybe she'll say something else. Just don't push too hard on it. If they had real suspicions, they could say something to the people they gave Little Paula to, warn them or something."

He hugged me and left.

I rose, washed my face in cold water, took a breath, and then went back downstairs. Nick and Trevor already had gone down to the basement, but there was still lots of cleaning up to do. Gabby was working like someone in a daze.

"I'll go clean up the barbecue and bring everything in," I told her.

She nodded and smiled. Critter was eating the leftovers, mostly mine.

"We'd better take him out soon, too," I said.

"Can you do it? I'm tired, and I'd like to just watch *Wives of the Rich and Famous.* Coming on soon."

"Okay," I said, sounding as cheerful as I could.

The barbecue was quite a mess, and there were beer cans everywhere, as well as ants enjoying the spilled sauce. I was surprised. Nick surely knew Big John wouldn't like this. Then I thought maybe Trevor had done it. In his little ways, he could be spiteful. He wanted to do anything that would annoy Big John. He wanted revenge for Little Paula. I just wanted her back. Besides, what more could we want to happen to him than what had happened in that truck accident?

I bagged the cans, cleaned and scrubbed the grill, and then went in to get Critter. Gabby was already sitting and watching television. I went to the basement door to listen. I could hear some music and both Nick and Trevor laughing.

So much was happening and changing so quickly that I could feel my head spin and that overwhelming feeling return. I put Critter's leash on him and took him out. It was what I thought must be the warmest night of spring. There were only wisps of clouds here and there, so thin they couldn't block the glittering of stars. I heard what sounded like two or more coyotes in the distance, their howls coming from closer to the lake. I walked Critter to the edge of the driveway and looked up and down the road. There wasn't a car at the moment. The silence was deep, disturbing. Critter did his business and then sat there looking at me. I was filled with crazy urges. I wanted to just start running down the road, crying as I ran.

Maybe it was because Trevor was so involved in what he was doing; maybe it was because Gabby wasn't really someone I wanted to talk to and sit beside to watch television. Maybe it was because when I looked up at the house, I saw the darker shadows and felt the emptiness. But all I wanted to do was run and run and run until I was out of breath and strength. I envisioned not just stopping but sinking and disappearing.

I had started to turn back to the house when I heard my name.

At first, he was just a shadow. I almost believed I was imagining him, but then he came closer.

"I thought it might be you," Lance said.

My mind spun so fast that I lost my footing.

He caught me in his arms.

EIGHT

"Hey," Lance said, seizing my arm to steady me. "You all right?"

"Yes, I just . . . thought you were a ghost."

He laughed. In the vague light of the partly cloudy night sky, I saw his familiar handsome smile. There was that confident look in his violet eyes, which seemed to seize and hold the twinkle of the stars. All the time between when I had last looked into them and now evaporated. But I gathered myself quickly, trying not to look happy to see him, and gently pulled my arm out of his grasp.

"Cute dog," he said, and knelt to pet Critter. "Golden retriever, right?"

"Yes."

He remained kneeling, looking up at me. When Mama had described how important the relationship between Trevor and me was, she'd said, "Love that's real reaches into places inside you that you didn't know were there, and once they are awakened, they never go back to sleep."

I wasn't thinking of Trevor right now.

"I was sorry to hear about your mother and now this news about your father. How terrible for you guys."

He stood. He looked taller and wider in the shoulders. More like a man than a high school boy. I tried not to look at him.

"Grandpa caught me up. Rather, his caretaker did. Nice lady. Mrs. Ireland. She's Irish, too. Name fits." He laughed.

"I didn't know your grandfather had a caretaker. I haven't seen him since . . . for quite a while."

"Yeah, he had a stroke about three weeks ago. My mother was up here for a while, and then they found Mrs. Ireland. He's not terrible, but he can't walk as well and lost most of his strength in his right arm. I think he's having sight problems, too, but none of this is as bad as what you're going through."

"I'm sure it is to him."

"Probably. He doesn't like being dependent on anyone. Keeps threatening to get rid of Mrs. Ireland. My mother asked me to spend some time with him, take the pressure off her. Not that there's much for me to do. He sleeps most of the time. So how's your dad?"

"He's bad," I said. "Paraplegia."

"What's that?"

"He's paralyzed from the hips down."

"Oh, crap."

"Yes, crap," I said. "He'll be in a wheelchair the rest of his life. My brother and my father's best friend, Nick, are preparing the house for him. Lots of changes."

"I bet." He paused, looked toward our house and then at me. "So how is Trevor?"

"He's very good. He goes to school. He's got lots of friends," I added spitefully.

"What about you? Don't you go to school, too?"

"Not yet," I said, and quickly turned. "I've got to get back. They'll be worrying about me."

"Don't go to school? Why not? Don't you have to? I mean, with your mother gone and all. And why would Trevor be going and you not? You're the smarter one."

Not when it came to you, I thought.

I started to walk away.

"Hey? Can I come over and see you guys?" he asked, following. "I'll be here a few more days, and I'm not exactly loaded with things to do. Mrs. Ireland does everything around the house. I don't even know why I'm here."

I spun on him. "You're here for your grandfather."

"Yeah, sure, but . . ."

"I don't know. We have things to do. Our lives are in turmoil."

"Sure. I'd like to help in any way I can. Sometimes just talking . . ."

"I'll ask Trevor. I've got to get back. We're working on the house, moving things around to accommodate my father."

I quickened my pace, and he stopped following.

"I'd like to visit, maybe play ball with Trevor, get some pizza," he called after me. "You have to relax, too."

I didn't respond. I think my heart was in my throat and I couldn't manage another word.

When I stepped into the house, I paused to catch my breath. Then I unhooked Critter's leash, and he hurried toward the den.

Gabby wasn't there, and the television was off. I could hear the music below and checked the living room. Gabby was probably upstairs, I thought. From what I could hear of the talking when I opened the door, she was not in the basement. I heard some laughter and then Trevor cursing over missing a shot. I called to him.

"What's up?" he responded, coming to the foot of the stairs. He had a bottle of beer in his right hand and the pool stick in his left. "You want to come down and play?"

"No. I took Critter out. I'm going up to do some reading."

I wanted to say more, even tell him about Lance and his grandfather, but I could see that Nick was close.

"All right. I'll be up soon. We're just going to finish this game," Trevor said.

I pointed to my mouth and then to him to indicate I had more to say.

"Okay," I said, and went up to the classroom to look out the window facing the front to see if Lance was still on the road. Two cars went by, and their headlights didn't show him. I was relieved, and yet I couldn't stop the surge of excitement that flowed from the memories of our short but intense romance. My only romance. Who else did I think of when I watched love scenes on television now, especially in Gabby's soap operas?

I would never say I didn't love Trevor. We were so much a part of each other that it would be like saying I didn't love myself. Even though Trevor and I had had sex and had Little Paula, there was still something unique about my feelings for Lance. There was an entirely different excitement, a different thrill.

I supposed it was true to say that Trevor and I had never had anything resembling a love affair. There was no poetry waiting in the wings, no music to be heard. Aside from saying "I love you" to each other, we really didn't say much more about our love. He would tell me I was pretty, but sometimes he sounded just the way Mama would sound when she would say it. And the way Gabby had compared her relationship with her brother to our relationship drove me to think that no one would consider us anything but a brother and sister. It was how we had grown up and lived together. A part of both of us now wanted to deny it so we could be Little Paula's parents, but there was a stronger part of us that said, *You'll never deny it. There's an invisible wall that keeps you from becoming anything else.*

But why was I even thinking about this? All my thoughts should be about Little Paula and getting her back. I wanted to resist any urges or even needs to do otherwise. Why be distracted now? And why make myself feel any worse? Gabby was right: I wouldn't be a teenager anymore. I wouldn't have crushes and dates. I'd never be on the phone, teasing and risking my true feelings with some boy. A part of me cried for it, but it was gone, probably forever. Lance was a ghost to me in more than one way.

Besides, he hurt you, I reminded myself, *hurt you deeply in that place where you are most vulnerable and at the same time trusting, that place where romantic love dwells.* It was Mama who had taught us, "People who love each other often hurt each other simply because they've dropped all the instinctive walls they keep high between them and other people. Love requires trust. It's like being willing to fall backward, believing and expecting your cherished love will always catch you."

Lance didn't catch me; he let me fall. *Why can't I remember that most of all? Why doesn't it stop me from thinking about his eyes, his sexy smile?* I rubbed my arm, not because it hurt but because that was where I had felt him touch me. It unleashed other sensual memories, especially of his kiss.

"I hate you, Lance," I whispered to the darkness outside the window. "I hate you because of all the pleasure and excitement you gave me. Now it only brings pain and, most of all, causes me to distrust myself. I will not dream of you tonight. I will not."

"Hey," Trevor said, appearing in the doorway. "Guess what?"

"What?" I asked, turning from the window and hoping he hadn't heard a whispered word.

"It is definitely the Couches who bought Little Paula. Nick didn't actually use the word 'bought,' but I read between the lines."

"Why did they do it, buy a baby?"

"He said some things, but we'll get more from the go-between."

"From what?"

"The person who told Mrs. Couch about Little Paula, who gave her the idea and told her how perfect it was. A secretly born baby. No birth certificate, no record; she could invent whatever she wanted, whatever her husband wanted. Despite all his riches, they're childless. Something about his wife being unable to conceive."

I stared at him. I knew what he was going to say. He was going to tell me who the go-between was. I doubted it would have been Big John meeting with a woman and her husband, at least not at the start. That left only one real choice.

"Why did she do it?"

He shrugged. "Putting aside any of the money she got, if she got any, she probably thought if she solved the problem he wanted solved, he'd marry her."

"Why was Little Paula a problem for him, anyway? We never asked him to do anything for her."

"You saw how he was around her. And what he always thought about us. To him, she was definitely an embarrassment. With Mama gone, I'm sure he believed everyone would blame him. How could he be so careless and let us make a baby? Stuff like that. Maybe he'd lose business. Who knows how he really thinks?"

"Nick told you all this about the sale of Little Paula? You got him to tell you?"

"I didn't go into detailed questions with him. I just let him talk, acting as if I was barely interested. If I asked questions, he would have heard my anger, and he would have stopped. We can find out from Gabby the details we need later. Maybe we'll tie her up and threaten to burn holes in her face until she tells us every little thing."

His words stopped me cold. I sat on the bed. He looked angry enough to carry out the threat.

"We're not going to do anything like that, Trevor."

"We'll see what we need to do," he said. "I got him drunk enough. I guess we can do that with her if need be. Don't let on how much you know yet."

"How can I look her in the face after what you're telling me about her role in all this, how much she did? How can I even talk to her, spend time with her? She always makes herself out to be so innocent. She's the victim. I'm the lucky one. If I hear that one more time . . ."

"You have to until it's the right time. You have to pretend you don't know anything and you're losing interest, just the way I do. Talk about wanting to go to school, anything. Just be careful about it."

"Really, how did you get him to tell you all this? You must have done or said something."

"He began babbling, and I let him believe I was grateful now that Little Paula was no longer an obligation, especially with Big John in a wheelchair. I did say, 'We have plenty to do just taking care of him.' He was too far gone to pick up any deceit. I told him to stay tonight rather than drive home tipsy, but these truck-driver types are arrogant. What's a car compared to an eighteen-wheeler?"

"So he left?"

"Yeah, he left. Stop worrying about Nick and Gabby. You should be happy about what I've learned. Forget about liking her, too, or how hard it is for you to tolerate her. She won't be here long, anyway. The better I make this house for Daddy, the quicker she'll be gone. He'll need her less and less. Of course, he'll always need us," he added, with that impish Trevor smile.

"I know how she thinks," I said. "She won't wait for you to change things. She'll be glad to leave as soon as she can. I don't think she's been faithful to Big John even before all this happened to him."

"So what do we care? It'll all be good, Faith."

He sat on the bed beside me and took my hand.

"Mama will be very happy and proud of us, too, proud of how we solved everything ourselves. We don't need anyone else's help."

I looked at him and then quickly turned to look out the window. I had almost said, *But she's dead. It's too late for her to be proud of anything.*

"What's wrong? You should be happy we're getting closer to bringing Little Paula home."

"I am."

"So? What's up? Something is."

I continued to look away. He touched me on the shoulder.

"What is it, Faith?"

"I took Critter out for a walk, and I was surprised."

"Surprised? How? Why?"

"Lance is back," I said. "For a visit. Mr. Longstreet had a stroke.

He has a caretaker, someone named Mrs. Ireland. He asked about you and wanted to visit."

Trevor rose as if I had set the bed on fire.

"That'll never happen," he said. "Mama . . ."

"What?"

"Would be very upset," he said. "You didn't invite him, did you?"

"No. I was as discouraging as I could be, saying we had too much to do. He offered to help."

"Help? He's the one . . ."

He stopped. Did he almost say, *He's the reason we had Little Paula?*

"What else did you tell him?"

"I told him I would tell you. He wanted to know why I wasn't in school, but I just walked away."

"So he doesn't know about Little Paula?"

"No. I'm sure Mr. Longstreet never knew. No one knew except Gabby, her friend Nina, and that doctor. I doubt she would have told anyone else. Big John would crush her like a roach."

He nodded.

"Even Nick would," I said. "He looks like he's looking for an excuse, anyway. How can they be brother and sister?"

"Yeah, I know. Good. We don't need Lance confusing things, especially now."

"But what if he just comes over?"

"Oh, I'll take care of that."

"But what if you're in school?"

"Don't answer the door. Be sure you don't tell him anything, Faith. He's a deceitful . . . just avoid him. He's too selfish to really care what happens to Little Paula and us. Just avoid him."

I nodded, but in my heart, I knew that was easier said than done.

"I'm going to take a shower. Mama was right about the basement. It makes me feel like I was crawling through wet earth with worms. I practically held my breath the whole time, but Nick never realized it. I beat him one game of eight-ball, too." He smiled. "He told me Big John would be proud."

He laughed.

"I've got him just where I want him," he bragged, and went to take his shower.

I couldn't help but think again how different Trevor was and was continuing to become. He wasn't just acting older, smarter; he was enjoying all this, the challenges, the tension, and especially how well he was manipulating everyone. Was he doing it out of love for Little Paula, or was he getting some sort of revenge?

It frightened me not to know for sure. We had always known everything about each other, anticipated each other's feelings and desires. Suddenly, when I looked at him, I saw a dark place in his thoughts, a wall that I couldn't pierce, at least confidently. I had a frightening thought. Was he manipulating me, too? Did he simply want to be in charge of everything, more like a father than even a brother, much less a lover? It was very rare for me to find even an iota of a reason not to trust him, but nothing was really normal now. Our world was topsy-turvy. What was true yesterday might be gone forever.

After he came to bed, Trevor fell asleep quickly. It made me jealous, because it took me quite a while to, hours, actually. How could he be so relaxed and secure after what he had learned and what I had told him? I tossed and turned, my mind rotating images of Little Paula and images of Lance. Exhausted, I finally fell asleep and slept later than usual.

When I woke, the house was quiet. Gazing at the clock, I realized Trevor must have risen, had breakfast, and left. I sat up and listened. The house was so silent, no floor or wall moaned, and no hinge creaked. Had Gabby left, too? I washed, dressed, and hurried down to the kitchen, where I found her sitting at the table, hovering over a cup of coffee as if she was in a daze. There were piles of Daddy's clothes in front of her.

She looked tired and disheveled, her hair not as neatly brushed as usual. She wore no makeup and was in one of Big John's flannel shirts and jeans. She looked up, realizing after a few moments that I was there.

Critter was lying at her feet, looking just as depressed.

"Why'd you sleep so late?" she asked, annoyed. "I was up working before Trevor left for school."

"Just tired, I guess. What is all this?"

"Some of John's clothes, remember? We told my brother that we're moving his things down. I thought you'd help organize them in that armoire in the den and in those drawers. The armoire's not as big as his closet. Maybe I brought down too much. I didn't know what to take and what to leave upstairs. Nick would like us to move the sofa bed out today also. He said we should slide it to the door. He'll slide it down the ramp and get it into the garage. There's no other place for it. Then we'll organize everything so we'll eventually get his bed organized in there."

"His bed? You mean from upstairs . . ."

"No, we can't move the one down from that old nursery. It wouldn't be good for what your father needs, and it's too big for the room, anyway. Nick says we're getting one that you can move up and down, a hospital bed. He took measurements and says it will fit perfectly. You can't oversleep now. There's so much to do."

"But there's time for all that. My father will be in the hospital recuperating and getting therapy, maybe for weeks. Why the rush?"

"Nick wants everything done so there's nothing to do the day we bring your father home," she said. "He's afraid he might get a long haul and not be able to help us. We might have to move John's favorite chair out of the den, too. We'll see. Nick is going to put the television on a bracket to make more space for a wheelchair and whatever else he needs beside him. He's going to the hardware store before he comes here to get all he needs. There are things to do in the bathroom, too," she said, her voice more shrill.

"Bathroom? What?"

"I don't know. A handicapped person's bathroom. I don't want to think about all that. Staying busy will help me keep from imagining what it will be like seeing John wheeling himself about, sleeping in a hospital bed, shrinking in front of me. He'll see it in my face; he'll see it."

She dabbed her eyes with a tissue.

"Besides, I don't have the strength my brother thinks I have or wants me to have for all this."

I got myself some orange juice and leaned against the counter. Critter rose and stood there staring at me.

"I think he has to go out," I said.

She didn't say anything. She sat there staring angrily at the table, her face full of self-pity. In a funny way, the more selfish she was, the more I felt sorry for Daddy, the man I should detest right now. There were so many conflicting emotions swirling in this house that I was sure even the spirits of the ancestors were confused.

Before I could say or ask anything, the front doorbell rang. Critter began to bark.

"Who could that be?" Gabby asked.

My heart raced. Was it Lance? He knew Trevor was in school.

"I don't know."

I walked slowly to the door, Gabby and Critter following. When I opened it, I faced a flower shop deliveryman holding out a bouquet with a variety of flowers and colors—yellow roses, white lilies, blue delphinium, and purple monte casino. I remembered ordering the same vase of flowers for Daddy to give Mama when he learned she had broken her ankle trying to fix a leak in the roof in the rain.

"What's this?" I asked, pulling Critter back.

"Delivery, ma'am," he said, holding it out to me.

"Oh, my gosh, how beautiful," Gabby said. She stepped ahead of me and took it.

The deliveryman tipped his hat and returned to his truck. I closed the door. Gabby put the vase on the table in the entryway and pulled out the card.

"It's a good-wishes card, expressing hope for Big John and comfort for . . . you and Trevor. Whoever this is doesn't know about me," she said, "or they'd have put my name on it, too."

She held out the card. I opened the envelope and took it out.

"So?"

Lance had sent it. I felt the blood rush to my face.

"We can't let Trevor see this," I said. "We'll dump it in the woods. It's from Lance."

"What?"

I started to reach for it, but she didn't move.

"Who is Lance? Why would that upset Trevor?"

"He's our neighbor's grandson. Mr. Longstreet. Mama didn't like him and chased him off our property."

She squinted. "Why didn't she like him? What did he do?"

"What difference does it make?" I moved past her and grabbed the vase.

"This is weird," she said. I didn't answer. She followed me to the back door, Critter so close to me I almost tripped over him. "Nick should know about this," she said when I opened the door.

I paused. "Why?"

"What did the boy do?" She stared at me so closely I had to look away. "Was he a boyfriend?"

"It's none of your business," I said, and walked out with the vase, Critter behind me.

She followed me, too. I was walking quickly toward the woods in the rear. I paused so Critter would do his business.

"Did you make love to him? Was he the father of your baby? And not Trevor?" she shouted from the doorway. "It's all like a soap opera—flowers, forbidden boyfriends, babies . . ."

I turned to her. She was smiling.

"You think all this is funny? You think selling my baby was funny?"

I looked at the flowers. I had no doubts that she would tell Nick about this and maybe even reveal it to Trevor. What was the point of smashing the vase on the rocks? I started back to the house.

"Your father knew, too, right? He probably wanted to break the boy's neck. Nick will make sure he doesn't come around here."

"He's not the father of my baby," I said. "I didn't make love to him . . . at least that far. Trevor doesn't want him coming around here because my mother didn't. You are only going to make more trouble for all of us. And if you thought living here was not going to be fun before, it will surely not be then."

I walked past her and into the house, Critter right behind me. I placed the vase on the kitchen table without the card on it, wondering how I would explain this to Trevor. She came in slowly behind me and looked at the flowers.

"I never had a boyfriend send me flowers like that. I know. I could say it came from a friend wishing me the best," she said. "I'll take them to my bedroom if you don't want them."

My grateful expression brought a smile. She picked up the vase.

"See? We can keep each other's secrets," she said. "Just like real friends or even loving sisters."

I watched her walk out with the vase.

"Start putting away John's clothes," she said. "I hate doing that stuff."

Was it just a coincidence? Lance coming into my life had brought so many changes and led to so much sadness. And here he was, doing it again.

I started on Daddy's clothes. Critter lay sprawled on the den floor, watching. Trevor was wrong. Daddy wouldn't want to get rid of him now. He probably would be a comfort for Big John, I thought.

Gabby didn't return until it was all done. She looked in the armoire and saw how neatly I had put socks and underwear in the drawers.

"Perfect," she said. "You could probably organize my things much better than I can. Oh, I'm tired already just imagining all this and what else we have to do. Let's think about lunch. Nick will be here about the same time as yesterday, so we'll have to have that sofa bed out on the ramp. It's heavy, but we can push it, I guess." She smiled. "But before that, you can tell me all the details about your banned boyfriend."

An idea came to me. If I acted on it, I knew I would be playing with fire. There was no doubt in my mind that Trevor would think so, but I believed that every day that passed was a day drawing Little Paula farther and farther away from me.

"Do you know what 'quid pro quo' means?" I asked her.

"What?" She laughed. "Hardly. What is it, French or something?"

"Latin. A common phrase," I said, smiling. "It basically means something for something. I'll give you the real details of my romance if you'll tell me how my baby was taken."

She grimaced. "You don't stop with that, do you? I do know a Latin expression: 'Don't look a gift horse in the mouth.' My father would say that."

"It's not Latin. I did have a hot romance," I said. Hot was what Gabby called the love affairs on her soap operas. "My first. That's why Mama wanted him off our property."

Her eyes widened with interest. "I'd love to hear all about that."

"I'm not supposed to talk about it, just like you're probably not supposed to talk about Little Paula. So we're equal if we both do it. Secret for secret."

She eyed me suspiciously, head tilting slightly as she studied me and thought.

"You did tell me we were going to keep each other's secrets, didn't you?" I asked. "Like sisters?"

She looked back at the rear door as if she was afraid Nick or my father would overhear.

"Well, I don't suppose it matters all that much to John right now, or ever."

"Probably not."

"You go first," she said, sitting at the table and leaning forward, her excitement blooming over her face like that of a little girl who was about to hear a new fairy tale.

"Okay," I said, shrugging and sitting across from her. "One day, when Trevor and I were in the woods, we heard this constant wood chopping and knew it was more than one person. I was more curious and went to the wall and looked at Mr. Longstreet's house. There was a tall, handsome boy splitting wood with him for his fireplace."

"*How* handsome?"

"He has these violet eyes and a lean, muscular body. But his smile almost made me . . ."

"What?"

"Want to have sex with him the first time I saw him."

"Oh," she said, sighing. "I had a boyfriend like that once." She thought a moment and smiled. "Maybe two or three. I almost had an orgasm on the spot. So?"

"Your turn," I said. "Quid pro quo. How did it happen? How were the arrangements for my baby made, and so fast?"

She smacked her lips, looked at the door, and leaned toward me.

"I was in Nora's salon. It's called Beauty Forever." She laughed. "Some of the women in there look like it's more Beauty Never. There's always a lot of gossip. I overheard talk about this rich woman who was unable to have a baby of her own but didn't like the idea of adopting. What she didn't like was everyone knowing all the details. I knew who she was, so I knew it was all true. It was easy to get a baby from another country, but when it comes to foreign children, she's very . . ."

"Bigoted?"

"Yeah, I think that's what someone said. She wanted a 'fresh, new American baby.' I heard she was willing to pay for it."

"And that was about the time I gave birth?"

"Yes. I told John about it. Even though she wasn't born yet, he was already complaining about what the baby's crying would be like and what things in general were going to be like. He blamed it all on your mother and said . . ."

She bit down on her lip as if she had to stop herself from speaking.

"Said what?"

"He didn't have to live with her insanity now. I told him that was not a nice thing to say, but he just fluffed me off."

"And so he sent you to make a deal? To negotiate the sale of my baby?"

"Yes, like I wanted to have that responsibility. But I didn't have much choice once I told him about Mrs. Couch."

"What was that like?"

"Easier than I thought. Big John had decided how much to ask for and said he wouldn't budge. He knew who they were, and he knew they were very rich. But here's the funny part."

"What?"

"He didn't like them."

"He sold Little Paula to someone he didn't like?"

"John says he enjoys taking money more from people he doesn't like than those he does like. That's a little silly, isn't it? Money is money."

"Silly isn't exactly the word I'd use," I said, and looked away so she wouldn't see the tears I was holding back.

"Okay, your turn," she said. "And I want the details so I'll know whether or not what you're telling me is the truth. Don't worry, I'll know. You do look too guilty for it to be nothing."

I could see my quid pro quo. The sexier I made it, the more she would tell me.

"There are good lies," Mama once told us. "Lies to help someone else."

Was I stepping into a pool of regret? Would I make everything worse?

NINE

"We really didn't talk much that first time we met," I said, "but from the way he was looking at me, I knew we would. He gave me the chills in a nice sort of way. I couldn't stop looking at him."

"Really? You were so lucky. Most of the men I met when I was your age were dull. I mean, you could either tell right away they wanted only one thing, or they looked unenthusiastic until I practically put words in their mouths. Almost all of Nick's friends are like that, but I don't hang around with him that often. Or at least, I didn't. Now I don't hang out anywhere, of course," she said, her eyes dripping with regret.

Here goes that self-pity thing, I thought. *Play to it.*

"Yes, it's unfortunate that when something terrible happens to people we're involved with, it really happens to us, too. People don't appreciate how much you can suffer as well."

Her eyes widened. "You're so much smarter than I was at your age. But really, how did you get into trouble? I mean, as dumb as I am, I never got pregnant. No one could talk me into that or get me so overwhelmed that I'd forget. My mother taught me the 'fail-safe' moment. One thing she never wanted to be was a grandmother; she hadn't wanted to be a mother. So what was it like, the moment?"

I knew what she wanted to hear, the compliments.

"You were lucky. You had more experience with men. You knew what buttons not to push," I said.

"Yes, that's true. I've had a football team's worth of experience, but tell me more about Lance. So what happened next?"

"He made friends with Trevor first."

"Clever," she said, nodding. "Some of Nick's friends tried that with me. I call it the Backdoor Approach."

"Backdoor or not, because of it, we gradually got to know each other more. I had never sent an email before I sent one to him. My whole world began to change."

"Oh," she said. "Fascinating. I forget that you didn't grow up with mobile phones. So then what happened?"

"He's from New York City and had many girlfriends, but he said he didn't have anyone at the time. I felt sorry for him, because his parents were in a nasty divorce and he was visiting his grandfather to get out of the battle zone."

"Oh. That was nice of you, but I'm sure he took advantage of your kindness. Most men I know would. At least, they tried that with me."

"Yes, when he kissed me, he apologized and said I was the first person to help him forget his trouble. Of course, that made me feel good. I thought he was sincere."

"Well, that was nice, even though it was probably a line he used on more than one girl."

"Probably."

"So? Then what?"

"Then he kissed me again but longer. I wanted to stop, but I felt sorry for him."

"Sure you did. You're just making excuses for yourself. I do the same all the time."

I smiled. "You're right. That's what I'm doing."

She looked so satisfied with herself.

"But maybe you were in the same situation," I said. "Recently."

"Recently? When?"

"With my baby. You were trying to be kind to this rich woman, right?" I asked.

"Oh, no. I didn't care about her. I just told John about her. I thought he'd be interested. And grateful. A friend of mine got word to her, and I met her for lunch at the Royal. She paid for everything. She even bought me a glass of very expensive champagne. She thought everything was perfect. John had told me the price for the baby, and she agreed right then and there. John was quite happy, I can tell you that. He's a better lover when he's happy, even better than when he's drunk."

"Then you took Little Paula to her?"

"No. They came here."

"What do you mean? When?"

"That morning, you slept. It was arranged. I brought your baby out to the limousine. She looked at her first and told her husband she thought the baby was beautiful. There was a nurse in the rear with her who examined the baby and said, 'She's perfect.' I knew she was colicky, but I didn't say anything. I don't know what they had expected to see, maybe a deformed child or something. I saw they had formula and diapers, everything. They were really prepared.

"Her husband didn't say anything. He seemed to just want to get it over with. John stood behind me to make sure it all went well. Her husband handed me the envelope with the money, and they drove off. Simple. No one was even driving by the whole time, so no one saw anything. The car would certainly have attracted interest."

"A limousine?"

"Big black one, with that emblem on the hood. John said he thought it was custom-made. Imagine having a car made especially for you. Anyway, you can be sure your baby will have everything. No need to worry. I told John I wished I was your baby. He didn't even laugh. He said, 'Forget this even happened.' He'd want to kill me if he found out I told you so much."

"He won't," I said. Lying was so easy when it came to her.

"So how far did you go with Lance? I want to hear all of it. Don't leave out any details. Was he smooth? Some men are made of hot butter."

I stared at her. The anger swirling within me started in my lower stomach and rose to my chest. How could she be so casual, almost indifferent to selling Little Paula and telling me not to worry?

"I don't feel well," I said. "My stomach and . . ." I put my hands on my breasts. "I need to lie down for a little while."

I rose before she could say anything and started away.

"Oh, well, we can talk later. We have lots of time together. Wait. What about lunch?"

"I'm not hungry. You eat."

"We've got to get that sofa bed out, remember. I promised Nick. Faith?"

"Later," I said. "I might throw up," I added, to get her to stop talking. But it wasn't too much of an exaggeration.

I hurried to the stairs. Suddenly, it was hard to breathe. When I looked up the steps, they seemed so steep and high. I held on to the banister and slowly began. I imagined myself falling backward, just the way Mama had, and toppling, smashing my head on the floor. If something happened to me, Trevor probably would give up, I thought.

I paused for a moment. I was imagining Mama standing there at the top. At least, I hoped I was imagining. She was beckoning, encouraging me to walk up. My hand felt sweaty on the banister. I was afraid it would slip off. When I looked up again, she was gone. Maybe I was simply wishing she was there, guiding and protecting me. Trevor would certainly believe she was there.

When I reached the top of the stairs, I did feel nauseous, however. Gabby's details were more upsetting than I had anticipated. How could we ever get Little Paula back from such rich and powerful people? Nurses, limousines, and all that money. We were just two adopted children. I knew when I told Trevor all that I had learned from Gabby and described how she had casually and happily told me, practically bragging, he would be even more enraged than I was.

I crawled into bed and clutched the blanket to my breasts. My heart felt as if it was being torn in three different directions. In a way, I had outsmarted myself. Thinking that the more detailed, romantic, and sexy I sounded, the more willing Gabby would be to reveal the details about Little Paula's being taken, I had unintentionally stirred up my own sleeping memories, memories I had successfully kept buried in the darker places of my mind.

Images of Lance's eyes and lips, the memory of his body against mine, his hands touching me in places I was afraid to touch myself, all came rushing back. I heard his soft, promising words of affection and felt the warmth rushing through my body. I envisioned myself turning to him, dropping all resistance, craving for him to go faster, further, and touch me inside.

"No!" I screamed into the pillow. To be a teenage girl in love, I certainly couldn't be a mother.

"Not to worry," Gabby had said. "She'll have everything."

I pressed down on those thoughts, thoughts that would certainly make me give up, willed and willed them gone, until I saw Little Paula's soft blue eyes and tiny nose and lips. I heard her gurgle and murmur and felt her tiny fingers in mine. I wasn't leaving her; I wasn't forgetting her.

And then, in my mind, there was Trevor as well, looking at me with such disappointment and pain because I would even think of it. I had to touch his face and reassure him. Nothing was lost; nothing was gone. We were as strong as we ever were. His smile returned.

I was afraid I would review and virtually relive it all again and again. More as an escape than anything, I fell asleep and woke to the sound of Nick downstairs berating Gabby for something, probably not moving the sleep sofa to the ramp. When they grew silent, I felt a little panic. They were whispering for sure. She had probably told him about the flowers and Lance. I doubted she could keep a secret even if she died with it. I rose, washed my face, and started down. Just as I had anticipated, Nick was dragging the sofa bed toward the door.

"There's a lot of dust in that room. I don't think this has been moved an inch for years. You two could have done this and gotten it cleaned up."

"I'll vacuum right now," I said, and went for it as he, with a little help from Gabby, turned the sofa and got it through the door. Then he closed the door behind him as he started pushing it down the ramp. He said once he had it down, he would wait for Trevor to carry it to the garage.

The den was very dusty. I think Mama had given up on it after a while. My father's cigar smoke was ingrained in the walls. She used to work hard to get the odors out, but surely she had decided it wasn't worth the effort. He certainly didn't want her doing it. The floor needed to be washed as well as the one window facing the rear of the property; however, Nick came in and wanted to work on the bracket to hang the television. He needed room to work.

"You can do the rest of it later."

He paused and looked at both of us. I held my breath. I could see he had something significant to tell us.

"I called the hospital before I came here," he said. "Did you?" he asked Gabby.

"No, I thought we should wait for you. We both did. Right, Faith?"

She looked at me for support, but I said nothing.

"They have him sitting up. He's doing better than the doctor expected."

"Then he'll walk again?" she quickly asked.

"No. Of course not. I meant everything else, all the bangs and bruises. Nothing else in his body is even fractured." He paused, looking like he was deciding whether to say any more.

"Then he's definitely crippled for life," Gabby said.

For a moment, I thought Nick was going to slap her.

"Don't *dare* call him crippled," he warned. "I told you. If you ever say that to him . . ."

She looked like she was going to cry. Her lips quivered.

"You can change the words, but you can't change what's happened to him," she said defiantly.

He shook his head.

"You better not make that mistake again," he warned, and went to work on the television bracket.

He was finished before Trevor returned, and the moment he heard him drive in, he went out to get him to help move the sofa. When Trevor did come in, I saw from the look on his face that he had lots to tell me, maybe more than I had to tell him.

"Going up to shower and change," he announced.

"I'm going to pick up some fried chicken for dinner," Nick said, poking his head in. He looked at Gabby. "Get everything set up, and clean up a little around here. You've got to do better, not worse, now."

He shut the door and left. You could have cut the air with a butter knife. Critter whined. I fed him while Gabby stood there biting down on her lip.

"How he talks to me," she said. "Like any of this was my fault."

"He's upset," I said.

"What am I?"

I didn't want to answer.

"I'm going to go up to shower and change, too," I said.

"Well, I feel fine the way I am," she said sullenly, her fiery look aimed at the door through which Nick had just gone. "After all, I'm just a maid. I don't have to look fancy for him, either, not that he ever cared."

I hurried upstairs before she could start another conversation of self-pity. Trevor was waiting excitedly for me.

"I didn't go to school today," he said.

"Not at all?"

"No. I was on a reconnaissance mission."

"What does that mean?"

"I went to the Couches' house. It's about three times the size of ours and on acres of land. There's a wire fence and a gate to the driveway. Driveway's long and circles in front of the house. I parked a little ways past it and walked back to watch from behind a heavy hickory tree just across from and to the right of the gate. About ten, the nurse came out with Little Paula in a carriage and sat for almost an hour in a garden area, rocking the carriage, feeding her, and reading. There was a nice fountain. Everything is so trim, the bushes, the lawns, you'd think the gardeners work with a pair of scissors."

"Why do you look so happy about it?"

"If it's a routine that the nurse follows, I—we—can lie in wait. I'm sure it is."

"You think we can kidnap Little Paula?"

"She's our baby. You don't kidnap your own baby, Faith."

I sat beside him. "How can we do it?"

"We'll do it," he insisted. "I'm going to come up with a plan now that I know the layout. Just forget about it for now. Nick is complaining a lot about Gabby. He was mumbling the whole time we moved the sofa bed. He says he spoiled her and she has no grit."

"Grit?"

"She can't take disappointments or deal with challenges. He said he had thought Daddy was the best thing for her, someone she couldn't manipulate, but now . . ."

"Now what?"

"He's beginning to think she's the worst thing for him. I think he loves Big John more than he loves his sister. He idolizes him, even in the condition he's in."

"Yeah. Great minds think alike," I said, and Trevor laughed.

I told him all the details I had gotten out of Gabby. As I had anticipated, his face reddened with anger.

"Is there any doubt now?" he asked, rising.

"Doubt about what?"

He turned in the doorway.

"That Mama got her revenge?"

He went to take his shower. I didn't know what to say. The more he said it, the guiltier I felt, but why should I? Daddy had arranged for the sale of Little Paula. Justice had been done. On the other hand, couldn't we just get her back without taking such joy in the terrible thing that had happened to him? Why did we have to bathe so in revenge?

I rose, and without knowing why, I looked out the window and saw Lance standing on the road and staring at our house. He was in a blue T-shirt and jeans. His hair fluttered in the breeze. I held my breath, my hands clutched between my breasts. If there was any wrong time for him to come knocking, it was right now, I thought. He seemed to hear me, and with his hands in his pockets, he turned and started back for his grandfather's house. I felt a mixture of relief and sadness. I don't know how long I stood there staring, almost willing him to turn back. Try as hard as I could, I couldn't fight back the remembered excitement.

"Your turn," Trevor said. He was wrapped in his bath towel.

"Thanks."

I had started for the bathroom when he seized my arm, almost exactly where Lance had held it.

"Don't be afraid," he said. "We're not alone. We're never alone. Not anymore. Not ever."

I smiled and nodded.

Later, we walked downstairs together. Gabby had done a decent job of setting the table and had even made some lemonade.

"I have a beauty salon appointment tomorrow with Nora herself working on me," she said, mostly to me. "We're returning to the hospital the day after, and I didn't want John to see me dragged out and sad. I could take you, too. Your hair could use a nice trim, some style. I mean, I could do it, but . . ."

"No, thank you. I'm fine."

Of course, I didn't want to say that Mama never went to a beauty salon. Besides, I knew what would happen if I ever did go with her. There would be all sorts of questions about school. How would I explain not being there now? Why didn't she anticipate all that?

"What do you think, Trevor? Shouldn't she go, too?"

"She's fine. All of us looking glamorous isn't going to help him. It will just make him feel worse."

"Well, it will help me, and everyone knows that if you don't feel good about yourself, you won't be able to make someone important to you happy."

"Glad he's still important to you," Trevor said.

She looked stunned for a moment and then smiled.

"Of course he's still important to me. I know it's sad, but we have to . . . deal with it." She looked at me. Maybe it was the expression on my face, but she didn't like either of our reactions. "My friends know how hard it is for me. They sent flowers today. Weren't they beautiful, Faith?"

Oh, boy, she could be mean, I thought.

I glanced at Trevor. Fortunately, he was uninterested in flowers.

"Yes," I said. It was clear she believed that she had something over me now. I envisioned having to do everything in this house, especially any chore Nick assigned her.

He arrived with the food.

"That's good about the beauty salon appointment," Trevor whispered while we stood by watching him take everything out of the bags. "When she goes to the hairdresser, I'll pick you up and show you where Little Paula is being kept. Maybe we'll see her brought out again to that garden."

"What about school for you?"

"If they call before I pick you up, just pretend you're Mama and say I have a flu. I called that in yesterday."

"Don't they know Mama is gone?"

He didn't answer. We sat to eat, Critter sprawling at Nick's feet as if he knew that he was sitting in for Daddy. I had little appetite but ate so as not to attract any attention. Nick didn't stay long afterward. He was going to a furniture store some distance away in the morning to order a hospital bed for Daddy.

"We need to make sure it's here before he arrives," he said. "We'll tell him about it this weekend, or I will. He's not going to like hearing it, so nobody else say anything about it," he added, looking directly at Gabby.

As soon as he left, I told her I would take care of the cleanup. She could go up to her bedroom and watch television. I wanted to make sure she didn't accidentally make a reference to Lance and the flowers.

Trevor surprised me. "I'm going for a ride," he said after she had started for the stairs. "I want to check things out at night."

"But . . ."

"Don't worry. I know what I'm doing—we're doing."

I was more nervous than ever and nearly dropped a dish. When I was finished, I went to the living room just to sit and calm my nerves. Critter sat quietly, as if he knew not to invade my thoughts.

Trevor and I had spent so much of our early days here sitting with Mama and hearing her stories about the house, her family, and her own youth. Returning to a place where you had warm memories helped you to relive them. It was just as Mama had said: words and deeds lingered, the walls absorbed them, and when you pressed hard to hear and see them, they returned.

I was so deep in thought that I didn't hear the gentle tapping on the front window until he had stopped and started it twice. For a moment, the sight of him standing in the glow of the front porch light did look ghostly. I gasped and immediately looked to the stairs to see if Gabby had heard. Confident that she was probably absorbed in one of her television shows, I rose and went to the door.

"What are you doing here, Lance?"

"I saw Trevor drive off. Everything all right?"

"What, were you watching our house?"

"No, I was taking a walk and saw him drive by. I tried to flag him, but he looked so intent on where he was going that I'm sure he didn't see me."

"I told you to wait until I asked him about you. He's still . . ."

"Angry." He laughed. "We don't have to do anything more than be friends for a while. I've had girlfriends who broke up with me or vice versa and still remained friends. Can you go for a walk, take your dog?"

I looked at Critter, who was wagging his tail as if he understood.

"Let me get his leash," I said. "But only for ten or so minutes."

"Great."

Trevor will be furious, I kept chanting to myself, but I didn't change my mind. I attached Critter's leash and walked out.

"We can just go up to my grandfather's house and back," he suggested, his hands in his pockets.

"All right," I said, and we started.

"So when do you see your father?"

"Day after tomorrow."

"Where is he?"

"Harrisburg. Close to where the accident happened."

He nodded. We walked for almost a minute in silence.

"I guess I owe you an apology for the way I left." He laughed. "I'll admit, your mother scared me to death that night. But," he said before I could respond, "I broke up with the girl I was seeing back in New York a week after I left here. It took a while for me to get you out of my mind, and I know she sensed it. She finally asked, 'Are you seeing someone in Pennsylvania?' I said yes, even though . . ."

I didn't say anything. I knew he was feeling uncomfortable, but I couldn't think of the right thing to say without encouraging him.

"During one of his better or clearer moments, my grandfather said he hadn't seen you since the day I left. I thought your mother liked him. From what I was told, your father should have thanked him a million times, even though . . ."

I shouldn't be on this walk, I told myself. *I'm going to get into trouble.*

"He really liked you guys. Likes, I mean."

"My mother didn't want me to be involved with your family," I said. It was partially true.

"I guess she was mad at you, too. It was my fault. I shouldn't have gone so fast. You had me . . . too far gone."

"Gone?"

"In love. You were, too, weren't you?" he asked.

"I'm not sure what I was."

Love? I thought. I was about to ask him what his definition of it was, but I didn't want to get too deeply into what had gone on between us. Once, when I was telling Mama about what I was reading in the novel she had given me, *Pride and Prejudice*, she stopped me and said, "Boys are more likely to mistake passion for love." She quickly added that Trevor was different.

"Right," Lance said, after a long moment of silence between us. "So why is Trevor in school and you're not?"

Critter was interested in something off to the right, so I followed him, drawing myself away from Lance.

"Does your father have a girlfriend already?" he asked, following me. "Mrs. Ireland seems to know everyone's business and said something about it when I mentioned I was going to visit."

"Yes, but I don't think for long," I said.

"Oh. Because of how he is after his accident?"

"Something like that."

"Sad. I guess it wasn't meant to be. Sometimes it is and overcomes what would ordinarily prevent it from happening. I mean, if you feel strongly enough about someone . . ."

"I've got to get back," I said, tugging Critter onto the road again.

I started walking. My heart was thumping. My whole body suddenly felt submerged in ice water.

"Hey, you're practically running," he said, keeping up with me. "We can be friends, maybe start again, but go slower. I was just impatient, but . . ."

I spun on him. All I could think of doing was getting rid of him, avoiding an inevitable confrontation with Trevor, but mostly probably to shut myself up, keep my secret longings buried deep inside myself. At least, those were the excuses I would use to justify it to myself. Trevor was going to be in a whole other world of hurt.

"I had a baby," I said.

I walked on. He didn't follow for a few moments and then ran to catch up.

"What?"

"Just what I said. I had a baby, a girl."

"Who . . . where is she?"

"My father sold her, but she will be back, and that's why I'm not in school."

I started to cry.

"But . . . no one thought she was mine, right?"

Of course that was what he would worry about, I thought. Maybe Gabby's advice and comments about men were wiser than I had thought.

"Right. No one blamed you."

"Then . . . I don't understand."

I spun on him again. "Do you want to do something nice for me? Do you want to really apologize?"

"Sure," he said, but he looked dazed.

"Then swear you'll never tell anyone what I just told you. Swear on your mother's life. Well?"

"Sure," he said. "I mean, why would I . . ."

I turned and kept walking.

"I won't tell!" he shouted after me.

Yes, I thought, *but you'll never want to see me again.* And maybe that was why I had done it . . .

TEN

Before Trevor returned, I fell asleep sitting in the living-room chair. I had been trembling when I sat and needed to put a blanket over me. It wasn't really cold, but my mind raged with fears that gave me the chills: *What have I done? Why did I tell Lance anything? Trevor will be so upset. Maybe it will spoil his plans for retrieving Little Paula. I cannot reveal any of this to him*, I thought, even though I realized that neither of us had ever been good at lying to the other.

When you grow up with someone else's face almost always before you, the last face you might see before you went to sleep and the first you might see when you awoke, you learn what every movement of his lips and eyes means; you anticipate the lift of his eyebrows and the slight tilt of his head when he thinks this or that.

It was surely the same for him, which was why we could tell each other so much without saying a word. I'd have to concentrate hard on not thinking about Lance when I was with Trevor.

Otherwise, I could almost hear him ask as soon as he saw me, *What have you done?*

Every time the flash of car headlights washed across our front windows, my body tightened. Critter, lying at my feet, would raise his head to look at me, as if he understood my tension. The anticipation eventually exhausted me. It was getting so late, too. Where was he? Had the Couch family discovered him spying? Had they called the police? Would they come knocking on our door to tell us?

They'd never call the police, I told myself, not after what they had done. How could they explain buying a child? That thought brought me some relief, and I dozed off again.

The sound of the rear door opening and closing woke me. Critter rose and ran to Trevor.

"What's going on?" he asked when he saw me sitting with a blanket wrapped around me on the sofa. "You didn't have to wait up."

"Why were you so long? Of course I would wait up. I worried. You might have gotten in trouble, been arrested," I said, putting him on the defensive before he could search my face for any other reason.

"I'm sorry. I'm sorry, but I didn't expect to discover what I did, so I spent more time on it."

He sat beside me, his face lit with excitement.

"What did you discover?"

"We don't have to worry about coming up with some fantastic plan to get Little Paula back. I was racking my brain about it until tonight."

"Why not? What changed tonight?"

"I found an opening in the fence around the Couches' property, a place they never repaired, probably because there was so much brush growing in that area. I walked along the side of the road carefully, never expecting to find it. I was worried about how to scale the fence, get Little Paula, and get back over it. Also, it's a lot of ground to cover from that garden to the fence. It would practically be impossible to distract the nurse, scoop Little Paula out of the carriage, and run without being caught.

"But both problems are solved," he said. He sat back, smiling. "I know you won't believe it the way I do, but it was like Mama was right beside me, almost as if she had taken my hand to lead me once I went through the opening."

"Lead you where? What did you do?"

"I went through the fence very carefully and stopped practically every three feet to be sure there were no alarms, no cameras focused on where I was. The house was quiet, lights on mainly downstairs and on the far side. When I drew closer, I saw that side was the section of the house where their living room was and where their kitchen and dining room were located."

He paused, the excitement lighting up his face, making his eyes sparkle, almost taking my breath away.

"Tell me!" I demanded, practically bouncing up and down.

"I am, I am. The lights were off on the near side, but the glow of them from the living room, dining room, and kitchen came through open doors. I saw there were two more cars parked in the driveway, so I figured they had guests. As I drew closer, I could hear the talk and the laughter. Crouched, practically crawling, I made my way to the windows on the near side. One was the nurse's bedroom. She had a dim desk lamp on and was bent over a desk, writing, probably a letter. I didn't see any computer. When she paused, I lowered myself to the ground and waited, being extra careful when I rose again, practically inch by inch. She had left her room. I moved down to the next window and looked in. She was there, leaning over the crib."

"Little Paula?"

"Yes. She fixed a blanket and stood there for a few moments, maybe a whole minute, staring down at her lovingly. I swear I could feel Mama's rage beside my own. She's our child; that's our family."

His anger gripped him so. He was staring right through me.

"What did you do?"

"What? Oh. She walked out. I was lucky she hadn't seen me. The crib is right below the window. For a while, maybe quite a while, I stood there peering in from the left corner of the window. I could see Little Paula clearly. She doesn't look like she's much bigger to me. Of course, it hasn't been that long since they took her, but maybe it was the crib. She looked lost in it. Everything has to be big for those very rich people."

Suddenly, it was I who couldn't talk. He had seen her. He had been inches away from her.

He took my hand. "So here's the good news, Faith. The window screen is easy to remove, and the window was slightly open. I suspect they keep it slightly open all the time now. All I have to do one night is take off the screen, open the window, lean in, and lift her from the crib. You'll be waiting beside me. I'll hand her to you. We'll bring one of her own blankets so I can bundle the one in the crib. Mama showed us the doll she had when she was a little girl, remember?"

"The doll?"

"Yes, it looked like it had real hair, just baby hair. It's perfect. It's still in the Forbidden Room on the dresser, right?"

"Yes," I said after a moment. How would I ever forget the way it had looked at me when Mama locked me in the room?

"She'd be so happy we'd use it like that."

"Like what?"

"Putting it in the blanket in the crib, making it look like she's still asleep."

"You told me once that you wanted to save that for Little Paula, that Mama told you to."

"I did, and we are. We're using it for Little Paula. It's still what Mama wanted. We're not changing that," he said firmly.

"Okay. Then what?"

"Then I'll close the window as far as it was and replace the screen while you walk back to the opening in the fence. I'll join you, and we'll get into Mama's car parked nearby and come home. Chances are it will be some time before they realize she's gone. She'll be safely and comfortably in her crib by then. Simple as that," he said.

"When would we do all that?"

"That's where we have to be patient. We have to follow the plan. We don't want to bring her back here until just after Daddy comes home."

"Why not?"

"Gabby would turn us in or do something. She'd be terrified and bring Nick into it."

"But the moment we sneak Little Paula back, she'll reveal it."

He smiled. "Just before Daddy comes home, she'll be planning on moving out. You'll see. Why would she stay here once the need for an adult supervising us is gone?"

"Guilt. Nick would make her. The only reason she remains here now is because of him and not because of some legal requirement, Trevor. She's afraid of her brother. There's a whole bottle of ugly family history that I don't want to open any more than it has been."

There was that Trevor shrug. "Worse comes to worse, we'll encourage her to leave."

"How?"

"You'll see, if it comes to that," he said. "For one thing, you could stop helping her with the house. Maybe I'll sabotage the television reception so she can't see her soap opera. She'll go into withdrawal." He laughed.

"You're almost diabolical," I said.

"Whatever it takes. That's what Mama would say."

He stood, stretched, and yawned.

"I'm tired. The excitement's worn me out. C'mon. Let's go to bed. I'll show you the house over the next few days after the hospital visit, and then we'll go there one of these nights soon. I'll take you to the window so you can see her."

"Go to the window?"

His eyes brightened. "That's it. We'll do a practice run, time it and everything."

"But if we get caught, we won't be able to go back."

"We won't get caught. We'll be protected. Wasn't I protected?"

"Protected? How?"

He smiled. "Let's get some sleep."

He started out and then stopped, turning back to me. I got up quickly to follow.

There was no doubt now. I would not tell him what I had told Lance.

I don't think I slept for an hour. He seemed to have passed out, but I lay there thinking and worrying until I saw the sunlight begin to break through the treetops. As if that brought me a sense of security, I relaxed and fell asleep. Trevor didn't wake me when he rose. For most of our lives until lately, we had woken up practically simultaneously. For him, it was like the mornings when Mama would come to our door and say, "Rise and shine, my lovelies."

By the time I went downstairs, both he and Gabby had left. He had returned to school, and she had gone to her beauty salon appointment. From the way Critter was whining and squirming, I gathered that neither of them had taken him out, so I did before I made any breakfast.

I stood there with my arms folded, watching him, but turned quickly when I heard and then saw a bright red convertible pull into our driveway. Lance got out quickly. He was in a turquoise T-shirt and black jeans with black and gray loafers. He took off his sunglasses and smiled.

"Hi. I'm on my way back to New York and saw you standing out here with your dog. I just wanted to say goodbye."

"Leaving? What about your grandfather?"

"Oh, he doesn't even realize I'm there half the time; the other half, he sleeps. My mother will be up next week. Mrs. Ireland has everything under control. Truthfully, I think I was getting in her way, playing the television too loud or messing up the kitchen. I'm good at that."

He came around his car, drawing closer. Months, days, hours folded into each other as he walked toward me, my body tingling in anticipation of his touch or his breath brushing across my face. So many books and even my instinctive awareness told me that first loves were destined to end unhappily. That was why they were first loves and not lasting loves. Perhaps that was what was different about Trevor and me. Ours was a lasting love but never a truly first love.

"Don't you have to be in school anyway? It's not yet summer," I asked, desperately trying to sound indifferent.

"I go to a private school now. It's easier to get away when I want." He looked at the house. "Anyone home?"

"No."

He looked hard at me, his eyes narrowing with the question I could almost hear forming in his mind.

"So you said your baby was coming back?"

"Did you tell Mrs. Ireland about her? That would open the dam, and the gossip and curiosity would circle our house like a hive of mad wasps and hornets. With what's happened to my father, that would be extra horrible now."

"Absolutely not, but eventually, people will know about it, right? I mean, if she's back and you're taking care of her and . . ."

"Eventually," I said, "when the time is right. But you swore not to tell."

"I didn't say anything. I'm just saying you can't keep that kind of thing secret forever."

"I don't intend to, but it's nobody else's business until the right time comes."

"Sure," he said, and shrugged just like Trevor and looked just as skeptical. "So when is she back?"

"Soon. Arrangements are being made."

I could see how he was struggling to break the tension.

"I'm sure she'll grow up to be as pretty as you. What's her name?"

"Paula. She's named after my mother."

"That's nice." He smiled. "I guess your father was quite surprised."

"Let's not talk about surprising anyone with secrets," I said. I looked down. I was sure it came out more harshly than I had intended.

He turned away, and then, when I looked at him, he put his sunglasses back on, probably so I couldn't see the anger and annoyance in his eyes.

"I don't see why either of you should be mad at me," he said. "I didn't put you into this situation."

"It's not a situation. Look," I said, softening my tone, "it's complicated right now, but for what it's worth to you, I'm not mad at you, at least not anymore."

He smiled. "I'm glad of that."

He paused and looked around as if he was leaving a place he loved.

"I'll be back, but not for a while. Unless something else happens to my grandfather. I'd just like to leave still being friends with you. I liked hanging with you guys. I hope it all works out for you. I really do. Say hello and goodbye to Trevor for me."

He started back to his car.

"Thanks," I said.

He turned with that smile. Everything in me that had wanted to be free and young, the teenager I had dreamed I'd be, came rushing back. I took a deep breath and started toward the house with Critter. At the door, I turned to watch him drive away. I wasn't sure why. Maybe it was because of Mama, but I felt sinful and guilty for being sorry to see him go.

Later Gabby returned, eager to show me not only her new hairdo but also a new dress that she had bought for visiting Daddy in the hospital tomorrow. She had bought matching shoes, too. She pulled everything out of the boxes and stripped down to her panties right there in the kitchen. She couldn't wait to put the outfit on to show me.

"Ta-da!" she said, turning like a model.

For a moment, I was speechless. This was the dress she wanted to wear to the hospital to visit Daddy? It was a spiral paisley shift, a good two or three inches above her knee. The pullover looked like an extra layer of skin so tight that I could clearly see the indentation of her belly button. A woman wearing this dress was surely a relief for men who lacked an imagination. There was nothing left to envision. With her not wearing a bra, her nipples looked like they might pop through.

"It's a little sexy, don't you think?" I asked.

Her smile froze. "Well, of course it is. Poor John has had a constant serving of middle-aged women dressed in sickly white uniforms. Most probably don't wear makeup. We're going to cheer him up, not add to the depression. I'm surprised you don't realize that's an important thing for me to do. You're so smart about everything else."

"But don't you think it might make him feel more frustrated?"

She smirked. "Exactly. The more frustrated and upset he becomes, the harder he'll work to get out of there. You didn't even say anything about my hair."

"It's very nice," I said without enthusiasm.

"It's called a shag." She turned so I could see the back of her head. "I think it's the perfect length for me. See how nicely it's layered? Someday you'll want to do something less ordinary with your hair. And when you do, think of this."

I was silent. My nonchalant reactions were obviously annoying her.

"Nick called," she said, closing the boxes sharply. "He bought Big John's hospital bed. It'll be coming next week, probably along with bedpans," she muttered. "And he's not coming for dinner tonight. It's just us."

"It'll be just us for quite a while, don't you think? I mean, Nick has to work, and it's not like Daddy's coming home in a few days, you know."

"Don't keep reminding me," she almost moaned, and then smiled. "Did you know that my brother has a girlfriend?"

"No."

"Sorta girlfriend. I think she's playing him. I know she goes out with other guys when he's on a trip, but most men refuse to face reality when it comes to their flaming love affairs."

"I never heard him mention her."

"He never actually told me, either, but I have ways of finding out things." She sighed. "He'll be here at eight tomorrow morning. Maybe you better be sure to wake me when you wake up."

She started away and then stopped.

"Oh. What do you think we should have for dinner? I have no idea."

"I'll make a pasta," I said.

"And a salad?"

"Yes."

"Good. I'm exhausted and can't think right now. I had something at the dress shop and don't have much of an appetite for lunch. I just need a good rest. I'm going up to my room," she said, and sauntered out with her boxes under her arms to go up-stairs.

With Daddy sleeping down here, that really was becoming her room, I thought. All of Mama's things had been put in the attic less than a week after she had died. Everything just made me more furious, especially her self-centered attitude. I no longer cared how diabolical Trevor was or could be. I wanted her out of our lives as soon as possible.

When Trevor returned from school, she was still up in her bedroom. I told him how she had acted, what she had bought for the hospital visit, and the things she had said about Nick.

"He never mentioned a serious girlfriend. She's just making things up to make herself look better," he said.

"She's already complaining about being alone with us. I'm so tired of hearing her 'poor me.'"

"Don't worry. It won't be much longer," he promised.

At dinner, maybe to show her how normal things were, he talked about school. Even I was surprised at his enthusiasm about his classes.

She asked him if he was in a sport or going out for one next year.

"I'm thinking about it," he said. "Basketball, maybe. My father and I used to shoot hoops a while ago. He said I was pretty good."

So did Lance, I thought, and wiped that out of my mind as soon as it occurred.

He looked at me, perhaps to say something encouraging and make his school life seem more attractive. Truthfully, I felt a little jealous, but when I thought about it, I came to the same realization I had whenever he mentioned anything about school. Unless we hired a nanny, I wasn't going to attend. Maybe when Little Paula started school herself, I could enter a junior college. I even dabbled with the idea of becoming a nurse.

Later, before we went to sleep, maybe because of the conversation at dinner, Trevor and I lay there imagining our future. When I talked about continuing my education, he surprised me.

"I don't want to go to college," he said.

"Why not? Mama would like that, wouldn't she?"

"Mama fell in love with a truck driver."

"So?"

"He barely had a high school diploma. It's not important. I want to become one, too, follow in Daddy's footsteps."

"But, like him, you'll be away so much."

"I'll keep it to reasonably short hauls until Little Paula is off to college. I have to build up to the eighteen-wheeler, of course. Unlike Mama, maybe you'll go along with me on some trips. We'll get to see things, find out the best restaurants to go to in the cities we have to pass through. It's the best way to see the country. You'd like that, right?"

"Yes," I said, but not enthusiastically. If he heard my hesitation, he ignored it and talked more about things to see, places to go. He recalled some of Daddy's stories and how we had both enjoyed hearing them. Even Mama had enjoyed them, although she hadn't liked his being so far away so often back then.

Why was it, I thought, before we both fell asleep, that all this sounded more like fantasy?

I did have to wake Gabby in the morning, but she took so long preparing herself that Nick said there was no time for her to have breakfast.

"Bring a candy bar or something," he snapped at her when she came down, and then he paused. He hadn't seen her in the new dress until then, of course. He did an almost comical double take. "Where did you get that dress?"

"I bought it yesterday for visiting John."

"You think that's proper to wear to a hospital?"

"I think I look good," she wailed. "And so did Faith. Right, Faith?"

I glanced at Trevor. I could see the smile under his apparent look of boredom. He easily transmitted his thought to me: *Plant the seed that will grow into her leaving.*

"I did say it was pretty sexy," I said.

The fury in her eyes looked like it would burn holes.

"That's exactly right," Nick said.

"Well then, you'll all have to wait until I find something else to wear." She started to turn away.

"Forget it!" Nick shouted. "We have a long ride. I know how long it takes you to dress. You'll spend an hour choosing shoes. Let's go."

She smiled at me like a child taking pleasure in getting the best of another and followed us out.

"Didn't you want to grab something to eat?" I asked her at the door, to show her I wasn't bothered by her grin of satisfaction. "You could grab one of the muffins I made a few days ago."

"I'm not hungry now. I'll wait for lunch."

Trevor and I sat in the rear, glanced at each other knowingly, and looked out the window. It was really only my second trip away from the house, and I wanted to relive every sight. The world out there, as I had thought of it all my life, streamed by like a ribbon of surprises once again. People, buildings, new colors, were all a visual feast, a buffet of the life I had seen mainly through books or on television.

Gabby sulked most of the way and was especially unhappy when Nick decided we wouldn't stop for lunch.

"There'll be plenty of time afterward," he said. "I'm sure the kids are anxious to see Big John."

"Yes," Trevor said. "I can't wait to tell him all the things we're doing for him."

"Exactly," Nick said. He turned to Gabby. "Let's not think of anything or anyone but him. Can you do that?"

She turned away sullenly and didn't say another word until we arrived.

I was frightened to see Daddy the first time we were here but was even more so now. By today, he surely knew everything about his future, and I couldn't imagine him being anything but enraged. Trevor looked as relaxed and pleased as he had the last time. Nick walked the fastest from the parking lot to the hospital entrance. Gabby seemed more interested in how many men looked at her. She threw her smiles like confetti.

We learned Daddy had been moved to his own room. When we arrived, he was sitting up in bed. Aside from some of the remaining black-and-blue marks on his face and neck, he looked just as he would sitting up in bed at home. He was cleanly shaven. I thought even his hair looked trimmed. If I closed my eyes, I could envision him at Sunday breakfast during those early days when we had been more of a family.

But the wheelchair beside the bed wiped away any hope of returning to even a semblance of that. Nick rushed to his bedside and clasped his hand. Gabby moved gingerly to the other side, and we stood at the foot of the bed. After Gabby kissed him on the cheek, he took her in with a look devoid of feeling.

"So how you doing?" Nick asked him.

"You followed up with the insurance company?"

"Yep. They should have the check in the mail before you come out."

"Yeah, come out," Daddy said dryly, and finally really looked at us. "You all behavin'?"

"They're doing great, John. Faith's been doing most of the cooking and cleaning, and Trevor's helped with making the house ready for you. I told you about most of it on the phone. What's the doctor saying?"

"What can he say? All I hear is the word 'therapy.'"

He looked at us again.

"You should be goin' to school, not cleanin' and cookin'," he told me. There wasn't even going to be a slight reference to Little Paula.

"School year's almost over, Daddy," Trevor said. "She might as well wait and help get things organized for you."

"Organized." He turned away.

"So will they have therapy after you're home?" Nick asked.

"They say. I don't need therapy to get myself in and out of that." He nodded at the wheelchair.

Nick described the ramp he and Trevor had built and how we were fixing up the den for him.

"And there's that special car you can get with everything at your fingertips. You'll figure it all out," Nick said, patting him on the shoulder.

Daddy focused on us again. The anger in his eyes felt like wind spiraling around us all.

"You don't have to pretend," he said. "Nothin's goin' to change when I get home. I'm still the head of this household."

"Oh, we're helping to make that a sure thing, Daddy," Trevor said.

Lucky he can't get out of bed, I thought. He looked enraged enough to throttle him for sounding so hopeful and even happy.

I glanced at Trevor. So this was part of his plan, I thought, to turn that knife in slowly with what sounded like hope and happiness. Maybe he was disabled and confined to a bed or a wheelchair, but Daddy still looked quite imposing to me.

Gabby complained about being hungry. She described how Nick had been so cruel to her by making her ride all the way here without so much as a cracker. It was about the only thing that brought a half smile to Daddy's face.

"You don't look like you're starving," he told her.

"Well, you can still be it without looking it, can't you?"

For some reason, she turned to me for reinforcement. I said nothing.

"Faith and I can take her to the hospital cafeteria," Trevor offered. "You and Nick can visit," he added, really sounding like he was giving Daddy permission.

"Oh, can you spare me for a few minutes?" Gabby asked Daddy. She kissed him on the cheek and turned to walk out before he could respond. He gave me a look that sent an arrow of ice through my heart. I quickly followed. Trevor mumbled something to the two men and joined us at the elevator.

In the cafeteria, Gabby gobbled her food. She made quite the show of choosing what to eat, asking this doctor or that male nurse for opinions as she went through the line. She was attracting a lot of attention in her dress, just as Nick and I had anticipated. Some of the female nurses shot darts from their eyes, but she was clearly enjoying it all.

"You can both see how difficult he's going to be," she said after we were at the table a few minutes. "He was hardly pleased to see me. Of course, I can understand why he's like that now. I'm just worried about what comes later."

"We'll help you," Trevor said.

"You're so sweet, both of you." She leaned toward us to whisper, "If truth be told, that's why I'm even still here. You're such devoted children."

I felt Trevor squeeze my leg under the table.

"And we so appreciate that," he said. He looked at me.

"Yes, Gabby," I said, rather robotically. "Thank you for being there for us."

She smiled and returned to her sandwich. Trevor began to eat just as enthusiastically. After seeing Daddy, it was clear to me that we had an unclear and dangerous future ahead of us. My stomach was so in knots with worry and fear I could hardly eat anything. I had no doubt, however, about where Trevor went to draw his courage and hope.

I was suddenly wishing that I could see and hear Mama as clearly as he could. Trevor simply assumed I did.

And then I wondered what Trevor would think of me if I admitted that I didn't.

And that maybe I didn't want to.

ELEVEN

An outsider definitely would find the different ways the four of us reacted to Daddy's impending release from the hospital curious, if not amusing.

Nick was looking forward to it the way a child looked forward to Christmas trees and presents. He followed through on a suggestion Trevor had made about a chair lift for the stairway down to the basement and had it installed. He went to a store that sold used medical equipment and bought a wheelchair for Daddy to have down there. He'd simply shift from the chair lift to the second wheelchair and do the same, shifting into his other wheelchair when he went back up. Daddy had already chosen a manual wheelchair.

"A man as big as John, even in a wheelchair, can play a mean game of pool as well as darts. After a while, he won't even notice the difference, but let's leave all this as a special surprise for him," he told us. "The quicker we get him back to do what he loves to do, the sooner he'll recover."

Even Critter looked excited when Nick spoke like that. Sometimes he even barked. It was just like he was talking.

"Recover?" Gabby said, barely above a whisper.

"Recover," Nick punctuated with his hands folded into fists. "If you think of him always the way he is right now, he'll never be even half himself. And you'll be to blame!"

She quickly looked away.

Gabby was clearly getting more and more depressed about what was to come. During the days before Daddy's arrival, she never said anything encouraging or expressed any delight. She sulked and watched television for hours. Whenever Nick was here, he continually warned her about her attitude and usually drove her to tears.

Trevor, on the other hand, certainly appeared as excited about Daddy's homecoming as Nick was. But clearly, to me, he was deliberately overexcited. He was too anxious to help. Sometimes it was obvious that he was doing it to annoy Gabby. He'd say things like, "We'll be here to assist your getting Daddy anything he wants or needs. I'm sure he'll require a lot in the beginning and, of course, have great issues and problems. You know how he can be. He'll be yelling, but we'll all get used to it."

Or he'd be deliberately detailed and say something like, "Neither of us is afraid to carry a urine bottle to the toilet if we have to, right, Faith?"

I'd glance at her and see how her lips would tremble. Trevor wore a serious expression, but I could discern the wry smile just beneath the surface.

Truthfully, my reaction to what was to come wasn't terribly different from hers. I, too, had trouble hiding my fear of what lay ahead beyond Daddy's arrival. I saw him pushing himself angrily in his wheelchair, banging into things, knocking things over, and lashing out in frustration. To avoid the images, I withdrew into housework, scrubbing places I had already scrubbed and reorganizing the pantry, even though it clearly didn't need it. There was no reason to put cans and boxes on different shelves. I even washed all the downstairs windows from the outside while Trevor was at school. I also had the front porch almost spotless.

Nick had gone on two short hauls during that time between our last visit and when we anticipated Daddy's release. When he returned from the second one, he was pleased with what Trevor and I had accomplished in the way of final preparations. All of Daddy's bathroom articles, razors, aftershave, and toothbrush had been moved down and put away in the bathroom near the den. Nick had installed the handicap railings for the toilet and tub-shower.

Wherever we could, Trevor and I lowered things to make them easier for Daddy to reach from a wheelchair. Trevor took Nick on a tour to show him everything we had rearranged. The hospital bed had arrived, and the den was well organized and immaculate. Trevor had bought a disinfectant used in hospitals, and sure enough, I heard Gabby whispering under her breath, saying things like, "It's even beginning to smell like a hospital."

If it wasn't for Nick, we would probably have known very little about Daddy's progress. Gabby didn't call him, and he certainly didn't call her. She spoke to him only when Nick was there and he handed her the phone. Her conversation was always short and, if anything, probably depressed him more. Before she returned the receiver to Nick, she always made a point, however, of giving us compliments.

Nevertheless, my anxieties only sharpened as the days ticked by. The actual release date was still unknown, but it loomed over us like an angry, dark storm cloud. Gabby became more withdrawn, leaving for longer periods during the day and even staying at her home a few nights when Nick was traveling. Of course, he didn't know.

Trevor's continual optimism oddly deepened my fears of Daddy sensing not only Trevor's underlying happiness but, more important, his anger over what he and Gabby had done with Little Paula. I was sure Daddy would be able to see through all this phony concern and joy eventually, if not right away.

Of course, I could easily see the vengeful pleasure Trevor was taking in every change that was made to accommodate Daddy. To him, it was truly like adding salt to a wound. I anticipated that if I told him to be more subtle, he would smile and once again tell me not to worry. We were protected. He was as confident of that as a monk was of God.

Mama had never talked to us that much about religion. She had said she had despised being forced to go to church when she was a child. We understood that she had attended only once or twice, not counting her own funeral.

"If you need God, you can find God right here," she would tell us if either of us even mentioned the word.

Trevor's confidence in Mama's spirit always being with us truly resembled what I understood to be someone's devotion to a higher power, a trust in what couldn't be seen and actually heard, a devoted belief impossible to challenge with facts or reality. I had no doubt that part of his faith was that I would not only understand it but eventually come to believe exactly what he did, and just as deeply and sincerely.

Ten days after we visited Daddy, when Gabby told us she might not be home that evening, Trevor decided it was time for our test run. Summer had made an early entrance in the Poconos of Pennsylvania. We had never had air-conditioning, even though Daddy had said a few times that he was going to install window units, especially in his den. The evenings had always been cool when we were growing up here, but lately they were more humid. It was still delightful to open a window and get the breeze, with the scent of rich, green maple, oak, and hickory trees and especially newly cut lawn.

Mama had said, "It's the same fresh air my ancestors breathed." She had often added, "And still do," which had made me wonder when I was little if spirits had to breathe.

I had asked Trevor what he thought, and he'd said, "If they don't, they might fall back into their graves."

It frightened me to recall all this so vividly, but Trevor enjoyed talking about the spirits and Mama's devotion to them, almost as much as he relished talking about his plan to get Little Paula back.

I was both excited and nervous about our test excursion. Trevor said we both had to wear dark clothes, including our shoes. The question that haunted me as we started away from our house was *How am I going to look at her and walk away?* I paid little attention to where we were going. We seemed to be sliding silently through the darkness. When Trevor parked near the Couches' house, I hesitated to open the door after he had opened his and stepped out. He poked his head back in.

"Why are you just sitting there, Faith? We're here."

I told him the question haunting me.

"Don't worry about that. You tell yourself it won't be much

longer. I know I've said that too much, but it's true. And you know
what, Faith? As soon as she's back in your arms, it will be as if she
had never left."

"How do you know all this?"

He was quiet.

"You sound so mature sometimes, Trevor. I know you haven't
read anything I haven't read. And you can't have learned something
like that at school talking to other kids."

"Mama told me," he said. "I hear her in my sleep every night,
her reassurance."

"You're just . . ."

"What?"

"Nothing. Maybe you're right."

I opened the door.

Trevor led me to the break in the fence. To me, the lawn we
had to cross looked like an ocean of green. The grass moved in the
breeze like the surface of the lake, rippling. The branches of trees
shuddered, and the few clouds above us seemed to be rushing across
stars, as if they were fleeing what was to come.

The house was so big it frightened me a little. People who lived
here had to be powerful and important. How insignificant we suddenly looked and felt to me. They'd suck us up and toss us like fish
onto a frying pan, left to gasp and struggle in an unwelcome dry world.
Like them, I wanted to get back to the comfort of my own home.

"C'mon," Trevor urged after he went through. He looked at a
pocket watch he'd pulled out, Mama's father's pocket watch.

I followed cautiously.

Even though we were still far away from the house, he whispered. "No cars tonight, no visitors. But it looks like they're on the
other side, probably watching television."

He paused every few feet, just as he had described doing the first time, and listened. I thought I heard laughter and music coming from their television, the hum of it leaking through open windows. Otherwise, it was cemetery-silent around us. No bird chirped. Everything that lived in nature was asleep.

"Looks good," he said, and moved faster to our left. When we were only a few feet from the house, he checked the pocket watch again. "Seems like a long time, but it's only been a minute and twenty seconds. When we go back next time with Little Paula, we'll get there in half the time. We'll go back fast tonight to see. But first . . ."

He beckoned and crouched more as we approached the dimly lit window. I didn't know whether my heart had stopped. I felt so faint, almost numb. We knelt below the window. Then he rose very slowly and peered into the room. I waited until he signaled that I should rise.

"Just stay in the corner of the window. Her blanket is down to her waist, so you can see her really well."

He stepped back so I could stand in his place. I would never have believed I could have forgotten any inch of her or be as fascinated and surprised as I was when I gazed down at her in the crib. She was a little bigger, like Trevor had described. For a moment, I wondered if it was indeed Little Paula. All her features looked more developed. I thought she was easily four or so pounds heavier, and she looked even longer. But the more I studied her, the more I felt she had been a part of me. She still tucked her mouth in slightly in the left corner the way I often did, and her tiny eyebrows were unforgettable. I'd gently run the tips of my fingers over them.

Suddenly, instead of fear, I felt so angry. These people were enjoying the changes in my baby. Everything Mama had said and Trevor had repeated about family came rushing in over me like a summer storm. She could grow up and never know us, could even pass us on a sidewalk without so much as a smile.

"I wish we could take her home now," I said.

"Daddy's coming home in two days," Trevor said. "We'll get her very soon after."

"Two days?"

"Nick called. He said he'll be bringing him home. He told me not to tell Gabby yet."

"So why didn't you tell *me*?"

"Shh," he said when the light within brightened. He beckoned for us to leave.

He checked his watch, and then we crossed back to the fence, running most of the way.

"Just as I thought. Thirty-two seconds," he said when we reached it.

We slipped through the opening and back to Mama's car.

"Well? Why didn't you tell me about Daddy?" I asked as soon as we were both seated.

"I wanted you to see her first and want to do this. With Daddy home, you might be afraid."

I was amazed. He was right. Daddy's presence, even in the state he was in, would be intimidating.

He started the engine and drove away with his headlights off for a few seconds.

"Of course I want to do this."

"But more now, huh?" he asked, smiling. "We've done a great job of hiding our true feelings, Faith. Neither Nick nor Gabby has the slightest suspicion. We're quite the team, huh?"

He was so happy and excited. I was feeling guilty about not telling him what I had said to Lance. What if Lance had lied to me and had told Mrs. Ireland? If the gossip trickled into the school and Trevor found out that way, he'd be so disappointed in me.

But suddenly, a colder feeling settled around my breasts, my heart. I realized that Trevor and I had changed in a very dramatic way.

We both could keep things from each other now.

As Mama once said, "With maturing comes greater powers of deceit."

I couldn't sleep for hours after we had gone to bed. Until we turned off the lights, he talked about Little Paula and how wonderful it was going to be to have her back.

"I don't know if you feel it like I do, Faith," he said, "but the house is so . . . empty and depressed since they took her. If I hear anything, it sounds like the family spirits are mourning and wailing. Once she's back home, everything will light up again. You'll see."

"Yes," I said, wishing I could be as certain about it all as he was.

"We'll have so much to teach her, to show her. You'll be like Mama. You'll set up the classroom for her, and I bet she'll be ahead of any other kid her age, as we are. She'll read before they do, and I'll take her out in nature and show her things just the way Mama showed us."

It was on my lips, but I didn't say it: *Don't you want to do more at school? Make new friends? Go to parties and join the basketball team, as you told Gabby? Don't you want to be a teenager?*

I told him all that in a different way. "Mama was much older than we are. She wasn't interested in much more than us, the house, and, even though it was less and less, Daddy. She had no real friends and left only when she had to get something or do something she couldn't put off. This was her world. She made sure it was ours, too."

"Oh, yeah," he said. "I know. But things will be better for Little Paula than they were for us. We'll take her for rides, go shopping with her, even go to that fun park Mama never took us to and have a picnic."

I said nothing. He either didn't understand or didn't want to, I thought. I watched him go to sleep so content. I did envy him for his faith. Not half the turmoil raged in him that did in me.

I knew that the mother in me had come too soon. Maybe I should have tried harder to prevent it, I thought, even though I didn't know how I could have. Whatever, it was too late now. I was who I was and forever would be. I was afraid to ask myself the same questions I had wanted to ask him. I'd feel guilty for even thinking of them. I felt ashamed for ruminating over Gabby's words in my memory, words telling me I should be grateful Little Paula was gone. When she said that, I imagined I could still be a teenager, have a romantic life, and maybe go to college. I saw boyfriends and parties, heard music, went to movies and on fun rides with all my friends in cars and in boats on the lake. In none of those fantasies was there a Little Paula.

I tucked them under everything else in my mind and, once again to escape, fell asleep.

When Gabby returned the next day, she looked like she was going to burst into tears. Trevor had left, and Critter was sitting beside me at the kitchen table. He had become so sensitive to any sound or any movement each of us made that he always had to be beside one of us. Did dogs really have that sixth sense? Was he anticipating Daddy's arrival?

Lately, I would drift into thinking more and more about our earlier years here and not realize how long I was sitting and staring at the wall. A part of me wanted to erase so much since then. I dreamed of returning to the past and then, with what I knew now, avoiding getting into trouble with Lance. The end of it all would be no Little Paula and maybe Daddy not disabled. He'd still be with Mama, and whether he liked it or not, she'd make him be more careful. The conflict raged inside me. I wanted my baby back, but I wanted to be a normal teenage girl, too. I wanted life to be at least something like it used to be.

I was tired of asking Gabby the same thing almost daily. I wanted to ignore her obvious unhappiness. Asking about it only kept it more alive. But the question forced itself out of me.

"What's wrong, Gabby?"

"Nick told me it would be wrong for me even to think about returning to work and leaving all the responsibility and work here for you. He says John is insisting you go to school, even if it's just for the end of the term. He says John doesn't want to have to depend on you or Trevor.

"I never said I loved him," she wailed. "We were having good times is all. I didn't mind babysitting you two as long as John and I were doing fun things together. But he never said he wanted to marry me or anything. Now, with you going to school, I'll have all the housework and the cooking and whatever he'll need me to do. I'm not a nurse. I never wanted to be one. I fainted once at the sight of blood. I mean, a big man like he is . . . he's going to smell and stuff. He won't like me bathing him as if he was a baby."

"Did you tell Nick all this?"

"Yes. He says I should think of it more as a favor to him, paying him back for all he's done for me. It's all right for him to go and live a life but not me!"

She was crying harder. "John's coming home tomorrow. It's all going to start tomorrow!"

Every fear and horror she had built up in her mind was exploding.

"I'm not going to start school. Trevor was right; it's too late for this year. After the summer . . ."

I let my words drift off. Of course, my real words were, *After Little Paula's back, that idea will die*, but I couldn't say it. I was almost as frustrated as Gabby was.

She plopped into a chair at the table, her hands over her eyes.

"I don't want to be the mean, unfeeling person," she said, still hiding behind her palms, "but it's not fair." She took her hands away. "Is it? I'm still a very young woman."

"Of course you are," I said. The Trevor in me was blooming like a flower in a video that was being fast-forwarded. I was suddenly just as conniving. "It's your brother who's being selfish."

"Yes," she said, sucking back her tears. "He is."

"You said he had a girlfriend, and he won't stop his work and travel after Daddy's brought home, right?"

"That's right."

"Maybe he doesn't believe you can do it."

"Do what?"

"Find a real life for yourself, be with someone who will provide for you, get you your own home, and make a family with you."

"He doesn't. He's always treated me like I was a child. I never asked him to do that, look after my health insurance, manage our money, and do everything that needed to be done with our house. He doesn't even let me write a check. He thinks he knows everything and I don't know anything."

"Can you get your job back?"

"I think so, or something just as good."

Another thought occurred to me, one that would be closer to the result Trevor wanted.

"Maybe you don't want to stay here. Maybe you want to travel or start brand-new. Do you have any friends in other places?"

She thought, and then her eyes brightened. "Yeah, I do. One of my best high school friends lives in Boston."

"I'd like to go to Boston," I said. "I'd like to go anywhere."

She stared at me.

"Eventually," she said, "you can find a nurse to stay with John so you can attend school, can't you?"

"Maybe. Probably. Thank you for staying with us until Daddy is home," I added. "But once he's here, even disabled, he's still the adult supervising. I think we can manage. You see how capable my brother is. There's nothing around here he can't do. It's how Mama brought us up."

"Yes, you two are far more mature than other kids your age. I've said that."

I shrugged, a Trevor shrug. "You shouldn't feel any guilt about leaving us, Gabby. It's the other way around, actually. If you're forced to stay here because of us, we'd feel terrible."

She still looked unsure, frightened, and incapable of making a big decision.

"Of course, you have to have some money to get your new start," I said. "Otherwise, this is just idle talk."

Her eyes widened. That money, or some of it, was as close as the envelope upstairs.

"If you have start money, you could call your girlfriend to see how she feels about your visiting her. You'd tell her you're thinking of reestablishing yourself there. Maybe she could begin looking for jobs for you. It's not like you're just driving off with nothing and no plan."

"Yes. That's right."

"Of course, Nick won't be happy, but maybe it's time you thought about your own happiness," I said. In my heart, I knew she never had thought about much else, but people who do that don't even admit it to themselves.

"Ordinarily, you should wait to have a family discussion with your brother, but . . ."

"But what?"

"Considering how fast things are happening here . . ." I stared at her a moment, and then, as casually as I could, I said, "I'd leave today if I were you. Let him know later, when he can't do much about it."

She stared, really looking beyond me, looking at the possibilities. Surely she had dreamed of doing this or something similar.

"I could go up and pack all my things that I have here. Nick's not home. I'll get whatever I need from there and leave before he knows it."

"Exactly. I won't say anything. When your brother asks about you, I'll say you left without telling me where you were going."

She rose slowly. "You won't feel like I'm deserting you?"

"Of course not." I smiled. "We'll be too busy to feel sorry for ourselves. So would you if you were here when Daddy arrives. You wouldn't have time to think of yourself."

That would be as close to tragedy for her as anything. She realized it, too. I saw the determination settle into her eyes.

"I'm going to do it."

"You need any help packing?"

"No, no, thanks," she said. She wiped away the residue of her self-pity tears and hurried to the stairs. I leaned down to tickle Critter behind his ears.

Trevor was going to be quite proud of me, I thought, even though I wasn't quite sure I should be proud of myself. Were Trevor and I going to be able to handle everything? Would both Nick and Daddy be so upset and angry that it would cause more trouble? Truthfully, it frightened me a bit to see how much influence I could have on someone like Gabby. When I reviewed the things I had told her, it was as if I was hearing Mama, word for word.

I was surprised at how quickly she came down with her two suitcases and her leather jacket over her arm.

"I called my friend. She is so excited."

"How wonderful for you, Gabby. Promise you'll call us once in a while to let us know how you're doing."

"Yes, I will."

She stood there looking at me, her lips trembling.

"You can do it," I said. I stepped forward and hugged her.

"I do love you guys," she said. "It's just that . . ."

"No need to explain. I understand. Trevor will understand, too. Have a safe ride, and don't look back."

She started for the door. Critter rose, as if he understood she was leaving for good. Her face began to weaken.

"You're not deserting a sinking ship," I said. "You know we're capable of handling it all."

She smiled. "Thank you, Faith. You have been like a little sister, only a wiser little sister."

She left, closing the door softly behind her.

I felt as if I had just set off a bomb. Then I turned and hurried up to her bedroom. The envelope was still in the drawer. I opened it and counted what was left. She had taken at least ten thousand dollars.

Her blood money reignited my rage. If it hadn't been for her,

Daddy might not have found any way to sell Little Paula. I thought about Nick's reaction and then Daddy's when they found out Gabby had left. I wasn't afraid of that anymore. I was looking forward to it.

It was easy to imagine Mama behind me, whispering, *You might enjoy all this as much as Trevor will.*

Later I went out back, sat at the bottom of the ramp, and watched Critter chase birds. He sniffed everything he could. Mama would say he looked like a child turned loose in a candy store. I held my breath when he approached Mama's Cemetery for Unhappiness. He started into it with his nose down, paused, and turned to run back to me.

What had he detected through his sense of smell? I petted him, and he settled at my feet like a child who had been frightened. It was how Trevor found us when he drove in, coming home from school.

"Hey," he said, getting out, clutching his book bag like a football under his right arm and carrying another bag in his left hand. "What's up?"

I stood.

"She's gone."

"What do you mean?"

"Gabby. She left to start a new life in Boston."

"What?" He smiled. "You're kidding."

"I talked her into it."

"You did? Wow, good for you, Faith."

"I know you're disappointed. You had so many plans for tormenting her."

He laughed.

"She took ten thousand dollars from the envelope."

He nodded. "I wasn't planning for us to give any of that money back to the Couches, anyway."

He looked back at the entrance to the driveway and then smiled at me.

"It will all be as perfect as it should be," he said.

"What's in the bag?"

"Did it in art class today. My teacher Mr. Longo's idea."

He put it down and took out a roll of paper. Then he threw it open.

WELCOME HOME, DADDY, it read in bright bubble letters.

Salt on a wound, I thought again, *salt on a wound.*

TWELVE

The phone rang just after I had fed Critter and we had sat down to dinner. Trevor had wanted Mama's favorite, chicken parmigiana. He said I seasoned it perfectly, almost as if she had been looking over my shoulder as I prepared it.

"Where's my sister?" Nick asked as soon as I had said hello.

"She's not here, Nick. She went somewhere."

Nick was silent. Then he said, "Did you see her leave?"

"Yes. She came downstairs with her suitcases, said goodbye, and left."

"And she didn't say where she was going?"

I looked at Trevor. He always said I was a better liar than he was, maybe because Mama had taught us that bending the truth was sometimes a good thing to do. "Nothing is really black and white in this world. We live most comfortably with shades," she had said.

"No, Nick. Did you try calling her mobile?"

He was silent again.

"Maybe she's in a dead spot or something," I suggested, well knowing why she wouldn't answer.

"She's in a dead spot, all right, especially when I get my hands on her. She blocked my number. What's going on with her? She took things out of our house and left her room a mess. And this, the night before John comes home?"

"Oh. Now that I think about it, I believe she was crying earlier. But she'd been doing that a lot lately. She's nervous about Daddy. Should I try to call her?"

"Oh, forget it," he said. "There's no time to worry about her right now. You two are on your own tonight. I've some things to do. Looks like you will have to get his clothes for him to wear when he's discharged. Pick out one of his nicest shirts and a pair of pants, underwear, socks, and shoes. I'll stop by in the morning to pick it up. If all goes all right, I should be arriving at the house with your father by about five or six tomorrow. Make him something he really likes for dinner, maybe a steak. I know he likes it rare. Your mother and I used to tease him and tell him he could take a bite out of a cow. We'll have a lot to talk about and do, I'm sure. I'll take care of telling him about Gabby."

"Okay, Nick. Thank you for being such a friend to all of us."

"Yeah." He paused. "On second thought, you call me if you speak to her or hear from her. She and me ain't finished by a long shot."

"I will."

"Wait."

"What?"

"Take his chairs away from the tables in the kitchen and in the dining room. His therapist told me we have to make things as smooth as possible at home without reminding him of his situation constantly. "

"Will do, Nick."

"Okay, Nick. I'm sorry about Gabby."

"Yeah. Me, too."

I heard him click off, but I held the receiver a moment or so. Trevor raised his eyebrows.

"So?"

"He can't reach her. She won't answer his calls, but he knows she left, maybe for good."

"Why don't I feel bad?" he said, and continued to eat.

"He wants me to pick out Daddy's clothes for his discharge and have them ready for him in the morning."

"Ah. I know just the shirt to give him, the one Mama bought him on his last birthday. I'll find it."

"He also asked us to take Daddy's chairs away from the tables before he gets here. It's more emotionally comfortable for him if he simply wheels up to his place without our having to remove it then or constantly."

"We'll put them in the corner of the kitchen and the dining room. We'll call it Time Out."

"Very funny. You know what I just realized, Trevor," I said when I sat again. "We're really going to be alone. I mean, Gabby left us for a night or two before, but this is different."

"What do you mean?"

"I mean, Daddy will be here but so restricted, unable to fix things around the house, and he'll be confined to the downstairs.

Now that Gabby's gone and with Nick going off on his trips frequently, we'll have to shop, care for the house, do everything. We're really alone."

He paused, lowering his fork.

"We're not alone, Faith. We're never alone."

"Yes, I know, but . . ."

"And we'll have Little Paula. She'll be our priority, not him."

"Yes, of course."

"We won't miss Gabby, or Nick when he's off on a job, either. Daddy's going to have to get used to the changes." He stared at me.

"What?"

I could tell when he was holding something back. Whatever it was brought laughter into his eyes.

"I bought something today," he said, rising. "With some of the money Gabby gave us the first time we went to the hospital."

He went toward the front of the house and returned with a bag.

"He's going to hate this," he said, smiling, and reached into it to take out two mobile phones. "They're all set up. I put one number on his to speed dial."

He turned the phones on and then pressed a number on one. The other rang.

"This is his, and this is mine," he said. "It'll be next to his bed, and when he wants something, he calls. I'll leave this one beside our bed in case I'm not here. Of course, don't rush if you're busy with Little Paula." He smiled and shook his head again. "He's going to hate it."

"Why should he hate it? That seems clever."

"It is clever, but he'll hate being dependent on us."

"Maybe he'll hire a nurse."

"A nurse? Not our Big John Eden. If I know him, by now he's

had his fill of nurses. I might suggest it once in a while, or you might, if and when he complains about us. Which you can be sure he will."

He smiled.

I didn't smile or laugh. I rose and began to clear off the table.

"You're not going to feel sorry for him, are you, Faith?"

"I'm sorry he sold Little Paula."

"That's right. That's the only thing you should care about now."

"Yes, but it's still difficult to be cruel to him, Trevor. He was a good daddy once. He used to bring us gifts and play with us. You wanted to go with him on long truck rides. Remember?"

"That was then; this is now. Besides, we're not just being cruel to him, Faith. How do you think he's going to take our bringing Little Paula home? If he's a little afraid of us, if he needs us, he'll just accept it."

I knew what he meant, but the idea of Daddy being afraid of us or dependent on us was still quite far-fetched to me, despite his injuries and condition.

And despite Trevor's optimism and confidence, I was not sure we would really bring Little Paula back. It looked possible but not as easy as Trevor made it seem. It was monumental to me. And what if we succeeded? What would happen afterward?

"And he's got to appreciate all we've done around this house and the grounds to make it easier for him."

"You enjoyed doing all that too much."

He laughed. "Remember Mama saying, 'I'm killing him with kindness'?"

"It won't be as easy as you're making it out to be, Trevor."

He gave me his shrug. "Just keep your smile, Faith. Say yes when he orders you to do something, and then take your time or don't do it. Maybe just say, 'I'll try.' Give him answers like that. Don't argue. I'm never going to lose my temper with him, no matter what he says or how much he yells. Calmness and patience always win in the end."

He rose.

"I'm taking Critter out. I think better out there. Me and Mother Nature."

I watched them leave and sat at the table for a while before doing the dishes and putting away the leftovers. I doubted that anyone who was about to walk out onto a stage to perform for a few thousand people would feel any more nervous than I did at the moment. Trevor and I had been convincing enough to alleviate any suspicions about us and our reaction to Little Paula being taken. Gabby, Nick, and even Daddy thought we had accepted it.

"But you're about to start the second act, Faith," I said aloud. "An act that will last years, if not almost all our lifetimes."

I rose to finish cleaning up the kitchen. Everything was nearly done when Critter came running in ahead of Trevor. From the look on Trevor's face, I knew something was wrong.

"What?"

"I heard the sirens and saw the lights, so I went up the road. There's an ambulance and a police car at Mr. Longstreet's house. I waited to see what was happening."

"And?"

"They brought him out on a stretcher."

"Oh."

"Completely covered."

"You mean he died?"

"Maybe he had a heart attack."

I nearly said it was probably a second stroke. How would I have known about the first? Maybe I was better at telling a lie or holding back the truth, but it wasn't easy to keep either from leaping out when you least expected it.

He was studying me.

"You don't look that surprised," he said.

Although we were both adopted, I had always believed that somehow Trevor's eyes were mirror images of Mama's whenever she scrutinized us suspiciously. It always felt as if she was looking right into me. It was not possible to lie to Mama successfully. I could try to convince myself that I had succeeded, but in the end, even though she didn't say so, she knew what was true and what wasn't. It was certainly like that when I lied about Lance.

"I'm sorry," I said.

I sat at the table. He didn't move. I could feel his gaze fixed on me. I was afraid to breathe too hard.

"Sorry? About what, Faith?"

I took a deep breath and looked away.

"Just say it," he said sharply, stepping closer and practically standing over me.

"I saw Lance one night when I was walking Critter. He came to visit with his grandfather because his grandfather had suffered a stroke. He apologized to me and wanted to visit, to see you. I told him I would speak to you. When I didn't respond, he sent flowers."

"Flowers? Where are they?"

"I was going to throw them out, but Gabby wanted them and said she would say they were from one of her friends who felt sorry for her because of what had happened to Daddy. They're still up in the bedroom, wilting. I'll throw them out."

"She was helping you cover up? What did you tell her?"

"Nothing about us and Little Paula. She knew Mama didn't like Lance. That's all."

"What did he do then? When you didn't respond to his flowers?"

"He saw you leave the night you went to learn about the Couches. He saw me again."

Trevor approached the table and sat. My thoughts spun around each other as I tried to phrase a way to tell him more without it being so painful for both of us.

"And?"

"He was full of questions, especially why you were in school and I wasn't. I didn't tell him anything, but . . ."

"But what?"

"He got me mad, so I blurted . . . I mean, I didn't think."

"You told him about Little Paula?"

"Yes."

Trevor looked more in pain than angry.

"Did he know she was gone, too?"

"Yes, but I said she was being brought back. He promised he wouldn't tell Mrs. Ireland."

"Who's that?"

"Mr. Longstreet's caretaker."

He sat back. "Who else did he promise he wouldn't tell? Did he list everyone in the world he knows?"

"He said he wouldn't tell, swore."

"Oh. That's reassuring."

"He stopped by when he left for home and said he wished we were all friends again. He liked hanging out with us, with you."

He was silent a moment.

"I was afraid to tell you. You've been so happy and confident . . ."

"This makes things different, Faith. It puts more pressure on us."

"Why?"

"Why? What if he told someone who lives here and that got back to the Couches? There might be an armed guard at that house by now."

"He really doesn't know anyone here."

"C'mon, Faith. You haven't seen him for some time. Do you know how long he was here?"

"Not long."

He thought and then nodded. "I'm not going to school tomorrow. I'll use Daddy's homecoming as an excuse. I'll scout the Couch house and property tonight after dinner and again tomorrow morning to be sure there's no added security."

"I'm . . ."

"Don't say you're sorry again, Faith." He rose. "I'll be right down."

"What are you going to do?"

"I'm going up to find that shirt Mama gave Daddy for his birthday."

"But . . ."

"We'll say Gabby put his things together. It was the last thoughtful thing she did for him. Nick will appreciate that and maybe even tell Daddy before he gives it all to him at the hospital. I'll lay it on the bed for you to pack, and then I'll get the money and hide it in our room, not that Daddy will ever get up there to search for it. If he asks for the envelope, we'll tell him it's gone. He'll think Gabby took it all. In fact, you can say you saw she had the envelope on her when she left. He was always easy to lie to. Okay?" He stared at me. "Okay?" he demanded.

"Okay."

He stood there, thinking. "Lance will return now for his grand-father's funeral."

He started away and then paused.

"I did like Mr. Longstreet. He was nice to Mama. But we're not going to his funeral, and don't do anything to encourage him to come here," he added quickly, and went upstairs.

I was surprised at myself for not feeling more terrible than I did. Whenever I disappointed Trevor, it used to haunt me for days. He tried so hard not to upset me. I hated upsetting him. Unlike others our age, we rarely argued. I couldn't think of many nights when we had gone to sleep angry at each other. I could still vaguely recall him crying when Mama had locked me in the Forbidden Room, drugged me, and brought him in to make Little Paula. I never blamed him, and we did often try to comfort each other afterward.

However, instead of sitting here and berating myself for keeping the secret of Lance from him, I thought about Lance. I told myself that was terrible, but I couldn't help envisioning those violet eyes when he took off his sunglasses to say goodbye. Fight it, forbid it, and vow to defy it though I might, I couldn't stop the excitement that returned whenever I recalled his smiling at me.

I wanted to slap myself silly. With all that was happening, the complexity of what we were about to do, how could I act, even only to myself, like a lovesick teenager? I was a mother, and Trevor and I were about to assume most if not all of the responsibility for this home and family. There was no time and no room here for any of those young woman feelings. I had been scooped up and carried beyond my teenage years.

I could almost see that part of myself rise out of me, walk to the door, wave goodbye with a mournful sigh, and leave forever.

And with it went everything I had wished for myself a little over a year ago.

Despite these thoughts of self-pity, I had to get up and go upstairs to apologize to Trevor in a way that would satisfy him. Critter rose when I did. I thought about bringing him up with me but then thought I should ask Trevor first.

"Just stay," I ordered at the foot of the stairs. He whined, but he didn't attempt the steps.

I walked up slowly. It was interesting how different parts of our house held different meanings and caused particular reactions now. Because Mama had had what would be a fatal fall off this stairway, it intimidated me. Since her death, I don't think I ever went up it slowly. It was always as if I had to pass through a dark cloud to get to the top. I hated every creak it made. Sometimes I dreamed Trevor and I tore it out and replaced it with a more modern, clean set of steps. I never stood at the top and looked down them anymore. Before I descended, I always closed my eyes for a moment and tightened my grip on the banister.

Trevor hadn't been standing up there at the time. He hadn't watched Mama fall like I had. I think that to him, it was still a stairway, although I never asked him about it or brought it up. Both of us avoided talking much about that fatal day. The only thing he had said recently about the stairs was "Now that Daddy can't go up and down, it'll last longer."

I turned toward our bedroom but stopped. What was I hearing? It sent a cold chill through my heart. I had imagined the spirits talking in our house, but I had never really heard them. Was I hearing them now? I listened harder, and then turned and walked slowly toward the Forbidden Room. It was coming from in there, the loud whispering.

I looked to Mama and Daddy's bedroom. The door was wide open, but I didn't see or hear Trevor in it. Surely he had taken the envelope of money by now, anyway. The whispering continued, but I could not make out the words. It was like gibberish, a child's make-believe language. I brought my ear to the door.

The whispering stopped, but before I could lean back and away from it, the door to the Forbidden Room swung open. Trevor stood there glaring at me. He looked so different for a moment, and then his face seemed to return.

"What are you doing?" he asked.

"I thought I heard . . . did you hide the envelope in there?"

"Yes. And guess where?"

I shook my head.

"Under the mattress in the crib." He smiled. "That's where Mama would have put it."

"Yes, good idea," I said. "Look, I'm sorry about—"

He put his hand up and smiled. "Don't worry. We cover for each other; we always have. I'll handle it, but don't see Lance without my being present, and certainly don't answer any emails, speak to him on the phone, or whatever."

We could hear Critter whining.

"I was going to bring him up, but . . ."

"Oh," Trevor said, thinking. "Bring Daddy's dog up every night?"

"We're not going to do that, Trevor. I just meant now."

"We'll see," he said. "Pets are important to handicapped people. His shirt's on the bed," he added as he turned toward the stairs. "Get the rest of his things together. Hey, Critter."

I watched him descend. Then I looked back into the Forbidden Room. Perhaps it was just the movement of the clouds over the now starry sky, but it looked to me like a shadow crossed the room. I closed the door and followed him down the stairs, my heart pounding harder with every step.

"Maybe I should go with you tonight to check on the security," I said when we went into the kitchen and sat down to talk.

"No. You'd better be here in case Nick calls with some last-minute request or idea. If there's no one here, he'll get suspicious or something."

We talked about preparing for Little Paula, getting things she would need and how we would reveal her to Daddy.

"I've been dreaming about that," Trevor said. "We'll wait for Nick to leave on his long haul. Without him here, Daddy won't have anyone to side with him. We'll just show him she's here.

"Stop looking so worried," he said. "You leave it to me. You don't say anything. When he asks, you have no details about retrieving Little Paula. You have to take care of her. That's all you know. You don't want to talk nonsense. You don't have time to waste with all he needs and with taking care of a baby." He thought a moment and smiled. "He'll be so involved in himself that he'll give up trying to figure it out."

"What about the Couch family?"

"Don't worry about them. I'll take care of all that."

He paused. Whenever Trevor stopped talking and looked down for a moment, I knew what he was going to say next would be most important, more shocking.

"As soon as Little Paula is home, I'm quitting school."

"What? Why? You have so little to go to finish the year."

"Why prolong the inevitable? I'm not going to college. There is no way I can leave you now for that long a time, months and months, until holidays and the ends of semesters, especially with Big John the way he is and will be. I told you. I'm going to start truck driving. There's a bigger and bigger demand for truck drivers.

Short hauls until Little Paula is older and you have everything under control, including him."

He put his hand up before I could start to speak.

"It's the way Mama wants it, would want it. Remember to get the rest of Daddy's clothes together for Nick if you haven't," he said, rising. "I'll take Critter for a walk to check on what activity is happening around Mr. Longstreet's house."

I couldn't stop the feeling of dread and nervousness that washed over me. I could see how determined he was. We didn't look at each other. I rose and went up to pack the rest of Daddy's things. I remembered that he wasn't particularly fond of the shirt Mama had bought him. I knew he didn't like those multicolored shirts for himself, and I thought Mama had been quite aware of that but had bought it for him anyway. He never had put it on. It was clear what Trevor was doing, but I didn't want to contradict him. It was easier to pretend Gabby had done it.

Suddenly, we were swimming in more and more lies. There didn't seem to be much reason or value in the truth.

The question was, would we drown in them?

I stepped quickly toward the front door when Trevor entered with Critter.

"It's just dark there. No one's come yet. I'll find out more about it all tomorrow. Maybe it's in the local paper. I know the breakfast place on the way to school, too. I'll stop in."

"But you're not going to school, right?"

"No. I'm going to where Little Paula is," he said, smiling. He looked down at Critter. "Let's give him a treat and let him sleep in our room tonight."

It was getting so I didn't recognize Trevor's smile. It was so full of glee.

THIRTEEN

So I began my day with a lie.

After Trevor left, I took Critter out for a while and then waited in the kitchen. The sound of the clock ticking had never seemed any louder. The house voiced its occasional creak, once sounding like footsteps through the hallway above. Despite all of Mama's stories and the way she would freeze suddenly when talking to us so Trevor and I could hear the spirits, twisting and turning sometimes, she said, because they were simply restless or impatient, I was never afraid of being alone in this house. If anything, I grew up here believing it was as protective as a shell for a turtle.

Mama had been adamant about all this.

"Most people grow up believing their homes are temporary

rest stations along their journeys. People don't respect their homes today. They buy and sell them the way they buy and sell their cars: get all they can out of them and peel them off. Who slept in them, who grew up in them, who washed and polished and repaired them with love and pride, no longer matters." She'd lean into us and say, "They're soulless structures, empty graves.

"But not our house, never our house."

I hadn't always listened as well and as intently as Trevor had to Mama, but suddenly, I was clinging to words I could recall, as if every syllable strengthened our life preserver while we floated about in this turmoil.

The sound of wheels over the gravel ripped me out of my musings.

I knew Nick would come to the rear door, so I sat at the kitchenette table facing it. He knocked and stepped in, a little surprised to see me just sitting there, waiting for him.

"Morning," he said.

"Morning." I rose quickly.

"Everything all right?"

"Yes, yes." I handed him the small overnight bag. "Gabby packed this for my father before she left."

"I'm surprised she could do that much. She hasn't called since, huh?"

"No."

"All right. I'll tell your father about her on the way home. I'll call just before we leave the hospital so you can figure on when to expect us. We'll get him settled in and have some dinner."

He looked past me into the house. "Trevor went to school?"

"Yes," I said. Second lie.

"Okay. See you later. It'll be fine. All will be fine," he assured me.

I watched him go to his car and then closed the door. I thought I heard a scream of fear and looked back toward the living room, realizing that the scream was inside me.

Trevor called from the car parked near the Couch residence later in the morning.

"Everything is calm here. I don't see any unusual cars. I saw Mr. Couch leave for his office."

"Did you get a local paper or stop in the breakfast place to find out about Mr. Longstreet?"

"Yeah. His funeral is in two days. They didn't say why or how he died. They listed his daughter and son and grandchildren. I can't imagine them keeping the house and land. We'll have new neighbors," he added, almost gleefully. "It's none of our business. All go all right with Nick?"

"Yes. He's calling when he leaves the hospital."

"I'll get my banner up when I get home. I can hear you worrying through the phone, Faith. It's going to be just great. You'll see."

"Okay. Be careful," I said.

"I will. It's a beautiful day. I want to see if the nanny takes Little Paula out as usual. They wouldn't let her if they had any fears."

"Okay."

The faster I stopped talking about that, the better, I thought. He'd said he wouldn't call anymore. He'd simply come home.

I paraded about the house, checking everything as if I expected Daddy would do a detailed inspection as soon as he arrived. I was trying to keep myself busy and not thinking about what was to come, but I paused practically every ten minutes to look at the clock. The face of it grew larger every time I did.

It's only when you continually think about something that is going to happen that time seems to move slowly. I paced about, dusting and straightening anything and everything, even moving some of Mama's family relics an inch or so in every direction: eighty-year-old ashtrays, framed pictures of great-uncles and great-aunts, and pictures of Trevor and me. There was one I remembered Trevor had taken of Mama and Big John a year or so after we had been brought here. I adjusted and readjusted it all, as if I thought Daddy would see something out of place and that would rouse all his suspicions. After a while, I realized how ridiculous I was being and stopped.

However, the silence in the house was getting to me. I put Critter's leash on him and took him out again, deciding to go along our well-worn paths Trevor had trimmed in the woods. I tried to convince myself I wasn't deliberately going to the wall to look at Mr. Longstreet's house. But that was exactly what I did. The sight of a new, expensive-looking car in the driveway triggered my stepping back into the shadows. I stood there watching, almost mesmerized. Critter tugged a little on the leash but eventually just sat and waited.

Suddenly, Lance came out of the house and went around to the trunk of the vehicle. He wore a white shirt and a dark tie with slacks instead of jeans. I watched him take out a small suitcase and then start back to the house. He paused after he had taken only a few steps. I held my breath when he turned and looked in my direction. Had he caught a glimpse of me, or was he reliving that moment when he had first seen me and Trevor? It was only a few seconds at most, but it sent my heart racing. When he clearly had reentered the house, I turned and hurried back through the woods.

Critter tracked in some dirt, so I cleaned it up and then washed the kitchen floor. I had just done it the day before.

This is madness, I told myself, and stopped working. I tried watching television but gave up after ten minutes because I couldn't get interested in anything. Besides, I felt like Gabby, hypnotized by her soap operas.

Soon after, I heard Trevor drive in. I opened the rear door and waited for him. Critter rushed out to join him. He knelt and played with him for a few moments and then continued to the house.

"She was outside with Little Paula and just as unconcerned as she was the first time I saw her. Nothing to worry about," he said. "Let's get the banner hung." He paused, eyeing me more closely. "Are you all right? Something wrong? Something break in the house? Gabby call? She's not coming back already, is she?"

"No, no. She didn't call. I'm just nervous."

"Everything's going to be fine," he said, hugging me. He stepped back and brushed strands of my hair off my forehead just as Mama would do. He smiled, really looking excited and confident.

I helped him hang the banner, and then we had lunch. He described the Couch house again and how easy it was all going to be to retrieve Little Paula.

"We'll do it all in less than ten minutes. You'll see."

Just before we finished eating, Nick called to say they were leaving the hospital.

"It's all going well," Nick told me. "He's excited about going home. I should have told you guys to get a cake."

"Don't worry. I'll bake his favorite, the vanilla with chocolate frosting," I said. Actually, I was glad to have something to do.

"That's a great idea," Trevor said when I told him. "We can write WELCOME HOME, DADDY on top. Mama showed us how to do that. Besides, I like that cake, too."

I got busy with it while he went to the garage to continue straightening it out, even though now there was plenty of space for Mama's car. Gabby's was gone. Hours later, I watched him write the words on the cake. He stood back and looked so proud that I almost believed he was truly happy Daddy was returning.

"Let's go sit out on the front porch. If they drive up while we're there, we'll look like we couldn't wait to see him arrive, like it's a big thing."

"It is a big thing, Trevor, definitely for him. He almost died."

"I guess," he said. He thought a moment and said, "It is definitely a big thing for us. It's the first step to our bringing Little Paula back. We couldn't do it until he was home. Nobody would have supported us, and there'd be so many problems with our living in this house by ourselves with a child until I turned eighteen."

"But he won't accept it, Trevor."

"We've been through all that, Faith. No, he won't accept it at first. But he will," he said, practically sang. I followed him out to the front porch.

I was even more nervous. However, he was full of energy and talked practically nonstop, describing school to explain why he wasn't going to miss it.

"I've made no friends, and I'm so ahead in every class that I just sit there doodling most of the time. The teachers who try to catch and embarrass me with a shotgun question usually end up with egg on their faces because I give them the answers so quickly that their heads spin. I'm just wasting time there.

"I found this driving school that specializes in teaching the driving of trucks. With that on my résumé, I could probably get a job easily. You know what's an interesting specialty? Driving hazardous materials. I can get a job like that when I turn eighteen in a few months. I bet Big John would even be proud of me."

"You say that like it matters to you."

He thought a moment.

"Twist him up a bit, don't you think? He'll be impressed and proud, but probably, at the same time, he'll be angry about us bringing Little Paula back. He'll just go out of his mind shut up here. That trucking business gave him a purpose for living. He's bound to go into a deeper and deeper depression, even with therapy. Besides, knowing him, I'm sure he'll avoid therapy. You heard Nick. He didn't sound hopeful he'd even call the doctor. If there's any problem, either you or I will have to do it."

"Is that good?"

"Sure," he said. "Good for us and good for Little Paula the more dependent on us he is. I doubt he'll say thank you very much, but we'll hear it."

"Do you really hate him now, Trevor?" I asked. "I know we have every reason to be angry at him, but . . ."

"How do you think Mama would feel about him now?"

"She did say that hate can eat away at your soul."

He looked at me, his eyes full of pain. "I don't think of it as hate. I think I'm just past caring about him. Maybe it's the same thing. For now, I smother it in what looks like kindness. Maybe it will change a while after Little Paula's back. That's the best we can hope for, Faith."

He looked out at the highway and then at his watch.

"They should be here soon, unless they were forced to stop on the way. I imagine getting Daddy in and out of a bathroom in a restaurant or a gas station isn't easy. He has no idea what he's coming home to," he said in almost a whisper.

My legs felt as if I had stepped in buckets of ice.

"I'd better get started on dinner preparations," I said. What I really wanted to do was flee. Trevor's glee was really beginning to annoy me.

"Need help?"

"No. The busier I am, the better."

"Oh, you'll be busy," Trevor said. "A little baby and a big baby to care for. Call me if you need me," he shouted.

As I began to work in the kitchen, I wondered if Trevor and I had ever loved Big John the way children should love their father. When we were first brought to live with Mama and him, we were both hungry for parental attention and also very curious about it. Neither of us really knew what to expect. Years from now, someone would surely wonder how we were so taken with and absorbed by the concept of family as to do and justify the things we had done and the things we were about to do.

Big John's acceptance of us either to please Mama or to fill his own need for progeny had been as welcomed as Mama's adoration of us. We had become someone, children with parents. Whether that fulfilled the definition of love for Big John or not, we did, at least in the early years, cherish the idea of our having a father. The words "Mama" and "Daddy" came late for us, but they came.

When Mama began to drift away from Big John or he from her, we began to drift away from him as well. After Mama's death, I was beginning to feel as if I had returned to the shadow of myself I had been in the foster home. To me, it seemed like we had been untethered and were drifting. Little Paula, as forced on us as she was, caused me to feel like I existed again. I was someone's mother.

Big John and Gabby, selfish and uninterested in the meaning Little Paula brought to my life, had taken that away from me and had taken away Trevor's joy in satisfying Mama. I didn't have to ask Trevor if he hated Big John. It was, as he was implying, almost irrelevant. This couldn't be a house with love in it as long as Little Paula was gone from it. Trevor was right about that. Every smile we gave, every seemingly kind word we said, any sympathy we showed, was all part of the deception that would enable us to restore what we had lost, a sense of being someone, a part of a family.

A little less than an hour later, Trevor shouted from the doorway to tell me he saw Nick's car approaching.

"Can't wait to see his expression when he sees the banner. C'mon," Trevor said.

He started down the steps to go around the house. I went to the rear door and saw them drive in, Nick pulling as close to the ramp as he could. Trevor stood on the side, and we watched Nick take out the wheelchair, unfold it, and help Daddy into it.

"Wow. Look at that banner. Nice work, you guys," Nick said.

Big John glanced at the banner but didn't say anything.

"Welcome home, Daddy!" I shouted when Nick wheeled him up the ramp and into the house.

Critter started barking and pressing himself toward Daddy, who looked dazed and confused. When the dog whined, Daddy lowered his hand for Critter to lick his fingers. Trevor came in behind them, carrying the bag of medicines issued at the hospital.

"We'll take care of the bathroom needs and then check on the new den, huh, John?"

"Yeah, sure," he said.

Nick wheeled him to the bathroom.

"Stop! I can handle it from here," Daddy told him sharply. When he spoke like that, I thought of a door slamming.

Nick let go of the handles of the wheelchair as if he was getting an electric shock. Daddy wheeled in and closed the door. Neither Trevor, I, nor Nick moved for a moment. Only Critter was whining and scratching at the bathroom door. Nick scooped him up.

"Put those things by the bed, Trevor," he said, referring to the medical materials he was holding.

Trevor moved quickly to the den. I turned to the stove.

"Nothing from you-know-who, huh? No calls?"

I shook my head.

"She won't last long out there on her own," he said. "She didn't have much money."

Trevor looked at me. Nick didn't know about the money? What did he know about the sale of Little Paula? Did he even know there was money involved? Would that have bothered him? Trevor shook his head at me before I could say anything. He quickly moved to show Nick the mobile phones.

"Great idea," Nick said. "You guys are going to be just fine."

Daddy came out of the bathroom. He saw his space at the kitchenette table.

"I think we're eating in the dining room, right, Faith?" Nick said, lowering Critter to the floor.

"Oh, yes. The table's been set." *All day, actually*, I almost added.

"Let's take a look, eh, John?"

Daddy wheeled himself ahead, Critter right alongside him. I finished work on the salad.

"Place looks pretty good, eh, John?" we heard Nick say.

"Good as it can," Daddy admitted. "Still oughta sell."

"Well, let's see how it goes," Nick said. "Oh, before we settle in for dinner, I have something to show you."

He wheeled Daddy back and opened the basement door.

"What the hell is that?"

"Chair lift, John. Trevor's idea, actually. Get you down to some pool and back up easily. There's a chair down there, as you can see."

Daddy looked at Trevor, who stood there smiling. Was he going to see it right away, I wondered, Trevor's deception?

Daddy nodded at him. "Well, they ain't stupid kids," he said. "Spoiled but not stupid."

Nick laughed. "I'm getting hungry now," he said. "I did recommend a steak."

Daddy grunted his agreement, and they returned to the dining room.

"I'm hungry, too," Trevor told me.

I brought in the salad and began to serve it. Critter sprawled beside Daddy's wheelchair.

"Dogs don't forget," Nick said. "Oh. I nearly forgot. No one move." He leaped up and hurried out through the kitchen.

"How was the ride, Daddy?" Trevor asked.

"Don't remember. Slept most of the way."

"Yeah, it's kind of boring, although there is some nice scenery. I've been fixing the pathway in the woods, widening it for you."

"Why the hell would I go into the woods?"

Trevor shrugged. "Change of scenery?"

Daddy grunted. "You keeping up the car?"

"Oh, yeah. Changed the oil last week and check the tires all the time. You're going to get a car, too, aren't you? That special kind of car. I did some research on it for you. The converted vehicle has a door that opens, and you swing out on your chair and just wheel off. Did they tell you about that? I think Nick was looking into it for you, right?"

Every syllable made Daddy wince.

"Don't worry about it."

"I'm not worrying. I'm excited for you, Daddy."

Daddy closed his eyes and turned away. Trevor's smile rippled across his face.

Nick returned with a bottle of wine.

"This is practically the only one you like, John," he said, show-ing it to him.

"Yeah."

"Goes great with steak. I'll get it open. Faith, can you get us some wineglasses?"

"I'll get them," Trevor said. He leaped up and went to the kitchen.

Nick opened the bottle and poured us all a glass, half as much for Trevor and me.

"A toast to better days," Nick said, raising his glass.

"Better days," Daddy muttered. "What kind of better days are in store for me?"

No one spoke.

He looked at us all and then said, "Forget it," and drank his wine.

Nick did most of the talking at dinner. He seemed terrified of a quiet moment. When he started to talk about looking into a con-verted vehicle for Daddy, Trevor sat with a smile on his face that re-minded me of a splashed egg yolk. Daddy didn't change the subject, probably because Nick went on and on about it, about places they could go (without mentioning provisions for the handicapped) and even the possibility of Daddy riding along with him on a haul. That was practically the only thing that made him perk up.

I had kept the cake hidden until it was time to bring it out. When Daddy saw it, his lips seemed to tremble, but like someone snap-grabbing a glass that almost fell to the floor and shattered, he turned his face back into the hard, chiseled non-expression that was his habit.

He did admit the cake was good.

Soon we could see he was getting very tired. I started to clear the table. Trevor sat there for a moment staring at him, until Daddy felt it and turned sharply to him.

"What's on your mind, boy?"

"Nothing. I'd better help Faith," he said, rising. "I can help you with anything you need, Daddy," he said, pausing. "School's almost over, too. I'll be here. Oh, I almost forgot," he said, then ran into the kitchen and returned with the mobile phones. "I got this set up for you."

Daddy looked at the phone. "What happened to mine?"

"Oh, I don't know. Nick?"

"Somewhere in the wreck, John. Trevor there came up with a good idea, though."

Trevor continued to explain it.

"We'll keep the other right close to us, especially when we go upstairs," Trevor said.

Daddy closed his eyes and breathed out.

"Yeah," he said.

He let Nick wheel him into the den. They closed the door.

Trevor stepped up beside me at the sink.

"Perfect homecoming," he said.

I looked at him to see if he was serious.

He was.

We worked in silence, washing and drying everything and putting it all away. Trevor cleared the table, and then Nick stepped out of the den and closed the door softly behind him.

"He's comfortably in bed," he said. "You guys did great. He's not in the mood to give anyone any compliments, but he appreciates everything, I'm sure. I'll check in with you tomorrow, but I think it's possible I got a new long haul. You have my mobile. He has his doctor's numbers and the number of a physical therapist and the other therapist. I was going to give it all to you, but he wants to hold on to all that for now. Thanks to Trevor, he's got a phone to use.

"However," he added, looking back at the den door, "his doctor at the hospital gave me this number for a doctor in the area who can handle any emergencies, whatever."

He handed Trevor the slip of paper.

"And," he said, looking at me, "you call me as soon as you hear from my sister."

"Okay, Nick. Thank you," I said.

"Yeah, thank you," Trevor said.

"It'll be a while yet; he's still got a lot of recovering to do, but once he's capable of it, I'll work on that car for him with all the controls on the steering wheel. Once he's able to get out and about, he'll be easier to live with. Great dinner, Faith."

"Thank you."

"All right. I'm going," he said.

We followed him out. At his car, he paused to look back at us standing together.

"I'm glad he has you two," he said, and got into his car. We watched him turn and drive away.

"Soon he'll have us three," Trevor said, smiling.

He went in, but I remained standing there, my arms folded across my chest, looking at the way the moonlight wove its way through the dark woods. Shadows seemed to ebb and flow as the moon made its way west. For a few moments, I thought one of them had taken the form of a person. It seemed to be torn apart as the silver light threaded through it.

Or was that Lance? I wondered, perhaps hoped. I listened. Unlike on most nights, the woods were deadly quiet. Nothing fluttered; nothing moved. It was as if the world had just gasped and held its breath.

"Hey," Trevor called. "Come on in. We have things to talk about and things to do."

"All right," I said. "Good night," I whispered to the shadows, turned, and reentered the house.

Trevor waited for me in the living room. He had a pen and a pad.

"What are we doing?"

"Let's put together the list of what we need for Little Paula's homecoming," he said. "I think we can bring her home sooner than I thought."

"Sooner? When?"

"If Nick gets a job tomorrow, like he believes he will . . . tomorrow night," Trevor said, smiling.

I wanted to be happy.

But I was trembling with a fear so deep that I had to sit.

"C'mon, Mama," Trevor said. "Dictate. We want everything new. We want it to be as if she never left."

FOURTEEN

Trevor thought it was no coincidence that Nick had to go on an important long haul the day after he had brought Daddy home.

"Remember," he said, "Mama told us, 'There's no such thing as a coincidence. Everything happens for a reason.'"

I didn't know if I ever believed that or believed it now. There was too much money involved for Nick to pass up any potentially lucrative continued business that he'd risk losing if he turned it down. But Trevor was so adamant about it being destiny that I couldn't disagree without upsetting him. Priests and rabbis didn't respect the words in the Bible more than Trevor respected Mama's.

Despite how good it was for him, Nick was feeling bad about

taking the job. He told Trevor he might find someone at the last minute to substitute for him, someone who wouldn't take advantage and capture his future opportunities and those that would have gone to Daddy, too.

"Oh, there's no reason to refuse to do it," Trevor assured him on the phone. "Daddy would want you to get the work, especially what would have been his. He's had a good night's sleep and already had his breakfast. I'm going to wheel him about outside so he can get some air. I wanted him to see the cleaned-up garage, too, and Faith is making one of his favorite dinners tonight, Cornish hens. We bought them a week ago anticipating when he'd come home," he added, looking at me. "So we're fine."

None of it was true.

"We'll call you on your mobile if anything changes or we need anything. You've done so much for us. Daddy wants you to do more for yourself, too. Have a safe trip. Thanks."

He hung up before Nick could say much more. Daddy was really just stirring in the den-turned-bedroom.

"Did he believe all that?"

"Of course. Even I believed it," Trevor said, smiling. "I've got to spend the day shopping for Little Paula's new things, the formula you want, and a cradle for downstairs. I'll pick up the groceries we need, too. As far as Daddy knows, I'm off to school. If he asks why I didn't take the day off, which I doubt he'll do, tell him we're having finals soon, so I had to go.

"But . . . if anyone from the school calls, tell them about Daddy and how I had to stay to help, making sure he doesn't overhear you, of course. Try to answer the phone in the living room rather than in the kitchen, just to be certain."

All these directions and warnings made me nervous.

He took my hand. "Don't be frightened. You're in charge. Don't let him order you around. Okay. Let's get started. We have a lot to do today." He knocked on Daddy's den door and then pressed his face close to it.

"Morning, Dad. I'm off to school. Faith's here to help you and get your breakfast going," he said. "I'll call her later to see if you need anything."

He looked at me. We didn't hear anything for a moment, then a gruff "Okay."

"See you later, dear," Trevor joked, kissed me on the cheek, and went out.

Critter whined when he closed the door on him. I still hadn't moved.

Daddy opened the den door, backed up in his wheelchair, and then started out. He glanced at me but headed for the bathroom without saying anything. I warmed the coffee and waited.

"You want some scrambled eggs?" I asked as soon as he opened the door. "We have some nice bagels, too."

"Okay," he said, and wheeled himself to the table. I poured his coffee quickly.

"Nick called to tell us that he had to leave to go on this—"

"I know. He called me on that phone Trevor bought. Where'd he get the money for that?"

I paused. A challenge for me to handle alone right away. I couldn't recall a time I had lied to him without Mama telling me not so much to do that as to hold back information. "He doesn't need to know," she would say.

"He always saved a little from whatever Mama and you gave him," I said. "Where could either of us go to spend any money ourselves?"

Daddy stared hard at me. I tried to keep my face from becoming a window on the truth, by staring back at him and holding my lips firm.

"I want you to do something for me this morning," he said. "I want you to go up to my room and look in the dresser drawers for a big envelope. There'll be only one. Just bring it down."

Could he hear my heart thumping? Trevor and I had discussed just how to answer this demand. We had assumed he would make it one day, although not so soon.

"Was it one of those manila envelopes, about nine by twelve inches, that Mama used to file our tests?"

He leaned back in his wheelchair and put the coffee cup down. "Yes. Why?"

"When Gabby left, I saw she had one sticking up out of her large purse."

His face blanched and then reddened with rage.

I continued as if I hadn't noticed anything. "I thought it was a little strange, because who just carries one tucked up under—"

"Wait on my breakfast. Go up and look for that envelope now," he ordered. "Go on!"

"Okay."

I turned and hurried to the stairs. I was as loud and as fast as I could be on the stairs. I thought about calling Trevor but decided I could do this myself. In Daddy's bedroom, I opened and slammed closed one drawer after another, hoping he would hear it. Then I waited a good thirty seconds and hurried back down to the kitchen.

"There's no envelope there," I said. "I took everything out of the drawers."

His lips trembled as his anger burned behind his eyes.

"What did she tell you? Where did she go?"

"She didn't say. She just said goodbye and wished me good luck."

"You tell me if she ever calls you, hear?"

"Yes, Daddy. Nick asked me to tell him, too."

He stared ahead, no longer looking at me.

"I'll make your eggs," I said, and went to do it.

"You're goin' to school," he said when I served him the eggs. "I don't need you babysittin' me."

"There are only a few days left. Trevor says finals are starting soon."

"Yeah, well, you plan on it for the next year."

I kept myself busy while he ate. When he was finished, I told him Trevor had said to tell him he'd wheel him about outside when he came home. He wanted to show him the work he had done in the garage.

Big John didn't say anything. The news about the envelope and getting himself up and out of bed appeared to have tired him. After all, he was only a day out of the hospital. He still looked pale and, despite his size and muscles, seemed weak. He squirmed a little in his chair, looking uncomfortable whenever he reached for something.

"Are you still in pain?" I asked.

"There are some deep aches."

"You have medicine for that, right?"

"I'm not goin' to become dependent on them damn pills," he said. He calmed a bit and added, "I'll take them when I have to."

"Are you going to have a therapist come?" I asked.

"We'll see," he said. "I'm goin' to make a few business calls."

"Do you need any help?"

"No," he said sharply.

He turned himself around and wheeled back into the den, closing the door behind him. Anger ate away at you as it was, I thought, but for him right now . . . it could make him very sick. What if he had a heart attack and died without my knowing anything and being unable to help? I thought, staring at the closed den door.

What would we do?

I tried to avoid thinking about it by reading and studying some of what Mama had left us to do before she died. I stayed as involved in it as I could until it was time to make Daddy some lunch. When I knocked on his door and he didn't respond, I started to panic. I knocked harder.

"I hear you!" he cried.

"Lunch, Daddy," I said.

That got him out of his den again. However, he was pouting and feeling sorry for himself most of the day and did little more than eat and sleep. I kept my distance. At one point, I knew Nick had called him from the road. I couldn't hear the whole conversation, but I heard enough to know that he had asked Nick to find Gabby, raising his voice to add, "You got to do it!"

Not more than ten minutes later, Nick called to ask again if I had heard from her or knew anything about where she had gone. For some reason, I had more difficulty lying to him than I did to Daddy. We had learned that he was basically innocent of the monetary arrangements regarding Little Paula. I wondered, though, if his conclusion about it being the best thing for us all would still have been the same if he knew.

Trevor returned about the time he would have if he had attended school. No one had called to see why he wasn't there. He entered the house from the front first so he could go immediately upstairs with the things we needed for Little Paula. He then went out to fetch the groceries and came in the rear door. Daddy was back in bed, resting. I told Trevor about Daddy's asking me to find the envelope and his pressuring Nick to find Gabby. None of it apparently gave him the slightest bit of trepidation. He looked as excited and as confident as when he had left in the morning.

"She couldn't have helped us more if we had asked."

He went into the den and offered to wheel Daddy about. Surprisingly, Daddy accepted and even let Trevor help him out of bed and into the wheelchair. While I started on dinner, he wheeled Daddy out, down the ramp, and to the garage. I even heard him start a conversation about his becoming a truck driver. When they returned, Daddy did look invigorated, and Trevor looked even more confident.

We set the kitchenette table for dinner. Trevor helped me with the preparations. When we began to eat, Trevor revealed Mr. Longstreet's death and the upcoming funeral.

"Well, he was helpful when it came to your mother," Daddy admitted. "She's the one who had me avoid any contact with him because she was so angry about that grandson and Faith. She had me do a lot of things I didn't want to do. She was as stubborn as a rusted nut and bolt when she made her mind up about somethin'," he added bitterly.

Trevor looked at me, his eyes sharp with anger at the negative tone toward Mama, and then as quickly as his rage had formed, it evaporated, and he smiled.

"I was thinking I should help Faith get her driver's license now, Daddy. Until you get your special vehicle, it'll be helpful if there are two drivers, don't you think? I can teach her the basics just driving around our yard."

"Yeah, sure," he said. "I was drivin' at twelve. Not legally, of course."

"Wow," Trevor said. "You never told us."

"Yeah, well. There's lots I never told nobody." His voice and posture softened. "This is very good," he added after another forkful of the Cornish hen. He thought while he chewed and then surprised us by saying, "I might contact that therapist this week."

"Good idea, Daddy," Trevor said. "We want you up and about as soon as possible."

"Up and about," he muttered.

For dessert, we had the rest of the cake I had made, and then, while I cleaned up, Trevor wheeled him into the living room to watch television. I joined them after, and we all watched one of Daddy's favorite detective programs until Daddy obviously grew very tired, fighting to keep his eyes open. Trevor suggested we might all go to bed.

"I've got finals coming up. I need to study a little before I go to sleep."

Daddy didn't resist.

After Big John was snugly in his bed, Trevor closed the door softly and looked at me with a look of determination that reminded me of Mama. My heart began to race.

"Go put on the dark clothes," he said. "Little Paula's coming home tonight."

Although I was too frightened to speak, I hurried to do what he said. I organized some of the things Trevor had bought for her so they would all be ready for her return, packed a small bag with a pacifier and some powders and creams, and then went down to find him sitting quietly in the living room. He had put out the lights in the kitchen. He nodded toward the front door, and, moving quickly and quietly, we slipped out of the house. I had brought along the new blanket for her and a bottle of formula, just in case. Neither of us spoke. We got into Mama's car, and he started the engine and drove out very slowly.

"What if he wakes up and calls for us?" I asked.

Trevor showed me the mobile phone.

"I'll tell him I'm in the bathroom and I will be down in a while, but I doubt he'll wake. He was exhausted and fell asleep almost before I left the room."

Although we had driven this way at night before, it felt different tonight. Lights in the windows of houses we passed looked brighter, and the oncoming headlights of cars were like flames illuminating the inside of our car. It wasn't until then that I realized Trevor was wearing a tight pair of clear plastic gloves.

"Why are you wearing those gloves?"

He lifted his right hand off the steering wheel and turned it as if he had just realized he was wearing them.

"Avoiding fingerprints on the screen window I'm going to remove and the window I'll push up. They'll think it was a professional kidnapper."

He put his left hand in his pocket and produced a folded slip of paper.

"What is it?"

"Don't worry. I made it with the computer and kept my fingerprints off it."

I took it and opened it to read: *We'll call in twenty-four hours and tell you how much.*

"Pretty good, huh? Who'd think two kids like us would do this, and successfully, too? I'm sure Daddy and Gabby made it sound like we were in perfect agreement with the sale of Little Paula. All that responsibility would be lifted from our lives, and we could be . . . teenagers. We'll be the last of the suspects that come to mind. It'll keep them off us for a while. Maybe. Maybe not, but why not prepare?"

"You amaze me," I said.

He smiled, but in the light of the next oncoming vehicle, his smile looked so devious. His light blue eyes were orbs of blue sapphire, two gems that captured the radiance and then sent it sizzling out.

"I amaze myself," he said, looking forward.

We glided onto the road to the Couches' house, Trevor putting out our headlights even before we stopped. Because there were no streetlights, the lights blazed around the property and in the house. We parked where we had previously. Trevor turned off the engine, but he didn't move. We could see that the side of the house where Little Paula's nursery was located was brighter than it had been the last time I was here with him.

"Why is it so lit up?"

"She's tending to her. You don't expect you'll be sleeping through the night for a while."

"Maybe the nurse is up with her because she still has colic," I said in a raspy whisper.

"We'll wait."

"Maybe it's something more serious—"

"Stop driving yourself crazy, Faith. Just relax."

Suddenly, car lights went on in front of the house. We watched a vehicle start down the driveway. All I could think was that if they turned right, they'd see us parked here.

"Easy," Trevor said.

The car turned left. I hadn't realized I had been holding my breath the whole time. My lungs ached.

And then the lights went off on Little Paula's side of the house, the windows only vaguely lit from the hallway.

"If we get caught, we'll never see her again," I whispered, realizing.

"We're not getting caught."

"But . . ."

"But if we did, we'd make such a stink about them buying her, they'd just let us go."

"They'd tell Daddy and . . ."

He held his hand up.

"Wait," Trevor said. "Don't do this, Faith. Don't think of all the negative possibilities. Take deep breaths."

The couple of minutes that passed seemed like hours, but then he opened his door slowly and nodded to me. We moved quickly to the torn opening in the fence.

"Just like before," Trevor said. "Do everything the way we rehearsed it."

He went through first and waited. I was so afraid my legs would just crumple, but I followed, and we made our way slowly across the wide lawn, pausing as we had done the last time and then rushing to Little Paula's window. It was slightly open, just as Trevor had said it would be. I waited while he peered in.

"Perfect," he said.

I stood and watched as he gently and very slowly began to take off the screen, using the screwdriver he had brought. Suddenly, it snapped out of the grooves. I thought the sound was as loud as a gunshot. He froze with the screen in his hands. Neither of us moved or breathed. A brighter light went on in the hallway outside Little Paula's room.

"Oh," I whispered. "Maybe they heard."

He quickly pressed the screen against the window, keeping the fingers of his left hand on it, and leaned against the wall, gesturing

for me to lower myself. We waited. Any moment, I expected someone to come running out of the house and toward us. No one did,
and the brighter hall light went off. Trevor still waited and then,
even more quietly than before, took the screen off the window and
carefully placed it on the ground. I saw him take a deep breath before starting on the window itself, carefully pushing it farther and
farther open, until it was about as far as it would go. He gestured
for me to stand and then boosted himself a little on the windowsill
and leaned in.

With surgical expertise that amazed me, he balanced himself
and reached into the crib. Little Paula didn't make a sound. It
seemed to take a half hour for him to get a secure grasp of her and,
with all his upper-body strength, hold her high enough for him to
back up and turn. Little Paula whimpered, but it was more like a
sound she might make during a dream. I took her gently into the
blanket and, for a moment, just stared at her.

"Go," Trevor whispered. "Go."

I turned and, pressing her snugly against my breasts, started to
walk as gracefully, but as quickly, as I could back across the lawn.
My heart was beating so fast and hard that I thought I might faint.
Behind me, Trevor lowered the window again and, as quickly as
he could, put the screen back in enough to stay. I imagined he had
tossed in the note he had written and left the doll in the crib. I
walked more quickly. Little Paula moaned. I pressed my lips to her
cheek and sped up even more, but slowed when I thought I was
jolting her awake.

"Go," Trevor said, coming up behind me. "Don't worry about
her crying now. We're too far from the house."

When we reached the opening in the fence, Little Paula finally
woke. She cried at being jerked out of her comfortable sleep. I

handed her to Trevor, who stood on the other side of the opening, and stepped through. She was crying more now.

"She's still colicky, Trevor," I said.

"We'll take care of her. We'll take care of her better than they did."

He opened the rear door, and I got in with her, reaching for the small bag I had brought in which there was a pacifier. She was kicking, making tight fists, and crying. Trevor hurried around, started the engine, and drove a dozen or so yards before turning on the headlights. Minutes later, we were on our way home.

She cried more and louder. I rocked her and spoke to her softly, kissing her warm, soft cheeks, and then brought her to my breast. I had read about starting breastfeeding after a gap. It was called relactation, and one of the tests for its success was whether your baby would take to it again after weeks on a bottle.

It was as if she had never stopped.

"Thank you, Gabby," I whispered. She had gotten me what I had needed to keep my breast milk from drying up. How ironic.

"She's feeding," I said.

Trevor was still too excited to speak. He drove carefully. Little Paula stopped feeding and fell asleep again.

"Did you hear me? I breastfed her. She took right to it."

"Sure. She knows she's going home," Trevor said.

I sat back with her in my arms, wondering if this was real.

When we arrived, we entered through the front door as quietly as we could and took her upstairs.

"Let's keep her in bed with us tonight," I said. "She'll surely wake before morning."

"Yes. For sure."

From the look on his face, despite all his confidence and planning, I was sure he was just as amazed at what we had done as I was.

Little Paula stirred and cried two hours later. I rocked her, rubbing her stomach until she calmed and fed again. Trevor opened his eyes and watched, smiling proudly. Then we all fell asleep and woke just after the sunlight broke through the curtains.

"I have to change her diaper," I said.

"I'll wait. We'll all go down together and give him the news."

"Maybe he'll call the Couches to tell them. He did make the deal."

"I don't think so," Trevor said.

"Why are you so confident?"

He opened a dresser drawer and held up the manila envelope.

"No need to hide it now."

We both washed and dressed.

And then, with Little Paula in my arms, where she should be when Daddy laid his eyes on her again, we started downstairs.

FIFTEEN

Daddy was already in the kitchen, making his own coffee, when we entered. He should thank Trevor, I thought, for making sure everything was within his reach. For a long moment, we all just stared at one another. He wheeled himself back and turned fully toward us, his face twisted in amazement and shock. Critter came over and waited, as if we were going to introduce him to Little Paula.

"What's that baby doin' here?" Daddy asked.

"This is where she lives, Daddy," Trevor said. "This is Little Paula."

He continued to stare, as if he had to convince himself that what he was seeing was true, his mouth slightly open.

"I was afraid you wouldn't recognize her," Trevor continued. "You saw so little of her."

"I know who she is. How did you get that baby back?" he asked, wheeling himself toward us. "What did you do?"

"Well, we never thought she left, Daddy," Trevor said. "We don't think of her as gone and now back."

"Never thought she left? What is this? Are you two crazy?"

"I'm not." Trevor turned to me. "Are you, Faith?"

Little Paula was amazingly quiet, just sucking on her pacifier, her colic subdued, even though Daddy's voice was echoing through the house and, as Mama would say, "could wake the sleeping dead."

Critter began to whine, as if he sensed it was a very tense moment.

"Don't be a wiseass with me, Trevor. I asked you a question. I want an answer, and now!"

"You might as well know everything, then, Daddy. First, I'm not going to bother with school anymore. I'm putting my finals on hold. You and Faith need me here to help, and I don't see college in my future. Second, neither Faith nor I was asked if we wanted to give up Little Paula. Mama wanted a granddaughter living in this house, her family house. This is where she was born, and this is where she belongs."

"I don't care if you don't go to school or college. But what did you two do? How did you get that baby back?"

"It doesn't matter how, Daddy. She's back," Trevor said.

Daddy pushed himself up in the wheelchair. His rage practically vibrated through his body. For a moment, he forgot his injury and tried to stand. The frustration made him angrier. He uttered an incoherent guttural sound and wheeled closer to the table so he could slam his fist on it. I thought it would shatter.

Critter whelped and cowered near the wall.

"You'll both be in big trouble for this."

"I don't think so, Daddy," Trevor said, still speaking in what, to Daddy, was obviously an annoyingly calm manner. "What we did was make sure *you* didn't get into any trouble."

"What? Me?"

"You can't buy and sell children these days. Actually, I think that stopped after the Civil War. Right, Faith?"

I looked at him and then at Daddy.

"Giving up a baby for a legal adoption is one thing. Putting a price on her head like some piece of furniture or something is another," Trevor added.

Daddy wheeled himself back a few inches. I could see in his eyes that our defiance and especially Trevor's coolness and poise heightened his frustration. Nevertheless, his rage was so raw that it nearly took my breath away. I surely would have endless nightmares of him rising out of that chair someday to beat us within an inch of our lives. The reality of his defeat settled over the rage. He nodded, his clenched fists looking like small sledgehammers.

"Did Gabby have somethin' to do with this? Is that why she ran off?"

"Not really. Well . . . indirectly, I guess. She confessed a lot of it to Faith, and we sort of took it from there. But that's all over with," Trevor said. "Best we think it all never happened."

"Never happened? You idiot. Couch will have the police at this door very soon. You'll be arrested for kidnappin'."

"Our own baby? I doubt it, Daddy. DNA tests will prove we're telling the truth, and besides, Mr. Couch will have a very hard time explaining this," he said, and brought his hand out from behind him, the envelope in his right hand.

Daddy's eyes looked like they would pop.

We're giving him a heart attack, I thought. *What good would that do us?*

He turned to me. "You told me she took that! You made a big thing of lookin' for it."

"I'm sorry, Daddy."

"Don't blame Faith. We weren't ready to tell you the truth, Daddy," Trevor said. "We wanted you to begin your recovery first. It wasn't easy for us to be patient, especially after we learned about this," he said, waving the envelope. "Mama's granddaughter sold? What could be more horrible?"

"Is the money . . ."

"Not all of it. She took some. About ten thousand?" Trevor asked me.

I nodded.

"The rest we'll keep safely for Little Paula. I'm sure she'll go to college someday, right, Faith? Oh. Gabby did tell us about Mama's will and all. We found those papers, too. We'll keep them safe. I'll visit her lawyer on my eighteenth birthday. Not much longer to wait," he said, smiling.

The air seemed to go out of Daddy's body. He sank deeper into his wheelchair, and his hands unclenched. He opened and closed his fists and sat forward again.

"So no one saw you swipe her, is that it?"

"We didn't swipe her. I told you. We brought her home."

"But no one saw you do that?"

Trevor just stared at him.

"This is not goin' to be as simple as you think, Trevor. Mark my words."

Trevor smiled as if Daddy was a child. I could see how much it irritated him, painfully swallowing all this information.

"So if there aren't any more questions, I'm going to go up and get the extra cradle I bought for Little Paula," Trevor said. "Faith will be able to keep her eye on her while she does things for you. This way, you can see her grow and be a part of everything. She's your granddaughter, too, you know. You should be happy, Daddy. Someday you will be, I'm sure."

Daddy nodded slowly, his eyes so focused on Trevor that I thought they'd drill holes in him.

"Don't come too close to me, Trevor. If I get my hands on you, I'll squeeze the life out of you."

"Well, we're not going to stay away from you, Daddy. I'll always try to help you. So will Faith. Right, Faith?"

I nodded. The moment of silence stung like a hornet flying next to our ears.

"What would you like for breakfast, Daddy?" I asked in a voice so soft that even I had trouble hearing it.

He looked at us with a shadow of frustration floating over him, turned his chair around, and wheeled himself back into the den, slamming the door.

"I guess he's not hungry. I am. I'll get that new cradle so you can prepare some breakfast," Trevor said. "Hey. I think it's a good day for some blueberry pancakes. Right? You like that. We'll enjoy breakfast."

"Once I pick my stomach up from the floor," I said.

He laughed. "It all went *well*," he said. "You can just feel how proud Mama is of us, can't you, Faith?" he asked, and went to get the cradle. Critter followed him to the bottom of the stairs. Embracing Little Paula in my right arm, I got the pancake mix out of the pantry and a mixing bowl out of the cabinet. Trevor came down, took Little Paula, and gently put her in the cradle, then placed it at the center of the kitchenette. He stepped back, as if he had accomplished something great.

Little Paula opened her eyes and watched me, glued to every move I made.

Trevor laughed. "See? I told you. She's comfortable. It's like she never left."

"Yes," I said. It *was* like that, I thought, or was I just hoping?

I started on preparing the pancakes, as if it was a Sunday morning with Mama. All of us would be around the table, laughing and talking, just the way we were in our early days, Trevor and I wearing the new Sunday clothes she had bought us.

"Little Paula's part of everything we do now," Trevor said. "We'll take her everywhere we go. I'll get you one of those baby carriers mothers wear in front."

"You sound like you've been doing more research than I have."

"Probably have. You're happy about it, right?"

"Yes, of course," I said. "Why wouldn't I be?"

Trevor put his hand on Little Paula's cradle and looked down at her with what I thought was surely as much pride as any father.

"Of course," he said in a voice barely more than a whisper. "Why wouldn't you be? It's like it's all really started. Just the way Mama said it would be. We really feel like a family now, don't we? Like we just became one?"

I nodded. It was true. This was truly the first day of whatever our lives would be.

Suddenly, we heard Daddy screaming. He had called Nick on the road and was describing everything we had done. We could hear him yelling at the top of his voice behind the den door, talking about the police and how all hell was going to break loose.

"I *am* trying to keep calm!" he shouted. "But how the hell *can* I keep calm?"

Trevor stepped up beside me.

"I'll take Nick's call when it comes," he said.

I held back on breakfast, expecting that phone call moments after Daddy's voice grew silent. We waited, not a sound coming from the den.

Then the phone rang. Trevor, as nonchalant as could be, said, "Hello." He listened, nodding and smiling at me. "Can't do that, Nick," he said, finally having an opportunity to speak. "I don't think you know that your sister and our father *sold* Little Paula. They didn't just find the perfect family for her. Gabby met with Mrs. Couch and gave her their demands. They received fifty thousand, ten thousand of which your sister took when she left. You know that's a crime, don't you, selling children, even to rich and important people?"

He stopped talking and shrugged, facing me. "He's not speaking. Stunned," he whispered. "Yes, Nick," he said, back into the phone. "No, we're not worried, and after a while, Daddy will get used to having a granddaughter. We'll be a family again."

He listened, pretending his ear was being burned.

"Sure, Nick. Call us whenever you want. Have a good trip," he said, and hung up, before Nick had finished, I thought. "At the end, he was at a loss for words and just cursed Gabby and started on a roll about her ingratitude, claiming she should have called him as soon as she realized our intention."

"Well, I don't think she ever did."

"True. You did a good job on her. Anyway, his relationship with his sister is not our problem now. Let's eat."

When the pancakes were ready, I knocked on Daddy's door and told him.

"They're just how you like them, too, Daddy," I said. I heard nothing.

Trevor and I sat at the table. Little Paula was asleep and looked quite content, and Critter was sprawled out near Trevor's feet. We had just begun eating when Daddy opened his door.

"You two are makin' a big mistake," he said. "You're too young to tie your lives up like this. I was just tryin' to make your lives easier. The money was for all of us."

"We're fine living up to our parental responsibilities, Daddy," Trevor said. "You always said we were more mature than kids our age. Gabby told us that practically every day."

"That ain't the point," Daddy said. His voice was a little hoarse.

Trevor cut a piece of pancake. "Hey, these are good. Almost as good as Mama's."

Daddy stared at us a moment and then looked at Little Paula. She had dozed off. I held my breath until he wheeled up to the table.

"How you feedin' her?"

"I'm back to breastfeeding her, Daddy."

"Yeah. Well, what if she gets sick? She was always cryin' before . . ."

"*Before* she was *sold*," Trevor said, smiling.

"She's just a little colicky still," I said. "But it will go away. She'll be fine."

"She's not getting any sicker," Trevor said. "If she does, we'll take her to a doctor. Faith knows more about being a mother than most women. You can believe that. There are plenty of sixteen-year-old mothers in this country, but none as good as Faith."

Daddy grunted. "You'll see this was a big mistake," he said.

I immediately served him some pancakes and gave him the

syrup I knew he loved. He looked at Little Paula sucking on her pacifier and shook his head.

"Just so you two know, I'm not defendin' you when they come for you," he said. "I'll tell them the truth, that I never knew what you were doin'. Now that I think of it, don't tell me what you did. I don't wanna know how you got her back here," he said, and began to eat.

Trevor started to talk about things he wanted to do around the house, as if nothing had occurred. After a minute or so, Daddy stopped glaring at us with rage. But despite how calm things seemed to become at the moment, I continually anticipated the sound of a car coming into our driveway, a knock on the door, and the arrival of the police or Mr. Couch.

Exhausted from his anger as well as his recovery and his medicines, Daddy slept on and off most of the day. Critter instinctively kept his distance from him. Trevor left to buy more groceries, warning me not to answer the door and to call him immediately if anyone came around.

"Not that they will," he insisted.

The afternoon had cleared to where there was only a wisp of a cloud here and there. All the windows were open, and the sound of passing automobiles reminded me of the swish of rain being blown across our windows.

At about three o'clock, almost as if he was trying to escape, Daddy emerged from the den, wheeled himself to the rear door, pulled it open, and went out and down the ramp. Holding Little Paula, I went to watch him as he struggled to move about the gravel driveway, cursing. At one point, he just gave up and lowered his head. Critter cautiously followed and stood beside him. When Trevor pulled in, he almost didn't see him.

"Sorry if I frightened you, Daddy. Never expected you out here," he said. "I'll be right out to help you."

He brought in the groceries and, smiling widely, took out a local newspaper, unfolded it on the kitchen counter, and slapped the front page. There at the top was the headline, *Couch Family Baby Kidnapped for Ransom*. I lowered Little Paula to her cradle and read.

"They're not looking for us," Trevor said. "They talk about a professional job, just as I had hoped."

"Don't show it to Daddy yet. You'll drive him to heart failure."

Trevor laughed. "Okay. Hide it. I'll help him get some fresh air. Looks like he's had enough exercise pushing himself around on his own. He's slumping in that thing."

I stood in the doorway and watched. Daddy was sullen, but he didn't resist Trevor's assistance, moving through the gravel and around the house, Trevor talking a mile a minute as he wheeled Daddy along. For a moment, the sight brought me some amused relief. When he brought him back in, with Critter following, Daddy looked ready for another nap. I started on dinner. Trevor held Little Paula and sang her one of Mama's favorite lullabies. I thought we were getting through the first day well, but we both froze when we heard a car turn into our driveway.

"Don't panic," he told me. He put Little Paula back in her cradle and went to the window.

"What?" I asked. "Who is it?"

"It's Lance," he said. He looked at me for my reaction.

"Don't be nasty to him, Trevor. He just had his grandfather's funeral."

He nodded and went to the front door. Little Paula started to cry, so I picked her up out of the cradle and joined him in the foyer. Critter approached Lance as soon as Trevor opened the door.

"We're so sorry about your grandfather," I said quickly.

Lance stood there in his jacket and tie, the tie loosened, and then knelt down to pet Critter. Despite what must have been a trying, sad day so far, he looked as handsome as ever, his eyes bright when he looked up at us.

"Thanks," he said.

Trevor extended his hand. Lance stood, and they shook.

"That's your baby, I guess."

"Yes," I said.

"Born almost bald, huh? My mother says I was born completely bald and didn't really grow any hair for weeks."

He looked at Trevor for some friendly sign, but Trevor just stared blankly at him.

"My family's over there discussing the sale of my grandfather's house and property. He's only been buried a few hours, and they started arguing about the price and stuff. I had to get out for a while."

"How long are you staying?" Trevor asked.

"My mother and I are leaving tonight. I'll be heading for California tomorrow. Going back to college. I made the basketball team," he told Trevor. "Not starting five but right up there. You still shoot a few?"

"Not for a while," Trevor said.

"Did you go out for the school team?"

"No."

"Well, maybe next year. You guys are dealing with a lot this year."

"No, I'm not going back to school," Trevor said.

"Oh?"

"I'm going to get into the work world, driving a truck."

"Taking over from your dad, huh?"

"Something like that. It takes a lot of time and training to become that sort of driver, especially driving an eighteen-wheeler. In the meantime, there's lots to do around here."

"I bet."

Trevor looked at me, looked at the way I was staring at Lance, I'm sure.

"Well, I just wanted to see you guys before we left. With the property being sold, I don't imagine I'll get around this way for some time."

"If ever," Trevor added.

"Yeah," Lance said, smiling. "If ever. How's your dad now?"

"He's sleeping," I said. "It's a long recovery, but I think we'll be fine."

Trevor smiled at my optimism. "Yeah, we'll be fine."

"Good," Lance said.

"Sorry we couldn't come to your grandfather's funeral," Trevor said, surprising me. "We did like him very much."

"Appreciate it. I should have spent more time with him. He was fun, and I learned a lot from him. Stuff I should have learned a long time ago, but my father is sort of a city guy. The only chopping he's done was in a supermarket."

He laughed at his own joke.

"At least you got to spend quality time with your grandfather," I said.

"Yeah."

The silence was a little uncomfortable, but I was afraid to say much more.

"Okay. Good luck with everything," he said, and turned to leave.

Trevor looked at me, and then approached and took Little Paula out of my arms.

"Go say goodbye," he said.

I didn't say anything. I just walked out after Lance.

"Hey," I called.

He was surprised.

"Looks like we're always saying goodbye," he said, smiling. "Doesn't mean I'll forget you. Every time I say goodbye to someone, I'll think of you." He laughed.

"Thanks for stopping by," I said. "Once again, sorry about your grandfather."

He nodded, and looked out toward the woods for a moment.

"It's funny how, despite everything, I felt a need to come here to see you one last time. It wasn't just me getting out of the house. We knew each other for such a short time, and yet I wouldn't go ten extra feet for some girls I've known for years like I would for you. I know I messed up."

"I don't regret the time we had together," I said.

He looked at the house. "You'll be a good mother, I'm sure. Not that I know much about it."

"I'm learning more every day."

He nodded, opened his car door, and paused. I wanted to run to him so I could be held one more time in his arms and kiss him one more time, but then I thought it would make his leaving more painful, because something precious of me would be leaving with him, too, something I would never regain.

He gave me that beautiful smile, got into his car, and drove out slowly. I watched him disappear down the road.

Trevor was out on the porch with Little Paula when I turned to go in.

"Thank you," I told him, and took Little Paula into my arms.

"Don't tell Mama," he said.

I wanted to laugh. I thought he was making a sick, dark joke, which, for some reason, would have endeared him to me more. But he didn't smile.

He meant it.

I followed him in, holding my breath like someone going underwater.

Daddy was too tired to sit at the table for dinner, so I made him a ham and cheese sandwich and brought it to him with a beer. He still looked quite stunned and defeated, and despite all the reason I had not to, I felt deeply sorry for him.

Trevor, however, seemed even more energized at dinner.

"We'll start teaching you how to drive tomorrow," he said to me. "We can put Little Paula in her cradle in the rear seat and strap it in. I know how to do it. We're just going to practice around here. You won't need me to help you learn the driving rules and laws. And then I'll take you for your driving test. Maybe we'll buy another car when I turn eighteen and can get my hands on more money. Okay?"

"I may be too nervous right now to do anything right."

"Naw, you'll be fine," he insisted. "The faster we get into our new lives, the better we'll both be, Faith."

About an hour after dinner, Nick called, because Daddy hadn't picked up his phone.

"He's sleeping. I think he's really exhausted," I said.

"Can't imagine him not being," Nick said sharply. "What a time for you to pull this stunt."

"It wasn't a stunt. Little Paula is our child."

"Yeah, yeah. You call that doctor if he gets worse, Faith."

"I will."

"Okay," he said. "I hope you guys know what you're doing. Couch can make a lot of trouble for you."

"We'll be fine," I insisted.

Trevor, standing by, smiled. When I hung up, I took a very deep breath.

"He warned me about Mr. Couch again."

"I think we all need a good night's rest," Trevor said, ignoring me. He looked at Critter. "Maybe until Daddy's settled a little more, we should bring him up with us. I'll set up his bed."

"Okay."

I was grateful that Little Paula kept me busy most of the night. Whenever I did try to sleep, I kept listening for the sound of a siren or a knock on the door. Once, when I woke up, I realized Trevor wasn't beside us. I listened hard and thought I could hear him talking. It sounded like he was in the Forbidden Room. I didn't have to wonder why.

He didn't come back to bed, but finally, exhaustion took over until the morning light. He was there beside me. I didn't ask him where he had gone.

When we went down, we found Daddy already had risen, dressed, and made coffee, and was at the table eating a toasted muffin and jelly. He looked up sharply. I was surprised at his energetic appearance. It was as if he had thought things over during the night and decided not to argue about Little Paula anymore.

But that realization didn't make me feel any better.

If anything, it made me feel worse.

Maybe, I thought, he knew that there was no reason to spend any more of his energy on this.

Shortly, this stunt, as Nick had put it, would be over.

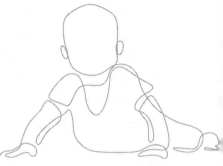

SIXTEEN

Not a waking hour passed during the days that followed that I
didn't hold my breath at the sound of an automobile or the
ring of the phone. Although I had no idea what she looked like,
I had nightmares about Mrs. Couch, a short woman in shadows
coming to our front door with a pair of policemen demanding the
return of Little Paula. I often paused anything I was doing and
peered out of a window, panning the driveway, even the woods,
looking for armed policemen approaching the house. I had never
paid as much attention to the sound of traffic in front of our
house. The beep of a horn would have me scurrying to look out
front.

Once Daddy caught me doing it and smiled coldly.

"They're comin'," he said. "You know it. You'd better convince Trevor and return that baby."

I quickly moved away from the window. Unlike Trevor, I didn't want to talk back to him, either sarcastically or coolly. It was easier to try to ignore him or quickly change the subject.

Between caring for Little Paula, cleaning the house, tending to Daddy, and learning how to drive, the days seemed to be ten or fifteen hours rather than twenty-four. Whenever Trevor went for things, he brought back a local paper. The Couch kidnapping story had moved off the front page. But a few days later, there was a headline pointing out that no one had called for any money, so the situation had grown even more serious. The last article I read mentioned that the Couch family had hired a private detective.

"It's all fine," Trevor insisted. "They'll just buy another baby."

He said that loud enough for Daddy to hear in the den.

Maybe Daddy had come to believe that himself finally. Often, when I was feeding and caring for Little Paula, I would see him watching. I wouldn't go so far as to say there was a smile on his face. Maybe it was more my wishful thinking, but he seemed to be impressed, not only with my mothering but with Little Paula's laugh and curiosity. One day, in an impulsive move when he was close by reading one of the mechanics magazines he had on subscription, I pretended to have to rush past him to turn down the stove and placed Little Paula in his lap.

"Just for a second," I said.

He winced, looked like he was going to toss her off him, and then carefully closed his big hands around her and her blanket to keep her from falling off.

"Thanks," I said.

"I don't know nothin' about babies," he said. "You think she sees me and knows I ain't no stranger?"

"Of course. When she starts talking, one of the first words will be 'Grandpa,'" I said, fiddling around with the stove and then returning to take her back.

He grunted and returned to his magazine.

"Well, she'll forget me soon enough, just like all kids forget their grandparents," he muttered.

"Do you remember your mother's parents?"

"No. They disowned her or vice versa. Never mentioned them." He realized he was talking about his past and quickly looked grouchy again. "You're makin' a mistake gettin' yourself so tied up with her. She'll forget you, too."

"Oh, no, Daddy. No matter what, that'll never be."

He didn't argue, but he didn't say it again, either.

To both my and Trevor's surprise, shortly afterward, Daddy did call the therapist, who turned out to be a stocky, five-foot-ten or so brunette woman named Claire Richards. I thought her forearms were as big as Daddy's. She was very pleasant, especially to us, but rather stern and businesslike with Daddy, who was clearly not sure he should let a woman provide him with therapy. Even though Trevor said I didn't have to, and, in fact, he didn't want me to, I took Little Paula upstairs when she arrived and didn't bring her down until she had left. As far as I knew, Daddy never mentioned her to the therapist, and, as if she knew she had to be quiet, Little Paula didn't go into any crying fits while the therapist was working with Daddy.

Aside from taking Little Paula out to be with us when I practiced driving, I didn't risk her being seen. No one but Lance and Nick knew that she was back at our house. However, Trevor talked about buying a carriage and a stroller and taking her shopping with us someday soon. I couldn't help but wonder why his confidence didn't wane. Daddy never stopped warning him, and I couldn't help but have my frightened moments in front of him.

If the headlights of a passing vehicle washed across our bedroom window, I froze and then sat up slowly, listening hard for any sound of someone coming to the house. Trevor slept through it, or he pretended to, because when I did it one night, he got out of bed, came around to my side, and held out his hand.

"What?"

"Get up and come with me," he said.

"What? Where?"

"Just for a few moments, Faith." He nodded at Little Paula. "She'll be fine."

He kept his hand out for me. I took it and rose. He led me to the Forbidden Room.

"Just stand here for a few minutes," he said. "You will feel Mama's energy, and that will give you strength so you don't lie awake worrying all night."

He held my hand snugly, as if he was afraid I would turn and rush back to our room, and then lowered his head as if in prayer. I did the same with my eyes closed. Of course, I recalled how seriously and often dramatically Mama had spoken of her ancestors, hearing their voices and feeling their presence. I did grow up with the belief that shadows were often not shadows, and that the wind wasn't what sounded like whispering, that there *was* whispering. Funnily enough, talking about it and imagining it never frightened me as much as it did at this moment. I didn't want to feel Mama's presence like this or hear her voice.

"Do you feel her?" Trevor asked after almost a complete minute.

I nodded, knowing if I didn't, he could very well keep us here the rest of the night until I said I did.

"See? She's always with us; she'll always protect us. Don't worry so much."

"Okay," I said. I was too tired to ask any questions or get into any sort of discussion about it.

He brought me back to bed and brushed my hair off my forehead before he kissed it, just the way Mama would. Little Paula was still asleep. I turned to face her. Trevor lay the same way on her other side. We looked at each other and smiled. This was our baby; this was the child we had made. Really, I thought, what harm was it doing for me to convince him I believed as he did? If he was comforted, surely I should be.

Two days later, while Trevor was out doing some shopping at the hardware store and the grocery and Daddy was in the den having therapy, the phone rang. I had just put Little Paula in her cradle. She closed her eyes and fell asleep almost immediately. I picked up the receiver in what had been Daddy and Mama's bedroom, still feeling tentative and cautious and afraid to say hello.

I was surprised to hear Gabby's voice.

"I was hoping you'd be the one to answer," she said. "Otherwise, I would have just hung up, especially if it was my brother."

"He's not here. He's been on the road, but he'll be here day after tomorrow."

She was silent. Why, I wondered, was she calling? Was she coming back?

"Where are you?"

"I'm still in Boston." She laughed. "It looks like I'll be here a long time."

"Why?" I asked, relieved.

"I met someone, someone considerate and loving, and I have a good job as an assistant manager in the lingerie section of a department store. I don't use my old phone anymore, so don't have anyone call it," she quickly warned.

"Have you spoken to Nick at all since you left?"

"No. I'm not ready for that," she said. "Maybe if I get engaged, which I think I will soon, I'll call him. But tell me how you are and what life is like with a handicapped Paul Bunyan."

"It's going all right now, Gabby. He's having therapy at this moment, actually."

"Good. You were always nice to me, so I thought I would call to see how you are. If things get bad, take some of that money and come to Boston. I'll help you find a job and a place to stay."

"But how would I contact you?" I asked, because her suggestion sounded so stupid to me now.

"Oh. Right. Well, when I'm engaged, I'll give you a telephone number."

"I wouldn't leave here, Gabby, even if Daddy became very difficult."

"Oh, you're such a martyr."

"No, Gabby, I'm a mother."

"You don't have to keep saying that and . . ."

"Little Paula is home, Gabby."

"What?"

"What you and Daddy did was a terrible thing and an illegal thing. Someday the police might come looking for you, and they won't need your telephone number."

She hung up. I listened to the sound for a moment and then cradled the receiver. Trevor was going to enjoy hearing about that conversation, I thought, but for now, I wouldn't tell anyone else.

Trevor returned before the therapist left. I heard them talking and then peered out the bedroom window to see her drive off. When she left, he went to Mama's car and took out a big box. He came back in and hurried up the stairs. I stepped out just as he put the big box on the hallway floor and took a deep breath.

"What's that?"

"A playpen. The way she's growing, I figured it wouldn't be too much longer. I have to put it together, which brings me to my next idea, Faith. I think we should move into the Forbidden Room and stop calling it that. It's bigger than our bedroom, and I want to throw out the crib that's there and replace it with Little Paula's own. If we're in that room, we'll be even more protected."

I didn't have to ask how or why, but it gave me a chill even to imagine sleeping in there again.

"Our room is brighter, and there's enough space to put a playpen in it. It really belongs downstairs, anyway, Trevor. You know I can't stay up here most of the day, and I'm not comfortable leaving her in that carry cradle. I don't trust Critter, either, if I put her on the floor. He'll lick her to death."

"Yeah, you're right." He thought a moment and then smiled. "Maybe I'll get another one for that."

"We don't need to put this one in the Forbidden Room."

He winced as if someone had dropped an icicle down his back.

"It's not just my idea," he said with that firm, deadly serious face that made me quickly visualize Mama's. "It was her original intention. You didn't know all that she had planned. She died before she could describe it to you, but she did describe it to me. It won't be the Forbidden Room anymore, either. You can stop calling it that."

There was a cold tone of anger in his voice, an anger that didn't even sound like him. Little Paula started to cry.

"See? She wants her new playpen in her new room," he said.

"I don't want to sleep in there," I told him as forcefully as I could. "There are too many unpleasant memories for me. You should know that and care. I won't do it."

He looked stunned. I turned and attended to Little Paula. Nevertheless, he put the playpen together in the Forbidden Room. I vowed to myself that I would never stop calling it that. Later, when he came downstairs, he pouted. Daddy quickly picked up on the anger Trevor was sending my way.

"Adam and Eve have an argument?" he asked, with a laugh building like a bubble about to pop.

"We don't argue," Trevor said, snapping back at him. It surprised him, and me as well. "We might disagree until the obvious truth comes out, but we're nothing like you and Mama were before she died."

"Well," Daddy said calmly, which was just as surprising, "I hope not."

He looked at Little Paula in her cradle. She was clearly looking at him and moving her arms frantically. Another surprise: Daddy smiled, put his thick right index finger against her left hand. She grabbed it.

"Wow, what a grip," he said, jiggling his finger. She released him. He looked at us as if he realized what he had done and then turned himself around quickly and wheeled himself into his den.

"Everything is going to be just fine, exactly as it's supposed to be. Family is back. I know it; I know it," Trevor said, looking after him. So often lately, he would talk as if I wasn't there. Whatever, he was still upset. We didn't talk about the playpen or the Forbidden Room the rest of the day.

I told him about Gabby's call and what she had done when

I snapped back at her and frightened her about the police. He laughed just as I thought he would. Then he took my hand, kissed me on the cheek, and said, "Mama knew you'd be strong. She had great confidence in us both."

"Should I tell Nick?"

"Not now. Why bring all that back into the house?"

He's right, I thought.

When Daddy came out for dinner, he was surprisingly calm, even gentle. He elaborated on some of the things Trevor had suggested be done around the house. Anyone listening would easily assume that he wanted us to keep living in it. He even played with Little Paula again.

I looked at Trevor, who smiled at me as if he'd known this would happen. Later that night, I woke, realizing Trevor had left the bed. I heard him talking and heard him laugh, too. Of course, I knew where he was. For some reason, tonight it frightened me more than ever. I was afraid I might hear voices, too, and know I was not imagining them. Like him, I had grown up here thinking that when that happened, it would be all right. Mama had said we'd be protected. We were part of them because we were her family, her spiritual children. It was comforting then.

But now I felt like a child who had believed in Santa Claus, even believed she had seen him, but growing older realized it was a fantasy. It hurt to be more of an adult.

And if you knew that a man in a red suit with a big white beard was a character for little children to believe in and strive to please, and then you saw a man dressed like that coming to your door or your window, you'd be afraid, ironically. Childhood fantasies and fairy tales become tales of terror for adults. So, too, after all that had happened, the same was true for Mama's stories

of spirits hovering in the walls and passing through us like traveling shadows.

For a moment, I couldn't move, but then, my heart racing, I
rose to listen at the door of the Forbidden Room to hear not only
what Trevor was saying but also, even though I feared it, maybe
what Mama was saying to him.

However, as soon as the floor creaked beneath my feet, he
stopped. Had he heard me coming? Or was it Mama's family's spirits who had warned him? "If you don't believe in them, they won't
believe in you," Mama had once said.

I returned to bed. When Trevor slipped in again, he said nothing. He didn't look at me and went back to sleep long before I did.
He didn't even wake when Little Paula cried to be fed. For the first
time in a long time, I went down before he did. Daddy was up. He
had wheeled himself into the living room, right up to the window
that looked out at the road that went past our house. He was so
quiet that at first I didn't see him there.

"What is it, Daddy?" I asked.

He turned and wheeled toward me.

"I told you two that you were up against a powerful man," he said.

I tightened my embrace on Little Paula.

"What did you do, Daddy?"

"I didn't have to do anything, Faith."

Little Paula started to cry. She could sense the tension in me,
for sure.

"TREVOR!" I screamed. "COME DOWN QUICKLY!
TREVOR!"

Little Paula cried louder. Critter started barking. Trevor appeared at the top of the stairs. He had put on his pants quickly and
was putting on his shirt.

"What is it?"

I looked at Daddy. He didn't have to say any more.

"They're coming," I said. "Mr. Couch and the police."

Trevor turned, went back to our room, and then started down the stairs, wearing a plastic glove and holding the manila envelope in his hand.

"That ain't gonna help ya," Daddy said. "These kinda people own the police, own the judges, own everythin'."

"They don't own Little Paula," Trevor said defiantly.

Daddy said nothing. He looked at me and turned to wheel himself back into the kitchen, where he poured himself another cup of coffee.

"Don't worry," Trevor said, but he did look a little shaken.

He followed Daddy into the kitchen.

"You finally called them, huh?" he asked. "Don't deny it, Daddy. We didn't hear any phone ring."

Daddy wheeled to the kitchenette and sipped his coffee.

"They woke me up," he said. "Called me on the mobile."

"Yeah, well, how'd they get your number?"

Daddy shook his head. "You're a smart kid, Trevor. Both of you are smart kids. But Franklin Couch has some pretty smart people workin' for him, too. Phones ain't hard to track. Nick calls me on it, don't he? You paid for them and hooked up the service. What names you use?"

Trevor winced. He glanced at me and surely saw the panic on my face.

"Yeah, well, I was never afraid of them knowing Little Paula was home."

"Yeah, well, home for that baby gets to be a debatable place, don't it?"

"No. Not when it comes to our family. Mama gave you a family. You should be happy. You shoulda protected it," he said, his voice quivering. He looked on the verge of tears, which only drove my panic higher.

"I worked hard to provide for you all. I did everythin' I could to make this old place safe and comfortable for all of you. What you brought on yourself you brought on yourself."

Trevor and I turned when we heard what sounded like more than one car pull in and over our gravel driveway. I couldn't keep the tears from coming. Neither Trevor nor Daddy nor I moved. We heard the car doors close and some voices, followed by footsteps on the front porch.

"They'll break the door down if they hafta," Daddy said.

Trevor looked at him and then moved quickly to the entryway when there was a loud rap of the door knocker. Before he could open the door, they rapped it again, and a deep voice said, "Police. Open up."

Critter began to bark madly, until Daddy yelled at him. He stood next to him, keeping a low growl.

Daddy wheeled up beside me, Critter moving gingerly behind him.

"What do you want?" we heard Trevor demand without opening the door.

"I'm Franklin Couch," we heard a man say. "We came here to get my child. You turn over the baby immediately."

Trevor opened the door and then quickly backed up to the doorway of the living room. A tall policeman, easily six foot three, almost as wide-shouldered as Daddy, appeared. He wore a light gray uniform shirt with black shoulder epaulets. A stocky man in a gray suit and tie, his dark brown hair seriously receding, came up beside him. He looked through the doorway at me, Little Paula, and then Daddy in his wheelchair. He had a soft, slightly plump face, with a thick mustache, and wasn't quite six feet tall. A woman in a blue nurse's outfit appeared. She looked to be in her forties, with light brown hair trimmed somewhat stylishly. Trevor retreated farther to stand defiantly in front of us.

The sight of the three of them seemed to take shape from one of my nightmares, emerging from the darkness. They looked invincible to me.

"The only baby here is our baby," Trevor said. "Her name is Paula. She's named after our mother. She's my and Faith's daughter. She was born in this house."

"Do you have a birth certificate?" Franklin Couch said with a curt smile.

Trevor didn't answer. Nina had never arranged for that, I thought. How did we not think of it?

"We're taking care of that," Trevor said. "It doesn't matter whether we have a piece of paper with a government stamp on it. Little Paula is our child. The nurse who assisted in her birth will testify to that." He turned to the nurse as if she was the only one who would understand and therefore back him up. "We'll even do DNA."

"We're not saying the baby wasn't born here," she said softly. "Maybe the baby is yours." She looked at me. "Maybe there's a different father."

"NO!" Trevor screamed back at her. "Mama . . . Mama made sure. He knows it, too," he said, nodding at Daddy. "You tell them, Faith. Go on."

"Trevor is my baby's father," I said, the trembling in my lips almost making it impossible to hear or understand what I was saying.

Franklin Couch's face seemed to turn to granite.

"We want this to go smoothly for everyone, John," he said to Daddy. "We're sorry for your trouble, your accident, but these kids are dangerously close to being incarcerated for what they've done. Just get everyone to be cooperative," he said, "and maybe we can keep this quiet so everyone can get on with his life."

His voice was deep and authoritative, the voice of someone used to giving orders.

"You can't buy and sell children," Trevor said, regaining his firmness and confidence. "I have proof right here that you did that. Your fingerprints are on this envelope. We have an eyewitness who saw you hand it to her yourself in exchange for our daughter." He looked at the policeman. "It's against the law to buy children. You should know that, too."

"We have all her adoption papers in order," Franklin Couch said. "You two are only going to make a lot more trouble for yourselves now."

"We don't want anyone to get hurt here," the policeman said. "It's best to be cooperative, young man."

We heard additional footsteps on the porch, and then a shorter, younger-looking policeman appeared behind them.

Little Paula started to cry.

"She's hungry," I said through my tears. "I've got to feed her," I told the nurse, who flashed a look of sympathy.

"John," Mr. Couch said. "You took that money. You told me these kids were brought up as a brother and a sister. This can get very ugly for them, for all of you. People will call this place a house of sin."

I backed up to the sofa, turned myself away from everyone, and brought Little Paula to my breast. Daddy watched me a moment and then wheeled himself forward.

"They were adopted, Franklin. There's no incest here. Don't go sayin' I said that."

"I don't care what you call it. Your girlfriend told my wife it was an unhealthy situation, that you thought so, too."

"Yeah, well, it got healthy," Daddy said.

Trevor turned sharply to him. I held my breath. What was he saying?

He wheeled himself more forward. "This was what my wife wanted for them, for all of us. I made a mistake. I'll confess to sellin' you the baby rather than go through legal adoption and take my chances in court. Trevor, give him back his money. We'll make up what's missin'."

Trevor extended his hand that held the envelope. Franklin Couch glared at it.

"Are you kidding me? I'm not going to admit I gave you that money for a child."

"That's what you did; that's what I took," Daddy said. "I even thought I'd get some work out of you back then, but as you can see, it don't matter much anymore. A lot of things don't matter anymore, but I guess the kid matters the most."

He wheeled himself clearly between me and them. There was a deep, silent pause. I was sure Trevor was holding his breath along with me.

"What do you want to do, Mr. Couch?" the policeman asked. "This could become very unpleasant."

Franklin Couch looked at the envelope dangling in front of him and then at us.

"Now that I see how nuts these people are, I think we're lucky," he said.

He turned, without taking the envelope, and started out, the others following. Even after the door closed behind them, no one spoke.

"Daddy," I began, my tears now tears of joy.

"What's for dinner tonight?" he said. "I'm gettin' up a good appetite." He turned before I could respond and wheeled himself toward his den, Critter following, his tail wagging like a windshield wiper.

"Trevor," I said. I wanted to ask if I was awake, if all this had just happened, but I didn't have to say any more.

Trevor nodded. "Mama was on that stairway watching the whole time. Daddy saw her, too. I'm sure of it," he said. "That's why he did what he did."

I waited. Was he going to ask if I had seen her?

He didn't, but it was clear to me by the way he had said it, he simply assumed I had.

SEVENTEEN

Trevor was so excited that he couldn't sleep. I don't know how many times he said, "We've done it." Before I fell asleep, probably exhausted from the tension, he lay down beside Little Paula and me. I was hoping he wouldn't talk too loudly or do anything to wake her. It had taken me hours to get her comfortable and satisfied enough to sleep. I put my index finger on my lips, and he whispered.

"You know, Mama told me once that you don't sleep after you die. You don't have a body to replenish, energy to restore. Your soul goes to where it was most comfortable and back with those you loved and who loved you. You can't change people, you can't make them do what they should, but you can influence them. You can get into them. I know when she's into me, and today she did a wonderful thing by getting into Daddy. You could see that, couldn't you, Faith?"

"Yes," I said. I was ready to say or do anything to get him to sleep and not wake Little Paula.

"Of course you could." He turned onto his back. "Of course you could."

In the starlight streaming through the window, I saw him finally fall asleep with a smile on his face. It was the same smile I had often seen when Mama had soothed him, comforted him, or described the wonderful things he would do for me and the family when he was older. It wasn't until I was much older that I realized Mama had never read us a bedtime story. Her soothing tales, repeated verbatim, were always stories about us when we would be grown-ups. To her, we were magical. As long as we were devoted to our family, we'd have the power and wisdom to slay dragons.

Later, when I would look back on our lives, I would realize that Trevor had always had a greater need to believe all that. A child psychologist would conclude that the tentacles of the creature that had gotten into him had originated in the early horrible years of his infancy, before his mother had given him up.

When the three of us woke in the morning, Trevor immediately went into a recitation of all the things he was going to do to improve the house and all the things he was going to buy to make Little Paula's and my life more comfortable. He avoided mentioning the Forbidden Room. I couldn't get a word in, but I was happy to see him so cheerful and energetic.

Our joyful mood didn't last long.

"There's a policeman comin' to see me this mornin'," Daddy said as soon as we went down for breakfast. He sat at the table, hovering over his coffee and a buttered English muffin as if he had to guard his food from someone or something that would steal it. Whatever had troubled or frightened him when he had awoken was still holding on to him with the tentacles of an octopus. His big hands looked more like claws.

Trevor had carried Critter, who was very afraid of walking down the stairs. He had him under his arm, with his dog bed grasped in his other hand. We had decided to have him sleep again near Daddy.

I gasped at Daddy's words. His tone was full of apprehension.

"They're coming back, even after what you did?" I asked. Wasn't his threat of confessing and bringing down the whole house of cards enough?

"It'd better not be about Little Paula again. I'll get in the car and drive right to the newspaper," Trevor threatened.

He lowered Critter to the floor, and Critter went right to Daddy, who reached down to pet him, his eyes fixed on Trevor.

"It's not about her. I suspect that's over completely. I'm sure Couch made up stories to tell his wife and get her off the baby," he said.

"Then why is a policeman coming?" I asked.

"It's about my truck, my accident that might not have been one," Daddy said. He gobbled the remainder of the muffin.

"Might not have been one?" I asked.

Both of us stood, waiting.

"Nick knew about the accident investigation goin' further," he continued, sounding angrier about Nick's holding back than what it could mean. "I spoke to him a while ago. He kept it from me. I wish he hadn't, but," he admitted reluctantly, "I wouldn't have been much help them early days. But my memory's comin' back a little more every day. I remember I did try to slow down, but I was pressin' down on air when that turn lay ahead. I had driven it many times and knew it was one of those eighteen-wheeler killers."

He flipped his hand.

"'Course, it could easily have been a malfunction. Mechanical things break down. I don't have any enemies. Not like that, anyway, what the cops are suggesting."

"It would be like attempted murder," I said.

Daddy nodded. "I imagine. Came pretty close. Nick'll be arrivin' this afternoon. We'll see what more he's got to say."

Little Paula started to cry, so I went about feeding her. Trevor fixed himself a bowl of cereal and sat across from Daddy. "I was thinking I should call about the septic tank," he said. That surprised me. He seemed to have plucked the thought out of the air to help change the subject.

It worked.

"Oh? It smell back there?"

"Yeah."

"Well, you're right, Trevor. It should be pumped. I think it's about time. The number for the honey dipper is in . . ."

"The book Mama kept in the top drawer next to the refrigerator. I know."

"That's good. Good thinkin'."

Trevor glanced at me, his face full of pride. He started to talk about other things, like the drip leak in the outside hose bib. Daddy seemed to relax again until we heard the sound of a car in the driveway.

Trevor rose to answer the door. I retreated to the dining room, because Little Paula was restless and needed me to rub her stomach.

"Hey there," I heard the policeman say. "Your dad around?"

"In the kitchen," Trevor said. "Waiting for you."

It was another Pennsylvania state policeman but with many

more medals on his shirt. Even with that little soothing, Little Paula had fallen asleep again and lay comfortably in my arms. The policeman smiled at me in the dining room and followed Trevor to the kitchen.

"Howdy do, Mr. Eden," the policeman said. "Lieutenant Siegler," he said, shaking Daddy's hand and sitting across from him.

Trevor stood back in the doorway between the kitchen and the dining room. I rose, gently put Little Paula in her cradle, and drew closer to him to hear the conversation. I was still suspicious. Maybe Mr. Couch was doing something sneaky. Maybe his wife wouldn't listen and insisted he keep pursuing us. My heart felt like a tiny fist slamming at the walls of my chest, anticipating hearing the Couch name, even though Daddy had sounded so definite when he said this meeting was about his truck.

"As you know, we've been investigating your accident. And as I suggested to you on the phone, forensics feels it was not an accident. They can do almost magical things these days when they examine wreckage and the tools that could have been involved. We've investigated the service station you bring your truck to periodically, and as of now we don't have anything suspicious to tell you. We went through all their equipment and checked the background of everyone working there. No one there had one bad word to say about you. Truth is, the place could have been your public relations department."

"Yeah, I like those guys. I never had a problem with them. Your forensics people might just be overstatin' it. Things might've just broken down," Daddy said. "Wouldn't be the first time. That truck's got miles on it, about twenty cross-country trips alone. It's been through all sorts of weather and roads. Once had to drive nearly a half mile over loosely packed gravel to make a delivery."

"Service guys say everything about your truck was tip-top, Mr. Eden. But as I said, there are ways to tell about these sorts of mishaps, and our people feel confident it looks like someone deliberately damaged your braking system.

"I know you're still recuperating, but if you can, try to recollect places you stopped before the accident and jot them down, especially places you've stopped at frequently. Over time, you might have formed an unpleasant relationship with someone there. It would be helpful to know any of that. It doesn't have to be that day, either. This could have been a slow brake failure, something sort of started, and then with the driving, bumping and grinding away like a slow . . . heart attack," he said, searching for the right words, "it did the deed.

"Also, it would help if you recall anyone competing with you relatively recently, perhaps. Some people like to eliminate their competition, if you get my drift."

"What exactly did these experts of yours find?"

"The brake was too clean. Those materials can be broken down under a microscope if found on tools used by someone under suspicion. It's kinda like traces of blood. A short while ago, we had a man, a housepainter, sabotage his competitor's ladder so that the top rungs snapped. They were always undercutting each other with potential customers. The planned accident nearly broke his neck. We located the hacksaw he used. Fragments of the ladder were in the teeth of it. Once we showed him the match, he confessed."

"Well, there's a few local competitors," Daddy said. "They might put in a bad word about someone else's driver or the company, but I didn't think they were this ruthless."

"Depends how desperate or ambitious they were. I'll call you in about a week to give you more time to think about it, and then

I'll stop by again. Oh," he said, looking at his notes, "we have the name of this friend of yours, Nick Damien. He's been following up, calling often to see if we've made any headway. Drives a truck, too, does he?"

"Yes."

"Same sort of vehicle?"

"Close," Daddy said. "He can carry anythin' I can. Anythin' I could've, I mean. He's comin' back today from a long haul."

"Don't take this wrong, but do you compete for work?"

Daddy was silent a long moment.

"I suppose in a way, but he's my best friend. We've split up some jobs. We usually look out for each other."

"What about the haul he's just done? Could it have been yours?"

"Nick wouldn't do somethin' like that."

"Understood. But you do expect him back today?"

"Yeah."

"Would you give him my card?" he said, placing it on the table. "Have him call me ASAP."

"You're barkin' up the wrong tree there," Daddy said firmly, just looking down at the card.

"Wouldn't be the first time I did, Mr. Eden, but if we didn't check every possibility, you'd have a right to complain."

"I'm not complainin'."

"Well, I won't bother you any more now. Looks like you have someone reliable looking after you," he said, smiling and looking at Trevor.

"Yeah, if he makes sure to look after himself."

The policeman laughed. "Okay. I'll be checking back with you, Mr. Eden. Whatever you remember . . ."

Trevor followed him out. Lieutenant Siegler paused when he caught sight of me and smiled. I nodded back, and he left, Trevor closing the door behind him. I joined him in the kitchen. Daddy was staring hard at the table.

"That was a mean thing he implied about Nick," Trevor said. "If he would have asked me . . ."

Daddy looked up sharply. "Let's not talk about it," he said.

Trevor shrugged. "Okay."

None of us mentioned a word about it the rest of the morning. Trevor called for the septic tank service and went out to greet them when they arrived. After lunch, Daddy wheeled himself onto the front porch. Critter followed and lay beside him. Daddy had been quiet and thoughtful since the state policeman had visited. I felt terrible about him placing suspicion on Nick. Daddy had lost so much. If he was going to lose his best friend, too, his depression could make him a total invalid. I envisioned him withering right before our eyes. To keep myself from thinking about it, I did laundry and vacuumed while Trevor shopped for things we needed. Nick pulled in before Trevor returned.

He was happy to see Daddy sitting out on the porch.

"Hey!" he cried, rushing up to him and grasping his hand so hard he pulled Daddy and his chair forward when he shook it. He carried a bag in his other hand. "Glad you're out and about."

"I don't think this is much *about*," Daddy said.

"Yeah, but it's a start. Got a six-pack of that Belgian beer you love, the one you pick up in Arizona. Actually, got a case of it in the trunk," he added, and looked at me standing in the doorway. "Hey, Faith."

"Hi, Nick."

"Where's Trevor?"

"Picking up some things."

"Heard you were learning how to drive?"

"Yes," I said, and looked at Daddy. It surprised me he would have told him.

Nick pulled a chair up to be closer to Daddy. He dug into his pocket and produced a bottle opener.

"So how's the therapy going?"

"It's goin'. I don't know where," Daddy said.

He still hadn't smiled. Nick looked at me and then opened the bottles and handed Daddy one. He took it but said nothing. Nick glanced at me again, his eyes full of questions and concern.

"So this was almost an uneventful haul. I missed a tornado east of Kansas by a day. I saw a coupla eighteen-wheelers that had been tossed like toys."

"Yeah, you know what that's like. I once drove through one."

"Right. I remember that. Somewhere in Illinois, wasn't it?"

"Texas," Daddy said, and drank some beer.

"Oh, right. Got some possibles for next month. Maybe we can get you strong enough to ride along. Could always use the company," Nick said. "You know how you get to talking to yourself on these trips. Got so I was believing there was someone next to me."

He laughed, expecting Daddy to say something, but Daddy sipped his beer and stared at the road. Nick could feel him avoiding his eyes. He looked at me again for some hint. I was afraid to move my head or even blink.

"You didn't need the doctor while I was away, did you?"

"Nope."

"I guess the confrontation with Couch was unpleasant."

Daddy turned to him. "You know I never wanted to deal with that bastard. If it wasn't for your sister . . ."

"Yeah, my sister."

"She called," I blurted. They both looked at me. "She's in Boston, and she might get engaged."

"Why didn't you say?" Daddy asked.

"I didn't want to disturb you any more than you were with all this."

"She didn't call me," Nick said.

"She said she won't until she's engaged."

"I pity that fool who wants to marry her," Nick said. "What else she tell you?"

"She works in a department store. She said she got rid of her phone, so don't bother calling that number, and she didn't give me a new number."

"Yeah, I found that out. Don't need the new number. I ain't gonna bother," Nick said.

Everyone was silent for a while.

"I was thinking I'd pick up some lobster tails for dinner with you all tonight. What do you think, John? I can set up that pot over the barbecue, and maybe Faith can whip up some of those fries she does so well."

"Whatever," Daddy said. He took another sip of beer. Without looking at Nick, he said, "A state cop was here today. They're pretty sure now I didn't have an accident. I was sabotaged."

"Yeah, I was afraid they'd conclude that. They have any ideas of who?"

"They want me to jot down every station I had any work done recently, practically any place I stayed overnight, and names of any competitors. He left his card. Faith'll give it to you. He wants you to call him ASAP."

"I call him often. I don't need his card. Has he got something to run by me?"

Daddy shook his head. Nick glanced at me. I closed my eyes and looked away.

"You had a bad to-do with that Wally Green in Granny's Tavern about a year ago."

"That was nothin', a bigmouth. He drives half the load in short hauls, anyway. He's no competitor. Not worth mentionin'."

We all turned when Trevor beeped his horn as he approached the house and saw Nick on the porch. Nick waved, and Trevor turned to go into our driveway. Nick took a long swig on his beer and stood.

"So I'd better go tend to some things and pick up the lobsters," he said. "Where's the baby?" he asked me.

"Sleeping."

"You'll have to tell me more about all that. Getting her back, I mean."

"Less said the better," Daddy interjected quickly.

"Sure. How's she doing?"

"She's still a bit colicky," I said.

"Yeah, babies. You have to live on their schedule," Nick said as Trevor came running up. "Hey, welcome back," Nick said, and embraced him before looking at Daddy. "I'm off to get some chores done and pick up some lobster for dinner."

"Coming back? Great. I wanna hear all about your trip," Trevor said.

Daddy's eyes grew small. I was sure he was remembering when Trevor would go running to him when he pulled in after a long trip, anxious to hear all about it.

"Yeah, we'll talk later. Come to my car with me. I have a case of beer for you to bring in with whatever you bought. See you all soon," he said, looking back.

Trevor glanced at me to read what everyone's mood was and then followed him excitedly.

Daddy stared out at the road again. I stepped up to him and put my hand on his arm.

"You can't possibly think anything bad about Nick, can you, Daddy?"

"From my eyes, Faith, everything in the world looks pretty dark. Your mother wouldn't be unhappy about it."

He spun his chair around and wheeled into the house.

I stood looking out at the road, tracing it with my eyes until it disappeared around a turn. Right now, that looked like a promise.

Later, before Nick returned, Trevor asked me if Daddy had said anything to him about the state policeman and the inquiry into the accident.

"He told him everything and told him to contact the police."

"Did he get mad about that?"

"More surprised than mad," I said.

"I'm with Daddy. They're barking up the wrong tree. Hey. It's nice out tonight. Why don't I set up the folding table and we have dinner outside like we used to? I'll help bring everything out. Daddy will probably like that. It'll be like a picnic."

"Okay," I said. Maybe he was right. Maybe doing something different and more fun would cheer up Daddy. And Nick as well, I thought.

Trevor wheeled Daddy out, and the two of them and Nick talked while Nick began with the lobsters. I could see how grown-up it all made Trevor feel, sipping the beer and laughing at Nick's jokes. Nick did get Daddy more relaxed. He told us more about his long haul, some of the places he had stopped to eat and sleep, and ranted about the traffic and the horrible driving going on around him. Before we were finished, he had Daddy describing some of his own close calls with drivers who had cut him off. Little Paula did better than I had expected, dozing in her cradle. If Nick had any more reluctance about our getting her back, that seemed gone tonight.

Just before dinner ended, while we were having some of the apple pie I had made earlier, Nick revealed he had called Lieutenant Siegler.

"I gave them permission to search my toolshed and take any tools they wanted to examine," he said.

It was like a thunderclap for a moment.

"I understand they have to explore every possibility. Whatever helps them in moving it along. We don't want this hanging over your head too much longer. Or mine," he added with a smile.

Daddy glanced at me and then nodded as if he had heard my thoughts: *Nick is your best friend.*

"What's your next trip?" Daddy asked him.

"There's that Nebraska delivery. About ten days, I think. Why?"

"Can't have you pulled over for talking to yourself," Daddy said.

Nick laughed. We all thought Little Paula was laughing, too, although it was probably just gas.

"Maybe we'll test out that stairway-to-the-basement chair to-morrow, eh?" Nick suggested. "See what kind of pool game you can manage."

"Whatever it is, it'll be enough to beat you," Daddy told him.

For a moment or two, it was as if nothing terrible had happened after Mama's death. I smiled at Trevor. He looked so lost in thought. He snapped out of whatever was occupying him and claimed he could beat them both.

I was so happy that Little Paula needed more sleep than usual that night. The emotional baggage of the day's events, the extra work I had done, and the tension I had anticipated at dinner exhausted me. I prayed I could get six or seven hours of sleep. Trevor looked tired, too, but he didn't come right to bed. As if he had to perform prayers regularly, he retreated to the Forbidden Room. I heard the mumbling begin, and just before I fell asleep, I thought I heard him crying.

Little Paula woke me about four thirty. For a moment, I was totally involved and didn't realize that Trevor was not in bed. I rose, picked her up, and went out to the hallway to listen near the Forbidden Room. I heard nothing, and the door was partially open. I peeked in but didn't see him. At the foot of the stairs, I listened. Perhaps he had gone down for a glass of milk or something, but it was dead quiet.

There are times in your life when you know something before you see or hear it, before you confirm that it isn't a dream; it's something that has festered in your heart, but you have kept it down, pressed it as far into the darkness as you could. You sensed these things when you were a child, but you clung to the belief that someone, somehow, would rescue you. You wouldn't get too sick, you wouldn't get too hurt, and you wouldn't be left alone and lost. Perhaps the worst thing about getting older is the realization that fantasy and hope are no match for reality.

I clung to Little Paula, whose whimper was more like one voiced in or because of a dream, and descended the stairs that I had never ceased to hate and fear. They always loomed to remind me that I would never stop seeing Mama's fall. I hated pausing at the top to look down and always marked my steps carefully, my eyes on my feet and one hand on the rail. This morning was no different.

I went to the window in the kitchen. Daddy had his den door open, but he was asleep. Critter lifted his head but didn't whimper or rise. I parted the curtains and looked out. The new moon was just over the treetops, the light more silver than amber. Everything looked black and white. There was little or no breeze. The trees were like sentinels with their eyes forward, their bodies indistinguishable from the structure they guarded. There were no night birds; nothing slinked along through the shadows. The world was holding its breath.

And then I looked to the left and saw him at the very center of the Cemetery for Unhappiness. He looked smaller, younger, a child digging slowly, pausing after each shovelful, like someone listening for further directions, and then nodding and starting again. After another half dozen thrusts into the earth, he stopped and reached behind himself to pick up what looked to be a cloth bag. He dropped it into the grave he had dug, looked up at what I knew were the windows of the Forbidden Room, and then began to fill in the hole. He patted it down, stood there with his head lowered, like someone saying a prayer over the dead, and then walked toward the garage with the shovel.

It felt like my legs had floated out from under me. Frightened I would fall with Little Paula, I moved as quickly as I could to the sofa in the living room and sat. She whimpered but remained asleep, so I set her beside me. Trevor seemed to move like a ghost, making no sound when he entered. He walked like someone walking in his sleep. The sliver of moonlight was strong enough to illuminate him moving toward the stairs.

"What did you do?" I asked in a loud whisper.

He heard me and stopped, but he didn't turn my way.

"Trevor. What did you do?" I said a little louder.

He turned slowly. I could barely see his face.

"What did you do?" I asked again.

He stepped toward me until he was fully in the light.

"You knew, Faith. You heard Daddy say it the first time we saw him in the hospital. 'Your mother did this to me.' You heard him."

"He was just angry, Trevor."

"No," he said, smiling. "He knew. But I can't let anyone else know. Mama would be so hurt. We don't betray Mama, Faith. Never."

"Mama didn't do this, Trevor. She was long gone."

"Mama's never gone," he said, the anger razor-sharp. "I know you refuse to believe it. I know you pretend, but you will. You will. Go to sleep. It's all okay now."

"But it wasn't Mama. It was you. Look what you've done."

"You were happy about it, Faith. You'll always be happy. You have Little Paula. We all have her now. Go to sleep."

"I'd never want you to do this, Trevor. Daddy would have helped us eventually."

"Mama helped us. Daddy knows it, too, now. Go to sleep, Faith."

"He doesn't know. It'll break his heart to know the truth. He could have died. What good would it have done? We wouldn't have been able to have Little Paula. We would have had no one."

"We always have someone. We don't betray Mama," he said more forcefully, and took a step toward me.

I was frightened, but then he paused and looked up, as if he had heard himself being called.

"I have to talk to Mama," he said. "She's not going to be happy with you. None of the family will be happy with you."

He turned and started up the stairs, moving slowly, moving like one hypnotized.

I heard him go to the Forbidden Room.

And in my heart of hearts, I knew, maybe I had always known, that he would never come out.

EPILOGUE

I waited for him all day. I told Daddy he wasn't feeling well. When I checked on him, went to the door of the Forbidden Room, I found it was locked. I called to him and heard him whispering, but he didn't come to the door, and at the moment, I didn't want to make a scene. I told Daddy he was sleeping. The more concerned about him he was, the guiltier I felt.

During the day, I did all that I could to keep busy, care for Little Paula, and prepare lunch for Daddy. Nick called, but I told him nothing. He said he would be over for dinner, because he and Daddy and Trevor had planned to play pool.

"He's ready to try that chair and get his mind off the rest of this," he said.

I didn't tell him that Trevor was sick, that he hadn't come down. I was hoping by then that he would, even though I wasn't sure how I would act or what I would say. It was warm; summer was rushing in, but I walked about in a sweater because my body felt frozen, numb. Daddy asked me about it and said maybe I was catching what Trevor had caught.

"Maybe you both need a doctor, some medicine," he said.

I had to avoid looking at him when I replied that we'd be fine. I returned to the door of the Forbidden Room almost every hour on the hour. Sometimes I heard nothing; sometimes I heard him whispering. Once I went up, leaving Little Paula with Daddy. I listened very hard, bringing my ear right up against the door, because some of the whispering did sound different. I dared think it: it sounded more like Mama. I ripped myself away from the door as if I had burned my ear on it. I couldn't help it, but I called for him more loudly, more desperately. It went quiet again, but when I went back down, walking that stairway as if I was walking through fire, I found Nick had arrived and was standing beside Daddy, who was still holding Little Paula. They had obviously been talking about Trevor.

"How is he?" Nick asked. "Does he have a fever? What's the problem?"

They were both staring at me so hard. Little Paula whimpered, but didn't wake.

"He's locked himself in the Forbidden Room," I said.

Neither of them spoke for a moment.

"What's he doin' in there?" Daddy asked.

Although my tears surprised me, I didn't wipe them off. I let them come, as if they were sparing me the trouble of revealing the truth.

"Faith?"

"He's talking to Mama," I said. "He often goes in there to talk to her."

"Jesus," Nick said.

"Why's he talkin' to her so long this time?" Daddy asked, his eyes sharp with suspicion.

I brought my hands to my face because my tears were thicker and coming faster. My heart felt like it was burning through my chest. I looked at Nick. He had instinctively put his right hand on Daddy's shoulder. *Where are you now, Mama?* I thought. *Where are you when I need you so much?*

"Early this morning, I realized he had gone out," I said. "I came down and saw him digging a grave for something in the Cemetery for Unhappiness."

"The what?" Nick said.

Daddy waved him off.

"What was he buryin', Faith?"

"I'm not sure, exactly. It was in a cloth satchel."

Little Paula woke and started to cry. I took her from Daddy and rocked her against me while I rubbed her back.

"Take us there," Daddy ordered. "Nick, wheel me out."

After he had dug up the satchel and spilled the tools out on the ground, Nick wanted to go up and smash in the door of the Forbidden Room, but Daddy told him no. They went back into the house and talked about it while I fed Little Paula. In the end, they called Lieutenant Siegler and put me on the phone with him to explain as best I could. When the police came, they brought someone from mental health. I tried to get Trevor to come out before they arrived. I told him what I had done, what I had revealed, but he didn't respond and didn't open the door.

I went back downstairs and waited with Nick and Daddy. I

went into the den to breastfeed Little Paula and then just lay there with her sleeping comfortably against my breasts while I hummed one of the lullabies Mama would hum to us. I heard them come in, Nick and Daddy meeting them, and heard them go up the stairs. They didn't break down the door; they managed to unlock it.

A while later, when I hadn't heard much, I rose and glanced out the kitchen window just as an ambulance pulled in. I practically collapsed onto a kitchen chair, clinging to Little Paula. I kept my back to the door and the activity and tried to shut the voices and sounds from my mind. I didn't look out the window, but I heard the ambulance doors being opened, someone shouting orders, and then I heard it pull out of the driveway, its siren starting when it turned onto the road.

I had no more tears to cry, so I just sat there holding Little Paula, until Daddy wheeled up and surprised me by taking my left hand into his surprisingly soft grip. Nick followed and leaned against the wall facing me. I had not yet turned around.

"It's all right," Daddy said. He told me how they had gotten the door unlocked because they couldn't get a response out of Trevor.

"And then?"

He looked at Nick.

"They found him curled up in that old crib with his thumb in his mouth, his eyes wide open. He was breathing all right."

"In the crib?"

"He wouldn't talk . . . he . . ."

"Just made baby sounds," Nick said. "I mean, they don't know what's going on yet, but . . ."

"He returned to Mama," I said.

Neither of them spoke.

"He won't be all right until she lets him go," I said.

They both looked shocked, looking at me with the kind of fear that easily turned big, grown men into little boys again. I smiled to relieve them.

"In his mind," I added.

"Are you all right?" Nick asked.

"Yes. No. But I think I will be. You're staying for dinner, right? I was thinking something Italian. Mama showed me this great way to prepare stuffed pasta shells."

What else would I do if I didn't keep myself busy, sit and think and cry?

Neither of them spoke. I put Little Paula in her cradle.

Maybe all three of us were just going through the motions, doing things we did at dinner almost mechanically, the two of them struggling to talk about something else or go off and whisper when they couldn't. Nick wheeled Daddy out after dinner, to get away from me, I know, but I was grateful.

Was it difficult going to sleep that night? It might have been one of the hardest things I had ever done or tried to do. I don't know how long I actually slept. I could have sworn that at times, Little Paula woke and looked to Trevor's side of the bed. She cried harder but was soothed and fell asleep again.

Days later, Lieutenant Siegler came to see Daddy and con-firmed what we knew. We already had learned where Trevor was being treated. I often wondered if he was basically catatonic out of guilt or anger at me. Nick took me to see him twice, but he didn't acknowledge I was there.

In the fall, Nick and Daddy took me to take my driving test. Daddy didn't want me driving Mama's car. He traded it in for a new vehicle with all the bells and whistles. And then, a month later, he practiced on a vehicle constructed for someone with his handicap and eventually bought it. For the first few months, nearly a year, actually, he wouldn't take a haul, long or short, with Nick because he didn't want to leave me alone. Eventually, he realized he could.

We were both enjoying Little Paula's development, her first steps, her attempts at words, and then, eventually, her first word, which both excited me and gave me a chill: "Mama."

Daddy sensed my reaction.

"Work on 'Mother,'" he suggested with a smile.

In time, she would call me that. I often wondered how much I would tell her about her grandmother, probably not much until she was much older. I found courses I could take and got my GED and then pursued more, thinking seriously of becoming a nurse. Daddy liked the idea.

"I'll have my own private nurse," he said.

Gabby eventually called to say she did more than get engaged; she'd eloped. I was short with her and told her to call Nick, not me.

"You'll be sorry if you don't hold on to some family, Gabby," I said. "Find ways to let the love that is in your blood return."

She didn't ask about Trevor or Daddy, and I didn't tell her anything. I know she sensed how little I cared to know about her now.

So many nights during the months and years that followed, I would sit on the front porch and watch the traffic as if I was waiting for someone.

Was I waiting for Trevor?

Was I waiting for Lance?

Or was I waiting to see myself, flourishing finally as my own person—a mother, yes, but also a more sophisticated young woman who knew in her heart that someday she would know who she really was, someone free of ghosts and spirits who could see the world solely through her own eyes?